T0113924

The Biography of George

BY MIKE ROBERTSON

authorHOUSE®

AuthorHouse™
1663 Liberty Drive
Bloomington, IN 47403
www.authorhouse.com
Phone: 833-262-8899

This is a work of fiction. All of the characters, names, incidents, organizations, and dialogue in this novel are either the products of the author's imagination or are used fictitiously.

Published by AuthorHouse 09/22/2020

ISBN: 978-1-6655-0079-1 (sc)
ISBN: 978-1-6655-0078-4 (e)

Library of Congress Control Number: 2020918412

Print information available on the last page.

The Introduction of George

His name was Daniel Small. He didn't like his name but at least he wasn't named after his father, whose Christian name was Hector. He often thought that he would have been mistreated a great deal more than he was had he been so titled. Fact was he was mistreated a great deal anyway, the term nerd seemed an appropriate moniker for a boy who sat in the front of the class in primary school and always seemed to be the teacher's favourite, whether he wanted to be or not and whoever the teacher was. He was now in his 30s and all that previous persecution had gone underground, gone but not forgotten. He was still strange, or so he thought others thought of him. Of that, there seemed to be no debate in his own mind. No one seemed to notice anyway. Or so he thought.

Despite a university degree in Arts with a major in Romantic literature, which he had admitted, at least to himself, was useless, at least as far as a future occupation was concerned. He was the only student in Arts that majored in a subject as esoteric as Romantic literature. As a result, he did not have any colleagues with whom to share his interests, which he had come to realize had faded years later. Still, he had not come to regret his choice in concentration even though most of people he knew thought he should have. Speaking of his job, he was now a humble administrative assistant, a position once called secretary but now sounding more officious, if not more sophisticated. He never understood the reason for the title change. He worked for a woman named Tessier, a director of a division in the recently renamed Department of Global Affairs, responsible, at least partially and along with the eleven people who worked under her, for certain elements of Canada's relations with the United States.

That was the background. In the foreground, Small was a collection of minor eccentricities, nothing dramatic or dangerous but noticeable nonetheless. Still, he was well regarded, capable and efficient in carrying out his duties, however minor they were, tasks like occasional typing, mailing letters, distributing internal communications, and making arrangements of one kind or another. He had no idea how a major in Romantic literature had anything to do with those activities but he managed to carry them out almost faultless.

He had joined the Department about four years ago, replacing an older woman named Beekman who was still remembered as reminiscent of an era when administrative assistants were called secretaries. She used to wear the kind of attire that was acceptable, if not fashionable thirty years ago, wearing actual dresses that had since been replaced by spandex and sweat pants, colourful hoodies and sweaters with drawings of animals on them. Mrs. Beekman was a formal individual who introduced herself as Mrs. Beekman right to the end of her career. She was the wife of Mr. Gerald Beekman, a middle manager who had retired from the Department of Finance several years before. Daniel Small was hardly acquainted with the woman personally but from what little he did know, she was a heroine to him. He was one of the few Department's adherents of Mrs. Beekman. She had been one of the few employees of a similar vintage left in the Department. There were two or three, one being an older man named Stewart who predictably enough was holding onto his career, such as it was, for dear life, which may have been declining in any event.

It was therefore not odd that Daniel was popular with older woman, of which there were fewer it seemed every year. They regarded him as unusually capable, an attitude that was not shared by most, if not all of the younger administrative assistants. They just thought that he was weird, a characterization that went unchallenged by pretty well everyone with whom he worked except of course for the older women. He displayed minor idiosyncrasies that were memorable enough to be repeatedly discussed by anyone who knew who he was. One particularly curious habit was his comportment during any meeting that involved the eleven people who worked in his division. Weekly meetings were de rigueur for the division despite the lack of enthusiasm of the division's director, the normally aloof Ms. Tessier. Daniel would sit silently at the table, apparently not really listening to his colleagues' blather but attentive enough to answer any question that was directed to him.

On social occasions, those divisional lunches that celebrated things like people's birthdays, Daniel would bring a paperback which he would read while the rest of his colleagues talked among themselves and ate lunch. People thought it the height of impertinence although some were mildly entertained by behaviour so delightfully peculiar, thinking it was intentional, simply to demonstrate his individuality. Further, he liked to decorate his desk with flowers, which he replaced each week. He was the only person in the department it was rumoured to place flowers on his desk. Finally, he occasionally brought fruit baskets into the office and made the contents available to everyone in the office. It was agreeable but admittedly odd. At times, it seemed that everybody in the building knew about Daniel's predilections. On the other hand, nobody thought that Daniel suspected that he was the subject of so much rumination, even though he was.

Despite such unconventional behaviour, his colleagues, including Director Tessier and people above her, had little, if any reason to complain about Daniel. Despite the opinion of the other administrative assistants, he was almost ridiculously competent, always willing and always able to deliver on whatever task he was asked, including by officers and managers to whom he did not report. As a result, he reminded most of his colleagues of the classic teacher's pet, pupils who, whether intentionally or not, seemed to ingratiate themselves through all manner of behaviour; e.g. enthusiastic participation in classroom studies, attracting compliments of teachers, excessive volunteering, or, most unfortunately, suspected snitching on classmates, of which it was never his intention but about which he was always suspected. Otherwise, Daniel spent his time at his desk either reading one of his treasured paperback books or making notes on short stories or even a novel that he was always planning to write. In that context, he had had literary ambitions since he was in high school, exemplary marks in English composition, an early indication of his future aspirations. In his last year of high school and several of his years in university, he was an occasional contributor to the literary magazines that both institutions published regularly. In his last year of high school, he wrote two short stories that were published in its literary magazine. In addition, while in university, having temporarily switched his literary pursuits to poetry, his work appeared in the campus magazine the "Adventure" at least once a year, the pinnacle of his campus literary career being a poem which unexpectedly won an award.

Such triumphs were hardly worth recalling, his efforts to continue his ambitions having faded into half forgotten reminiscence. After university, it seemed that his every attempt to replicate his previous literary achievements usually ended in failure, his interest in each planned story or poem or even a novel turned out to him to be hardly worth pursuing. So his interest in literary matters were hardly known to anyone in the office. He seemed the type his colleagues thought might fit into the so-called literati, a group with which most, if not all of those colleagues had little familiarity. Still, they hardly gave him any such thought, particularly since the only other person in the entire branch that might fit that description seemed to be a much more appropriate choice, Director General Allison Coleman, the boss of Daniel's immediate boss Tessier. Ms. Coleman was remarkably young for her position. She was a thirty eight year old woman who also had literary ambitions, having published several stories in various local literary anthologies.

Or so it was understood.

She was aware of his background, having had a lengthy conversation with him regarding his university studies at last year's Christmas gathering. The party was held, as it usually was, in the fourth floor boardroom. Aside from trays of vegetables, attendees were permitted one glass of wine or beer. Daniel, who felt he was compelled as usual to take part in the festivity, was seated against the far wall holding a napkin of carrots and reading a paperback. For reasons that went unexplained, Ms. Coleman sat down beside him and immediately informed him that she was aware of his scholastic background, claiming that she had heard from someone that he had a degree in Arts with a specialty in Romantic literature. She inquired about his choice and then asked him about his other interests. He mentioned his occasional literary successes in university, such as they were, triumphs that immediately prompted Ms. Coleman to admit her own literary interests. She admitted that while they had not resulted in any awards, they did result in occasional publication. Daniel asked if she was working on anything specific at that time. She mentioned that she was thinking of starting on a story, its ultimate direction, format or plot unknown at this point. He asked whether she had any specific plans aside from the ambition of a story. She said that she had a short introduction and little else. She asked if he would be willing to take a look at it. He was surprised. Of course, he agreed.

It was after Christmas, more than two weeks later, when Director General Coleman walked across the third floor to give Daniel Small two sheets of paper, on which she had produced the opening of her story, which was titled "His Name Is George". That was unusual in and of itself. People thought it strange, wondering about what had motivated Coleman to ask an administrative assistant that didn't work for her to presumably perform duties that she could easily ask others to perform. Although they weren't aware of any agreement between Director General Coleman and Daniel Small, they assumed that Mr. Small was working for Ms. Coleman on some unknown project related to work. One theory was that the administrative assistants who worked for Ms. Coleman were incompetent and therefore she preferred Mr. Small to do whatever she had decided was important enough to be done properly. At least one officer from Tessier's division thought that maybe Ms. Coleman and Mr. Small were closer than people otherwise thought. That drew big laughs from everyone.

A man from Tessier's division named Nolan actually observed the two of them that day. He reported that although they spoke, their conversation was surprisingly brief. He said that she handed him a couple of sheets of paper and left. He folded the sheets, put them in his crumbled briefcase, an unusual accessory for an administrative assistant, and headed for the elevators. Nolan said he got the impression that Small knew she was coming, an e-mail message likely notifying him of her arrival. For reasons that he could not explain even to himself, a couple of days after he had first saw Small take the sheets of paper from Coleman and put them in his briefcase, Nolan considered following him out the building. But he never did.

Daniel had remembered that first time he had read the text that he had received from Director General Allison Colemen. In the message attached to her text, she had informed him that it was the introduction to a novel she was planning a novel about a neighbourhood vagrant who lived in a shack in a suburban town west of Montreal. She was planning the story for reasons that she did not explain. Not that it mattered. To Daniel, there was never any reasons for considering a story. They just came to you. He thought, in fact was almost convinced that the subject of her story, as preliminary as it was, was someone about whom she had been aware when she was growing up or had heard about him from someone who actually knew him or knew someone who was like him. He almost immediately realized that she was intending, as she claimed, to write some sort of biography, a story of the man's life. Fairly standard stuff although from the style in which it was written, it could be a horror story. He started to read the text. There were only several paragraphs.

His Name Is George

The neighbourhood, whoever they were, never saw his scar ridden, frightening, menacing looking face which looked like he belonged on death row. To almost anyone who saw him, he was the source of nightmares, a characterization that had stood still like a tombstone. He lived in a ramshackle shack that was located, like an ancient warning, on a corner lot that had been undisturbed for years. People thought it looked like a forgotten graveyard. People crept by his shack like they were expecting capture, their pace quickening, their pulse sometimes pounding, their fear of capture a possibility. Even people who passed his place every day, even people who were familiar with him, even people who thought of his fearful reputation as a neighbourhood myth, could still occasionally create anxiety in the back of their minds. He was dread.

Some people called him Dead End George although most called him Old George, both titles seemed darkly appropriate. No one knew who bestowed on him those monikers, no one knew how he got to that dead end, wherever that meant, but people did think that he was old even though he wasn't. His age seemed indeterminate. The neighbourhood kids, and their occasionally fearful parents, were persuaded somehow that George, however dead end or old he was, was actually a character out of a ghost story, someone to scare you when you could not fall asleep, the soul of Halloween. Few people ventured on to his property, few people inspected his primitive dwelling, the place that sheltered him from his own torments. His estate was littered with junk, abandoned furniture, rusted tools, useless appliances, and even an automobile that looked like it hadn't been driven or even moved in decades. The vehicle was likely new thirty years ago, perhaps longer. Behind his shack were three large trees, sending foreboding shadows to the street. All that was left if it were a film script was disquieting music in the background. The entire scene sat in the neighbourhood like a permanent warning of future melancholy or worse.

No one really knew much about George aside from the fright that the thought of him usually inspired. For example, the only obvious income he could possibly receive came from the local community association that paid him cash to do odd jobs around the city parks. Although he did his jobs competently, no one ever saw him actually performing them, the suggestion being that he exclusively worked at night. The community association was, however, seriously divided as to the efficacy of having a unsavoury individual like George taking care of facilities providing recreation mainly to children, even though they seldom saw him. The head of the community association was a hard drinking man named Barnes, who worked for an advertising company. He was easily the most enthusiastic advocate for hiring George to take care of the rinks for example, reasoning that there was no one else for the job. Previously, the members of community association took care of keeping the park chalet clean, the ice on the three skating rinks well frozen and free of snow. Barnes and his associates had grown tired of maintaining the rinks. However, the rest of the association membership, three men named Lewis, McCarthy, and Richards respectively, were reluctant about hiring George. On the other hand, they could not think of anyone else.

Barnes had allowed himself to be appointed the emissary to contact and negotiate another deal with George. He did not think that it was a guarantee that George would agree to take another city job.

Both McCarthy and Richards suggested that George might well already have sufficient income. Aside from the other casual city jobs, the possibility of selling used tools, old appliances and perhaps liquor that he had cooked up in his shack was being offered as evidence. He also frequented a local office that hired day labour. There was also rumours, at least from the oldest Barnes kid, an eighteen year old named Patrick that George was also selling weed. This kind of information, whether it was accurate or not, made all four of the community association members nervous about hiring George. Barnes said he would approach George at his shack on his way home *from work, after he disembarked from 5:30 out of Windsor Station. It was 6:15 when he arrived at George's place, the decrepit, two room dwelling with a roof that looked like it was about to fall down. He knocked on the front door and two fairly large paint flecks fell off. He heard a loud but sinister sounding voice emanating from a place that looked more like a cave than a habitat.*

"Who are you and what the hell do you want?", a guttural voice emerging from inside the shack. Barnes stood at the door, waiting for George to answer it, suddenly realizing that he did not know George's family name. "George, my name is Don Barnes. I want to talk to you." There was a pause. "I'm sorry but I don't know your family name." There was a silence within George's shack, the only thing Barnes could hear was George lighting a cigarette with a wooden match. Finally, there was a reply. "Why the hell do you want to know what my goddamn family name is?" Barnes was standing with his face unseen, close to the door frame, it being open a couple of inches. "I like to know the full name of people who I am doing business with." Loud, chilling laughter came from inside the shack and then the voice. "Gagnon, my last name is Gagnon."

Preface

He was mildly fascinated, if not entertained with the beginning of Ms. Coleman's story. It did read, however, more like the opening of a horror story than some sort of biography. The novels and stories of Stephen King were obvious sources. It seemed predictable, therefore, that she intended to produce several paragraphs suggesting the dread that seemed to her to surround George Gagnon, at least in the few paragraphs that she had provided him. Whether she had a plan that would result in Old George doing something despicable, perhaps abusing or even murdering one of the kids who regularly hung around the rink, the rink that Mr. Barnes would pay George to look after, was foreseeable, if not entirely predictable. After reading and then rereading those few paragraphs, Daniel thought that George Gagnon would need a biographical narrative that might explain his ultimate destination to a decrepit old shack in a suburb outside Montreal. Daniel thought of a story that would start at the beginning and explain Mr. Gagnon's unfortunate journey to that dump on Donegani Avenue in Pointe Claire. It came to his head like the emergence of a waking dream, a dream that he could not get out of his head. He was sitting in front of his computer screen with Ms. Coleman's text in his hand. He started to type. He didn't really have a title or even a story. But he was starting the tale of George. He wondered what she was envisaging for those few paragraphs. He wondered whether they would become an inspiration to him.

Maybe a day later, he stopped Ms. Coleman in the hallway outside her office, having loitered part of the morning until he spotted her walking alone, possibly toward the elevators. He discretely stopped her and made a proposal that might attract her. He had been contemplating the proposal. He mentioned his critical admiration for her nascent story about Old George and then suggested he might start on what Daniel called a "back story" to the five introductory paragraphs that Ms. Coleman had provided him and that she could have something to say about anything he wrote. Ms. Coleman replied to Daniel's recommendation. "You know, that seems like a good idea. I know I probably don't have the time to write anything substantial on the life of George anyway, whatever that means. Anyway, I would be more than happy to give you my opinion on anything you intend to write. "That sounds like a good idea to me. Why don't we try it?" Ms. Coleman just nodded and then smiled. She stepped back as she saw a colleague walking toward the two of them. Then, she quickly agreed with Daniel's proposition. "Let's try it. It could be interesting. I will send you an e-mail about this later." With that, she walked toward the elevators.

In her e-mail, Allison suggested that he write the first chapter of the "back story" to George and she would comment. As she understood it, as explained in her e-mail, he was a more experienced writer than her, having authored she understood a myriad of literary products, ranging from poems through to short stories to outlines and fragments of several novels. As far as subject matter was concerned, Daniel still thought that she had imagined something about George Gagnon. It may not have been much but he thought that maybe it was enough to give him a start. He would probably need her advice.

Old George Arrives

He did not have a name. He arrived on the steps of the Notre-Dame Orphanage on Decarie Boulevard in Montreal in January 1949. He was a newborn infant boy wrapped in a cliche of swaddling clothes and a blanket in a wicker basket, abandoned, possibly destitute, alone. Someone, and no one ever was able to identify anyone, had left the infant around eight o'clock in the evening, knocked on the large oak front entrance and abandoned the baby in the basket before anyone could answer the door. Sister Marguerite, who had been walking by the lobby on her way to the girls' dormitory, had some premeditation that someone was or had been at the entrance. She went to the door, opened it and found the infant in a wicker basket. It was cold out. Sister Marguerite therefore hoped that the infant had not been outside too long. It came as no surprise that the infant did not have any identification on him, no indication whatsoever as to who the baby was or who had left him. Sister Marguerite had called out to Sister Denise and the two of them brought the infant into the lobby. After a few minutes, Sister Denise started calling him Moses. Sister Marguerite summoned the wit to note that the city bordered the Saint Lawrence River and not the Nile. Sister Denise quietly giggled to herself but only for a moment.

They were soon on their way to inform Mother Superior Therese, a stern looking sister who usually scared the grey nuns who lived in the Notre-Dame Orphanage as well as those who resided in the adjoining the Sisters of Charity convent. They were relatively certain that Mother Superior Therese would be in her office at this hour, often working as she did until at least ten o'clock in the evening. She did not look up from her desk. She appeared to be reading a magazine, the most recent copy of *The Catholic Register* it was, and smoking a cigarette, a vice that usually embarrassed her, that is if she was discovered, which was seldom. Even though Mother Superior Therese thought it was a venal sin at best, she remained uneasy about the smoking. So when the infant Moses let out a small cry and the Mother Superior looked up, she immediately put out her cigarette and could not help but to allow a guilty look to materialize on her face. She saw the baby and then looked up with a dumbfounded look on her face. Sisters Denise and Marguerite both took a couple of steps into her office and stood silent, waiting for the Mother Superior to say something, the only sound in the room the still crying baby.

Mother Superior then spoke. "Did someone leave the baby? Do you know if anyone left it?" She now had a puzzled look on her face, as if she was attempting to determine the situation. Sister Marguerite had to answer. "Someone, someone we don't know, left little Moses --- Sister Denise and I started calling him Moses because we found him in a wicker basket. We found on the steps to the front entrance. There was no note, no clue as to the baby's identity, nothing but the baby in the basket." Mother Superior pushed herself out from behind the desk, stood up and came around to the front of the desk to study the baby. She looked uncomfortable, which was curious since the Notre-Dame Orphanage included a nursery in which half a dozen infants currently resided. "So are you bringing the infant to the nursery?" The two sisters nodded. "Let me know how the baby fits in, won't you? Sister Monique will be pleased. She loves every new gift from our Lord, doesn't she?" She paused for a moment and made a last comment. "Moses, right?" And then she smirked, a beatific smirk with which every nun in Notre-Dame was well familiar.

The sisters walked out and headed down to the nursery. Sister Monique was leaning over one of the cribs when the two of them entered. She turned and brought her finger to her lips, cautioning them to be quiet, five of the six babies apparently asleep. Sister Monique then motioned the two sisters and their small passenger over to an empty crib, which was always prepared to host a new guest. There were a dozen cribs in the room, six of them occupied by infants, four boys and two girls, two cribs prepared to accept new inhabitants, and four empty cribs leaning up the back wall. There had never been more than ten babies occupying cribs in the nursery in the Notre-Dame Orphanage. That was several years ago, before Sister Monique took charge of the nursery. Back then, every nun in the place had associated the increase in the incidence of baby orphans with the end of World War II, suddenly unwanted births not particularly surprisingly. The infant Moses was, however, the only unnamed foundling who ever came into the care of the Notre-Dame Orphanage. Every other baby left with the orphanage seemed to come with a name. At least that was the history of the place. Moses did not a name.

"What's the baby's name?" asked Sister Monique, stepping away from the crib and walking toward the sisters and their passenger. She leaned over the baby, looked up at them and smiled, one hand over the crucifix around her neck. She then assured the two nuns. "We're ready. We have a crib for her or him." She paused and asked again for the baby's name. The two sisters introduced infant Moses.

"Whoever left him, they didn't leave his name. So we decided to call him Moses, you know, like in the bible. And yes, he is a boy." Sister Monique brought her hands to her cheeks. "Oh my goodness, you found the poor dear ..." Sister Marguerite then completed the sentence. "....in a basket. He was left in a wicker basket on the front steps." Sister Denise added an obvious detail. "And there was no one there with the basket. Whoever left Moses just knocked on the front door and disappeared. I found him and the two of us immediately brought him to see the Mother Superior and now you." Sister Monique then threw her arms out and beckoned for the baby. "As I said, I have a crib all ready for him." Sister Monique took Moses from Sister Marguerite, carried him in her arms, was handed a milk bottle from Sister Denise and then fed Moses his evening repast. Sister Monique stood over his crib cradling the baby for a while, stared at the picture of the Virgin Mary above his crib, and then gently placed Moses in his new billet. Sisters Denise and Marguerite then left the nursery. Sister Monique walked back to her desk and turned down the lights in the room. No one was crying. It was a celestial moment.

The next day Mother Superior Therese Granville called

several nuns into her office to discuss the next adoption presentation at the Notre-Dame Orphanage. Every three months, the Grey Nuns invited parishes in the Montreal area to inform prospective parents interested in adopting a child. Such parents would have to be recommended by their parishes. They would then come to the Notre-Dame Orphanage to view orphans who may be available for adoption. The sisters would bring every child in their care down to the building foyer for viewing and allow prospective parents to select their next son or daughter, almost as if they were choosing a piece of furniture or their next automobile. Usually but not always, there would be several dozen boys and girls brought into the foyer. The hopeful parents would wander through the crowd of boys and girls, talk to the occasional child if they were capable of conversation and then inform Mother Superior Granville of a possible selection. If parents wanted a baby, children under one year old qualifying, they were always preferable it seemed, they would be escorted into the nursery and given a choice there.

If a baby managed to reside in the nursery for a year, which was unusual for the most part, he or she would then be transferred to one of the two dormitories. It was they who would be paraded before prospective parents. Aside from the infants, the most probable of the residents to be adopted were the ones between one and four years old, after which it became more difficult. The oldest orphan residing in the Notre-Dame Orphanage at the time of the arrival of Moses was a boy named Ronald. He was six years old and was scheduled to be transferred to either an institution or one of the many foster or group homes in the city. The older their residents were, the less likely they were to be adopted. Several years previously, when the orphanage had few, if any vacancies, the orphanage was host to a pair of twins who were apparently almost ten years old. The twins eventually ran away, destination unknown, a predictable outcome given the number of children left to wander around Montreal without parents. In such circumstances, there were orphans without shelter and orphanage or any of the other such places without vacancies. It was a sad truth, the reality of single unwed mothers maybe thirty years in the future.

The first presentation at which little Moses appeared attracted a dozen potential parents, all holding carbon copies of written recommendations from their parish priests, the originals having already been sent to the orphanage. The recommendations basically certified that the approved parents were members in good standing with their parishes and would be upstanding parents if they were to adopt one of their orphans. It was a Saturday morning in June at nine o'clock when the first set of applicant parents arrived in the orphanage foyer for the presentation. Prospective parents were waiting for Sisters Denise, Marguerite, Monique, and a novitiate named Anne, fresh from the Grey Nuns convent on Sherbrooke Street. Mother Superior Granville was there to supervise proceedings. Generally, sex, appearance and general demeanour were the principal determinants for most parents although characteristics like eye and hair colour presumably were sometimes factors in their decisions.

The dozen potential parents walked around the foyer trying to talk to the children who were old enough to possibly engage in conversation. On the other hand, the infants, the most popular of the possibly adopted were sequestered in the nursery where future parents were ushered through by the sisters. Two of the couples who were looking for infants selected two of them, one girl and one boy respectively, leaving five in the nursery, including the most recently arrived Moses. Seven of the remaining couples seeking to arrange adoptions selected five girls and three boys, with one of the couples, a young couple named Kelly from Saint Thomas More Parish in Ville LaSalle saying they wanted two children, a boy and a girl, one named Frederick and the other named April. The six couples who wanted single children were approved by Mother Superior Granville without much discussion among her and her advisors, two older nuns named Sisters Grace and Jeanne. There was, however, considerable discussion among the sisters about the efficacy of allowing one couple to adopt two children simultaneously. It was understood that a visit to the Kelly home in Ville LaSalle had been arranged. The three sisters had been satisfied.

On the other hand, the three of the dozen visitors who were rejected as adopting parents were subject to considerable deliberation among the three wise nuns, a designation that most of the other sisters quietly employed as a guilty amusement. The three parents, they were named Audet, Harrison and McCarthy, had come under doubt basically due to Mother Superior Granville's intuition, a capability that she often used to judge people's characters. She used it to judge prospective parents, the nuns and the novitiates under her care, the priests who provided them with religious services, the caretakers, custodians and other workers who worked in the Notre-Dame Orphanage, and even administrators from the Catholic Diocese of Montreal, including Archbishop Larose. With regard to the Diocese, some colleagues from the Grey Nuns thought that Mother Superior Granville was really running the Diocese. In any event, after the sisters spoke to the pastors from the three parishes from which the couples had managed to obtain recommendations, Mother Superior Granville informed the three couples that they could not adopt a child from Notre-Dame. It was a situation that seldom occurred.

Moses was adopted in the spring of the next year. He was more than a year old when the orphanage agreed to the adoption of Moses to James and Thelma Gagnon of Saint Willibrord's Parish in Verdun outside downtown Montreal. Not only had the orphanage been assured by Father O'Grady that the Gagnons were parishioners of the highest order, noting in particular that James Gagnon was being considered for a church warden, normally a post occupied by a much older person, and Thelma Gagnon helped out during the church's rummage sales and its Sunday breakfast program. Father O'Grady also informed Mother Superior Granville that the Gagnons regularly went to confession, at least once weekly, a classic recommendation for adoption approval. Once approved by the orphanage, Moses became George Richard Gagnon, the first name after his father and the second name after his mother's father. A little more than one year old, George Richard Gagnon was now the older child of James and Thelma Gagnon. He now lived on Brown Boulevard in Verdun. Coincidentally enough, another couple, an older couple named Talbot, were also interested in adopting Moses. They did not seem to have the same bona fides as the Gagnons, religious reasons or not. The Talbots were, however, approved for another adoption, a boy named Robert was adopted as their son three months later.

For the first few weeks after George arrived at his new home on Brown Boulevard, he sat on the coffee table in the living room, either staring out through the front window or ripping out pages out of old catalogues of the T. Eaton Company, where his new father worked as a salesmen in the appliance department. Within a week of his arrival, he was introduced to his father's mother, Elle, as well as his father's three brothers, Hector, Richard, and Donald, now his uncles and his father's sister and his aunt Helen. The family exhibited a fair amount of enthusiasm meeting George, even Elle suggesting at some point that little George looked like a Gagnon, a strange observation that raised eyebrows and was immediately forgotten. Once they got home after the meeting with the Gagnon family, Thelma proposed that they travel to Toronto to introduce George to her family. James thought it a good idea, recommending that they drive there the first week of July to meet Thelma's side of the family, her parents, her four sisters, her two brothers and their multitude of children.

Farther O'Grady regularly inquired about domestic life at the Gagnons now that George was a member of the family. For reasons that the good father thought spiritually prescient, Thelma started bringing the baby to Saint Willibrord's practically every day, the eight o'clock mass the only weekday service. She also began to go to confession every second day, hardly necessary given that Thelma and the baby were as unblemished as most of the nuns he knew. In fact, it was Father O'Grady's experience that nuns seldom entered the confessional more than once a week, implying that Thelma was as devout as any parishioner in or outside Saint Willibrord's or any other church. So Father O'Grady wondered about the effect that the arrival of little George had had on Thelma. Before his arrival, Thelma was a regular church goer but had not joined the dozen daily congregants, the elderly women who thought that the more they prayed, the closer they came to heaven. But for reasons that he could not, despite his years of scholastic training, comprehend, the arrival of her adopted son had changed her entire religious outlook. Predictably, however, her husband did not join her in her increased devotions, his work schedule the obstacle. He accompanied both Thelma and George on most Sundays but not all. It was clear that they were going in opposite directions. Father O'Grady pondered the question often, particularly when he was sequestered in the confessional with one of his elderly regulars and there was nothing more interesting to consider.

The next three years were an exercise in almost bucolic bliss. Thelma and George had become a paradigm, going to church, to the grocery story, walking through the community, passing the elementary school, passing the high school, passing the Verdun Arena, passing along the Verdun canal, playing in the park, and talking to the neighbours on Brown Boulevard. Most of their neighbours seem to know the two of them. Predictably, James Gagnon was seldom seen with Thelma and George, certainly not during the week. He did, however, accompany his family to church most Sundays and the occasional picnic on Saturday, every second Saturday being his day off.

The Gagnons lived in the bottom half of a recently built duplex. It was owned by the Boorman family. Their names were Mark and Shirley. They had four children ranging in age between thirteen and seven. Shirley was quite friendly with the Gagnons while Mark not so much. Shirley, Thelma and the Boorman children spent a fair amount of time together, either in the backyard of the duplex or in the park although the two oldest Boorman children were not that interested in spending time in the park with their mother. The oldest Boorman kid, a thirteen year old named Bob sometimes liked to linger around there in the evening when older kids invaded the place to smoke cigarettes and pursue other teenage activities. As for eleven year old Peter Boorman, he was more interested in staying in the house, mainly to read comic books, of which his mother disapproved and about which his father didn't care.

Once school started again, George was the only child left to entertain Shirley and Thelma in the park and elsewhere. Their routine was fairly predictable, walks to the park and around the neighbourhood the usual fare. George seemed to be about the only child left on the street who was not going to school. He was therefore well known in the area by other park people and the staff at their regular haunts, the Atwater Market and Kresge's in particular. In addition, there was an older man, doubtlessly retired, a craggy faced senior who visited the park regularly. He sat on a bench on the edge of the park, on the Church Street side, smoking a pipe and reading the *Montreal Gazette*. He greeted George and his mother every time he saw them, warmly calling out to them. George seemed to be pleased to see the man but his mother Thelma was not so comfortable with him, sharing her reservations about him with some of her fellow walkers. One of the ladies, who lived across Brown Boulevard, who apparently lived on the street for over thirty years, told Thelma that the old man with the pipe was a former police officer who was fired from the force for reasons that were never made clear to anyone, including most particularly the neighbourhood gossips. The general view was that the man was corrupt, which was a common failing among the local police force in those days. Apparently, the man with the pipe was too corrupt, something that was difficult to believe said Mrs. Gibson, who was a thirty year veteran of the neighbourhood. She also claimed that the old man's name was Legault, Sergeant Legatee, a member of the Verdun police force before, during and after the war. Mrs. Gibson opined that if the good Sergeant had not been fired, he would have retired within three or four years anyway. Mrs. Gibson also claimed that Legault lived on Armstrong Street, a less prosperous area of Verdun. In fact, it was a slum.

Thelma began to try to avoid the man on the park bench, her irrational intuition being that the old man was possibly a danger to both her and her son.

The Accident

He had turned six years old that spring, at least according to the good sisters at the Notre-Dame Orphanage although there was still no official confirmation of his exact date of birth. He was therefore ready for grade one at St. Gabriel Elementary School on Dublin Avenue in Verdun the following September. His mother had accompanied him to the school in April to register for grade one in September. There were dozens of neophytes, girls in one line and boys in another, waiting for their mothers to sign them up for their introduction into their education. Some of them in both lines were weeping, a hint of what was to come in several months. George was not one of them although he was told the reason for their tears, an explanation that his mother repeated to him several times. Somehow, though, he was frightened.

George forgot about his future first day at school and started to go back to playing the carefree six year old. Then something happened that was not so carefree. It was a Tuesday morning, close to lunch time, and George was out on Brown Boulevard playing airplane, an entertainment that involved running across the street pretending to fly, producing the sound of a propeller and spreading his arms spread out like the wings of an airplane. For some unpredictable reason, as most six year olds seem to have no reasons, George turned across the street at an inopportune moment and hit a slow moving passing car, his head bouncing off the front passenger door of a navy blue 1955 Pontiac Pathfinder like a rubber ball. The car, which was driven by an insurance salesman named Allan Price, slammed on its brakes, then its motor was turned off. Price immediately opened his door, ran around the front of the car, almost hysterically yelling at George who was sitting on the east side of Brown Boulevard. He was a little dazed but otherwise seemed to be alright. "Are you okay?" Mr. Price was still yelling, repeatedly, like reciting a prayer. It was scaring George. He looked at Price with a strange smile on his face. He had a cut on his forehead. He was bleeding. Price examined George, wiping blood off his forehead with his handkerchief. He then asked where he lived. George pointed at his house up the block on the other side of the street. Mr. Price, his handkerchief still dabbing, helped the boy up and then into the passenger side of the car. Price got in the driver's side, started the car and headed toward George's house on the other side of the street.

They were in front of the house. Allan Price led George up the stairs and knocked on the door. Thelma Gagnon, George's mother, answered the door, saw the gash on her son's head, and looked with some alarm at his chaperone, Mr. Price. He immediately explained the incident to his mother, an unusual accident to say the least, the idea that a six year old boy hit an automobile as opposed to an automobile hitting a six year old boy. It was the kind of thing that the any newspaper, the *Montreal Star*, the *Miontreal Gazette* or more likely the *Montreal Post*, would likely place in its local section. In addition, local French language weekly *Allo Police,* which usually specialized in stories about crime, might well want to pick up a story like that, episodes of peculiar circumstances of particular interest. George's mother stood almost stupefied, so transfixed by Allan Price's account that he had to repeat it. As she cuddled George, she thought for an instant of asking him about the incident. Surprisingly, George did not seem affected, not the least bit traumatized by an incident that would normally bring a six year old boy to tears. It didn't. He just stepped back from his mother's embrace and went into the house.

As George went to his room, his mother offered Allan Price lunch and invited him into the kitchen. She was still somewhat nervous but she was still able to guide him into the kitchen. She offered him a cup of tea. She was planning tomato soup and egg salad sandwiches. She thought she had enough to serve the three of them. She turned to the stairs and asked George to come down for lunch. George was a little surprised to see Mr. Price sitting in the kitchen, a cup for tea before him. George thought that maybe he was in trouble, convinced that hitting some man's automobile with his head was not exactly an innocuous incident. He sat down at the kitchen table, a soup, an egg salad sandwich and some potato chips before him. Across from him was Mr. Price, who looked a little anxious. Price was tapping a cup of tea that Mrs. Gagnon had placed before him and staring at his soup and sandwich. Then Mrs. Gagnon sat down and starting to talk with Mr. Price. She asked him to again recount the story of her son hitting his car. Once she heard the story a third time, this time without the emotion that he had exhibited when he brought her son to the front door moments ago, it started to sound humorous, particularly when Price informed Thelma that George's head had left a small dent in the passenger door of his car. She patted Price's arm and softly smiled. Mr. Price and Mrs. Gagnon were relieved. George was eating his lunch and ignoring them. He had the impression, in so far a six year old could form an impression, that the two of them were enjoying themselves.

George finished his lunch and asked for a couple of biscuits from the cookie tin on the counter. Thelma opened the tin and handed him three cookies. "Try not to leave any crumbs, George." With that admonition, George went upstairs, to his room. Once in his room, George ate his cookies, checking for cookie crumbs, while reading or trying to read for the hundredth time it seemed, one of his favourite books, *Goodnight Moon*, which he got for Christmas two years before. His mother had read the book to him dozens of times since he had received it, which pretty well explained how he was able to read or at least try to read the book. He finished the cookies, put down the book and started to play with his cast iron dinkies, miniature cars that his father occasionally brought home from the toy department in the T. Eaton Co. While he played with the toy cars, arranging them in straight lines consistent with the contours of the carpet in his room, he continued to hear his mother and Mr. Price talking, almost whispering, the occasional chuckle emanating from the kitchen. He was confounded and surprised that Mr. Price was still talking to his mother. When he feel asleep, Price was still in the kitchen talking to his mother. At least he thought so. By the time he awoke,

Mr. Price was gone. He went downstairs and took a glass of milk offered by his mother. She looked at him and observed. "You know, Mr. Price is a nice man, isn't he?" She then told George, in an almost conspiratorial whisper, not to mention the accident to his father. He did not know why she made that observation about Mr. Price and why she asked him to conceal news of the accident from his father.

When his father came home, his usual time of 5:45 in the evening, he went though his routine, a perfunctory greeting to Thelma and George, removal of his suit jacket, a trip to the kitchen for a beer, and his usual seating in the living room with his beer and the *Montreal Star* newspaper. Thelma had dinner, a meal of liver, mashed potatoes, and carrots, on the table within fifteen minutes, at which point his father sat down and started to issue his usual complaints about the liver, which he never really liked but did understand that liver fit into the family budget. The three of them ate in silence for maybe five minutes when his father noticed the cut on his forehead. He understandably asked about it, which his mother claimed that George had injured himself in the park, having fallen she said trying climbing up to the top of the slide, a rusty structure about which most of the neighbourhood parents had complained. That might have included James Gagnon if he knew about the old slide. Some even suggested going to one of the borough councillors. Nevertheless, his father took the opportunity to blame his wife for George's injury, accusing her, as he often did, of not being a good mother, not being attentive enough in looking after their son. George had often heard his father make such comments to his mother. Although he did not really understand his feelings, he did not agree with his father. Although it took him years to understand, he knew his father's comments to his mother made him sad.

It was a week later when Allan Price knocked on the front door of the Gagnon house on Brown Boulevard. It was just before lunch. George, who had fiddling with his dinkies in his room, crept to the top of the stairs. He watched his mother answer the door and Mr. Price came in. He had a grey fedora in his hand, a fashion accessory he had noticed him wearing during last week's incident. He could imagine his mother placing her hand on her cheeks and then then a finger to her lips, signifying to her unexpected visitor that he should be quiet, the reason unknown to George. He was almost at the bottom of the stairs when George saw his mother take Mr. Price's hat, place it on peg by the door and led him into the kitchen.

"Thelma, I hope I'm not disturbing you." he said, quietly as instructed. "I don't have any appointments for lunch today, so I thought I'd drop by to see how George is getting along." By this point, George was peering into the kitchen, on his elbows like he was watching television. Mr. Price's back was to him and his mother was looking up at Price like he was fascinating somehow. It reminded George of the look that was occasionally on his mother's face when they went to church. "I really hope that you don't mind." Mr. Price continued. His mother stepped forward to shake his proffered hand. George managed to see Mr. Price place his left hand over their shaking hands. They then walked into

the kitchen. "I was just about to serve Georgie and I lunch ---
we're having cheese sandwiches. I think we will have enough
for the three of us, if you want. Would you also like some tea?
Either tea or some lemonade, that's for George." With that,
Thelma called out for George, announcing lunch. George,
who was hiding at the bottom of the stairs, immediately
responded and then realized that both of them might have
guessed that he was eavesdropping outside the kitchen. He
didn't think that either of them would have appreciated
that. It reminded George of the times that he happened to
overhear a conversation between his parents, or his parents
thought he had overheard one of their conversations. Most,
if not all those conversations seemed, at least to George,
total gibberish, like he was listening to the relatives discuss
housing prices in the neighbourhood. He got to his feet and
came into the kitchen. Mr. Price, who had seated himself
at the kitchen table, said hello, slightly tousled his hair and
then inspected the remnants of the gash on his forehead,
a scab having been formed, marks of a band aid plain as a
tattoo. Price then looked across the kitchen at Thelma who
was busily preparing cheese sandwiches. She looked over
her shoulder and looked at Price. "I think George's forehead
looks okay to me. It stopped bleeding that afternoon. Does
it look okay to you?" she asked. Price nodded, looked at
George, smiled and answered Thelma. "Yes, it looks almost
healed. It's amazing really. He hits my car and I think my
car is in worse shape than George is. Amazing, absolutely
amazing!" Then, both Allan and Thelma gently laughed,
leaving George to wonder why the adults were laughing at
all. Then, his mother placed a cheese sandwich and a glass
of lemonade in front of him. Mr. Price and his mother now

had their sandwiches and their teas in front of them. Adult conversations began. George stopped listening to them and finished his lunch. He was back in his room and his dinky toys before his mother and her visitor were half finished their lunches.

For the next thirty minutes or so, Allan Price and his mother finished their lunch, smoked cigarettes and whispered to each other in the kitchen. George could not hear anything they said although judging by the tone, they were discussing something serious, something adult, something that George could not possibly be interested in. He heard his mother bid farewell to Mr. Price in a strangely soft voice. For some reason, he had been trying to listen the entire time they had been talking but really didn't hear a thing.

It became an unexpected routine for George, a routine that would soon be interrupted permanently by the first week of September, when first grade would become the opening of a future which would likely lead to a life not dissimilar to the one his parents now navigated. He was downstairs waiting for his mother to pour him a bowl of cereal for breakfast, corn flakes a prominent choice. His parents were sitting over plates of scrambled eggs and pancakes, behind cups of coffee, and smoking cigarettes, his father always looking like he couldn't wait to leave the house, his fedora and briefcase sitting by the front door ready. He would listen listlessly to her report on her plans for the day, which was not surprising since she and George often seemed to do the same thing every day. For his part, his father hardly said a thing, his only contribution a terse recitation of the anticipated weather for the day and the latest traffic conditions on St. Catherine's Street. He hardly, if ever, mentioned anything about his responsibilities at the T. Eaton Co., something that Thelma initially thought was an oversight but soon concluded it was deliberate, an action she was certain was some sort of job requirement. She was also certain that the other wives probably thought the same way.

It had become a practice for most Wednesdays and if not Wednesday, Thursday. After a walk around the neighbourhood, an interlude at the park, and maybe a stop at the grocery store, their standard custom, Mr. Price would visit. George was still only six years old but suspected, if not knew that something was amiss, something was unusual. He would arrive just before lunch, have lunch and George would be asked to "go play in his room". George then would climb the stairs to his room, play with his dinkies or look at one of his picture books, at least for fifteen minutes or so, before creeping to the top of the stairs to listen to the two of them whisper to each other. He could never explain his curiosity, even after reflection years, if not decades later, an inclination that was understandably explicable given the future relationship between Mr. Price and his mother. Occasionally, he would manage to catch sight of the two of them sitting close to each other, a condition that grew more prevalent as the weekly visits went by.

By the time George reported for his first day at the newly constructed St. Gabriel Elementary School, the two looked like they were holding hands as they sat at the kitchen table. On one occasion, less than two weeks before his first day at school, George thought he saw his mother kiss Mr. Price as he left the house. It didn't seem like a friendly kiss, not like the cordial peck that a grandmother would apply to his cheek every time he saw her. She was a crotchety old bird, a characterization that his father usually used after she and his grandfather, an elderly man named Horace, left the house after a visit. He passed away two years ago and the grandmother moved to Toronto to live with his aunt. Although he didn't realize it, he somehow knew that there was something strange going on between his mother and Mr. Price. He was puzzled and would remain puzzled until he was much older and even then, he wasn't that sure.

It was the first Tuesday in September of the year 1955 when Thelma Gagnon escorted her son George to his first day as a student in grade one at St. Gabriel Elementary School on Dublin Avenue. While he was determined not to cry at the prospect of his first day of attendance in school, he found himself, like pretty well every other first time student, weeping. His mother said goodbye, she too may have been crying, and then she was gone, her first days without George in almost five years now ahead of her. George was told, by the grade one teacher, an apparently elderly woman who wasn't elderly and may not have been a woman, that every first grade one student cried. The teacher's name was Miss McCarthy. She stood in front of her new students, all boys of course, with a wooden ruler in one hand and what could have been a prayer book in the other. She told them to fall into two columns graduated by height. One boy, whose name George later discovered was Patrick, stepped out of line to make some sort of comment to a presumed friend, and was immediately hit on the head by Miss McCarthy's ruler, action that provoked Patrick to let out a loud yelp. It was followed by Patrick bringing both hands to his head, pain the obvious cause. Like every other student in the two columns, George then followed Miss McCarthy into the school with a certain fear in his heart, his tears still wet on his face.

Aside from the whack on the Patrick's head, that first day was hardly memorable, at least to George whose impression of that day was so forgettable that he could hardly provide his mother with any details of it, the situation between Patrick and Miss McCarthy confidential. She had joined most of the other mothers in waiting for their sons to finish their first school day. Again like the other mothers, she was there to walk him home, talking the same route that they had employed that morning. This time though, he was not anxious, no tears, the grip on his mother's hand not as secure as it had been that morning. She told him that she would walk him to and from school for the rest of the month, after which time he would be expected to travel to and from school on his own. She pointed out to him that the school was only three blocks away. Besides, as she helpfully added, it was likely that there would be at least one or two of some of his classmates who lived either on Brown Boulevard or on an adjacent street, Parkdale on one side or Willow on the other. He could walk with them.

Within a week or so, his mother's prophecy came true, at least for the most part. He had become accustomed to the three block walk from home to school every day, no apprehension, no fear, no sense of dread, walking happily to and from school as if he could not remember why he he was ever scared of school in the first place. In addition, he had become fast friends with a boy named Peter who, although he did not live on either Brown Boulevard or Parkdale or

Willow Avenues, lived close enough to accompany George on his walks to and from school. Peter lived on Rielle Avenue, which was two streets west of Brown Boulevard in a less prosperous area of Verdun. A boy named Gregory also accompanied the two of them on the way home, his father driving him to school every morning. The two other boys initially thought that Gregory's father drove a taxicab, a vision that survived until Gregory informed them that taxicabs usually had yellow lights on their roofs. Gregory's father did not have a car with a yellow light on its roof.

George usually took his lunch to school, cheese and walnut, peanut butter and jelly, egg and onion or bologna sandwiches, an apple, a cookie, and a thermos of milk the usual fare, all packed in a metal lunch pail with a picture of the Lone Ranger on the side. They usually ate in the cafeteria on the boys' side of the school. All seven grades were crowded in a room about half the size of the gymnasium. They were supervised by several teachers whose main duties it seemed was to prevent or break up fights and to ensure that the students did not throw food at each other. The girls had their own cafeteria on the other side of the building. The gymnasium was in the middle of the school.

George ate his lunch with most of his classmates, a practice that was followed by most of the other classes, students in grades six or seven sometimes mixing but not always. George usually had lunch sitting with his two friends with whom he walked to school. They sometimes traded the contents of their lunches, cookies, cakes and fruit deserts the usual source of barter. Peter particularly liked George's sandwiches although he was hesitant about his mother's cheese slice and walnut repast while Gregory liked Peter's desserts, store bought confections. Gregory usually accepted whatever he was offered by the other two. After lunch, which was thirty minutes in duration unless the principal, a tough, serious-minded man named Chartrand, had some sort of announcement to make, a declaration that the boys in grades one through three usually did not understand, the students were let out to spend some quality time in the school playground. Such time almost always consisted of watching the older boys fight with each other, playing games in which they would chase each other around the yard or try to talk with the students on the girl's side of the yard.

George and his friends, the number of which varied depending on what they were doing, would often wonder about their futures. Peter had an older brother who was in grade seven and could be seen participating in the very activities in which they would invest so much of their time in the future. One of their more constant fascinations involved the combative adventures of an older boy named Jumbo, a nickname that was an ironic reminder of the fact that Jumbo, whose real name was Andre, was a dwarf, or a midget as he was more atypically referred. He would routinely do battle with a classmate named Clifford, a normal sized boy who had a strong dislike for Jumbo, his apparent crime the fact that Jumbo was French and Clifford was English. Although George and his friends had no idea regarding the historical origins of the enmity between the two groups, the boys somehow knew that it was an existential fact, kind of like the weather, antagonism that had existed for centuries it seemed and would likely continue although not for nearly as long. As for the fight between the two of them, a teacher, at least one anyway, would intervene and the confrontation would be over before any real damage could be done. George would often think about Jumbo, even thinking about him years later for reasons he could never quite comprehend. He remembered the discussions between his friends. They seemed the same every time they anticipated any Jumbo/Clifford match. But for the some reason, he always remembered particular days for fights between the two combatants. It was during lunch period on a Friday. George could not say which Friday although he knew it was not during the winter.

"Jumbo should lose every time they fight." observed Gregory, as he did practically every time they witnessed the two of them about to go at it. "He's so small and Clifford's so big. Clifford should pound him every time." Gregory said that all the time. He volunteered to demonstrate.

George pushed him a bit, like he was dramatizing the fight himself. Gregory took a fumbling swing in retaliation, missed and Peter took the brunt of the blow. George laughed. "You know Jumbo. He's tough, tougher than Clifford who's a bit of a baby anyway. I mean, every time they fight, Clifford looks like he's going to lose before Mr. Clark or Mr. French stops it." Peter, having recovered from Gregory's half hearted punch, added a comment. "You mean Monsieur French." All three of them giggled. Then silence would fall over the three of them as they waited for the metaphorical bell to ring. It was still lunch time and the audience was ready. It looked like half the students in the school were waiting for the bout, clapping, yelling and waiting for the rumble to begin. That included George, Gregory, and Peter although the three of them, like most of their classmates except a tall boy named Stanley, who Miss McCarthy called a lummox and his colleagues in grade one wondered what she was calling him. There were a number of interesting derogatory comments the three of them were to hear about Stanley over the next few months, their favourites being clodhopper and lout. But by the time all of them were in grade four, their favourite appellations about Stanley had been either forgotten or transferred to some other classmate, the candidates being boys who had failed one or more of their previous grades.

Mr. Price

It was the first Tuesday of December, in the morning. Miss McCarthy was conducting a presentation on the alphabet, part of her literacy class, using her wooden ruler for something other than smacking her students for various infractions. George was feeling somewhat sick, ill he thought from the breakfast served that morning by his mother, bacon and eggs with the greasy bacon the likely culprit. He was sitting at his desk trying not to throw up, the idea of vomiting in class as frightening as being ordered to Principal Chartrand's office. He finally found himself putting his hand up for Miss McCarthy's attention. She was pointing to the letter M and providing a number of words that started with that letter. She had turned to the class, looked at George with an annoyed look on her face, and took a step toward him.

For a moment. George thought that she was about to hit him. "Mr. Gagnon, George Gagnon, what is it?" she asked, her voice automatically reaching a higher volume. She seemed to be staring at him, eyes wide and demanding, presumably waiting for a response. George slowly stood up, nearly shaking as the entire class it seemed was preparing it seemed to watch the moment. The kid who sat beside him, a bespectacled boy named Douglas Pope, sat looking up at George as if he were about to sing the national anthem or something.

Miss McCarthy took in a breath and made a second inquiry. "Well, George, what do you want? We are waiting." George was now actually trembling, forcing his voice to be heard above the silence that had descended on the class like some sort of cloud. "I feel sick. I might have to throw up." With that, a murmur arose in the room. Miss McCarthy was taken aback somewhat, stepping back as if she expected George to immediately make good on his warning. She then told him, in a stern voice, to go to the rest room, using the term toilet, and then pointed to the door. Then there was a quiet hoot rising from the class. Miss McCarthy then turned her gaze, which was more like a stare, to the class as George hurriedly headed for the classroom door. He was discretely out the door as Miss McCarthy reminded him to come back as soon as he was done, asking him to take care not to spew on his shoes, using a term with which he was not familiar. With that, there was another hoot from the class.

The corridor was hushed but for the echoing of someone walking away from him, an occasional locker being opened and then closed, and the sound of the school intercom being switched on and then off, faint static in the air. As a result, George was frightened, never having been alone in the school hallway, worried that someone or something would suddenly appear. Fortunately, the washroom was halfway down the hall on the left, less than twenty steps away. He crept into the washroom, slowly pushing its door open to see a much older, bigger boy at one of the urinals, with a lit cigarette in his mouth. George stood at the door, fear now adding to the nausea already warehousing in his turbulent stomach. The older boy turned to look at George with a sneer on his face, still depositing a morning's urine in the ceramic latrine. His face was pockmarked with the genesis of whiskers on his upper lip. He had sideboards, brilliantine black hair with a generous spray of bangs. The sneer still on his face, the older boy asked for an explanation of his purpose. George sheepishly told the older boy that he was there to throw up, prompting him to point out that he had done his throwing up earlier that morning, the consequence he said of drinking too many beers the previous evening. "Well, go ahead, but don't make too much of a racket, I've had a damn headache all morning." With that implied threat, or at least what George thought was an implied threat, he hurried into the first toilet stall, bouncing off one of the walls, and heaved into the bowl from his knees, almost hitting his head on the porcelain. He could hear the older boy clapping his hands and then slapping the door to the stall as he left the washroom. There was a cloud of smoke hanging in the air as he left the room.

George stayed on his knees in the stall, lightheaded and empty. It felt like twenty minutes although it might have been only five. He was suddenly sleepy, almost putting his head down on the lid. He was worried that Miss McCarthy would come down the hall, burst into the boys' washroom and order him back to the class. He got to his feet, as shaky as if he had just got out of bed after dozen hours of sleep, and wobbled back to his class. Miss McCarthy had almost finished her trip through the alphabet, her wooden ruler currently pointing at the letter W and explaining its use in the word "word", an interestingly ironic choice that a class full of first graders would not, could not actually appreciate. As soon as he managed to lurch through the door, Miss McCarthy lowered her ruler and turned to look at him. So did the rest of the class, staring at him. "George, you look like you're really sick. You're pale as a ghost." she said, paused and then continued to her diagnosis with a question. She asked in a surprisingly calm, if not kindly tone, a miracle coming from Miss McCarthy. "Were you sick? In the washroom?" she asked. George nodded awkwardly, embarrassed, the class quietly producing a quiet muttering, never having seen Miss McCarthy act like someone's mother rather than their custodian. Miss McCarthy walked over to George, stood beside him, placed her hand, her spindly old lady hand on his forehead, and gave her medical opinion. "You definitely have a temperature. I think you should go home."

Miss McCarthy then walked over to the intercom, pressed a button and spoke into the speaker. It was the first time, in more than two months that they spent sitting behind their desks in grade one, that the class saw anyone speak into the intercom. Normally, they would heard Principal Chartrand or his secretary Miss Desjardin make some sort of announcement to the school. This time, Miss McCarthy asked Miss Desjardin if she could walk one of her pupils home. She said that his name was George Gagnon, he was sick, he needed to go home and he lived on Brown Boulevard. Miss Desjardin said that she would have to check with Principal Chartrand although she did not think it would be a problem. She also assured Miss McCarthy that George's mother was at home, just like every other mother of every other grade one student in St. Gabriel Elementary School. Miss McCarthy then turned back to the class, taking up the letter she called the most unusual in the alphabet --- "X". George was waiting by the door while she brought up the word "xylophone", which she then explained was a musical instrument that people played with wooden blocks like the drums. Miss Desjardin, who George had never met and in fact had never really seen, arrived at the classroom door and asked for him. It was eleven o'clock in the morning.

Miss Desjardin, who had taken his hand and guided him down the corridor past, right past her desk in the principal's office, and out the front door of the school. George's hand was warm in hers. He looked up at her. She was smiling, surprising him. She looked younger than he thought she would look, younger than his mother and most, if not all the ladies in his neighbourhood. She was wearing lipstick, a much brighter colour than George usually saw on most other ladies. They walked down Dublin Street, turned right on Beurling Avenue and then right again on to Brown Boulevard. They were soon at the front door of 1612 Brown Boulevard. They climbed up the stairs and knocked on the door. The two of them stood on the veranda to the house and listened while someone said something to someone else. Miss Desjardin looked down at George, a surprised look on her face, and asked. "Is your father home?" George shook his head and, for some reason, took one step closer to his escort. In addition, he tightened his grip in Miss Desjardin's hand and waited.

A couple of minutes went by with both of them weaving slightly on their feet and wondering when someone would answer the door. Within a couple of minutes or so, George's mother opened the front door slightly, peering out through the crack in the door like she was expecting someone she normally did not want to greet, if not allow in the house. As soon as she recognized her son, she looked up at Miss

The Biography of George

Desjardin and nervously asked, "Who are you? Is something wrong?" George immediately noticed that his mother was wearing a nice dress, not a duster or house dress that she usually wore during the day. Miss Desjardin didn't seem to take notice of her outfit. George was sure that she had never met his mother and certainly would not have been familiar with his mother's normal attire. "I'm sorry, Mrs Gagnon, your son has been feeling ill this morning and his teacher, Miss McCarthy, thought it best that he be sent home." Miss Desjardin paused and then continued with her explanation. "And we couldn't just send him home alone. That's why I'm here. I'm Miss Desjardin, Principal Chartrand's secretary." Thelma looked a little concerned and then shook Miss Desjardin's hand. A face then appeared behind Thelma, obviously curious about events at the door. It was Mr. Price, dressed in a shirt and tie and holding a cup of something. George looked up at his mother who then introduced Mr. Price to Miss Desjardin and invited the George and Miss Desjardin into the house. It was obvious that the two of them were having an early lunch, sandwiches and coffee. Thelma led George and Miss Desjardin into the kitchen and asked if she wanted something to eat or drink.

George wondered what Mr. Price was doing in their house. He said he wanted some chocolate milk. His mother poured him a glass of chocolate milk. It was made from powered milk to which George had become accustomed. His mother then asked him to go upstairs and take a nap. Miss Desjardin had been provided a cup of coffee and Allan Price had sat down. Thelma still looked a little nervous, like she wanted Miss Desjardin to leave. Miss Desjardin assumed as much, took a couple of sips of coffee, and said goodbye to Thelma and Mr. Price. She had to return to school, Principal Chartrand expecting her back by lunch. By the time Miss Desjardin left the house, Mr. Price and his mother were sitting at the kitchen table and George was laying at the top of stairs, pretending to have a nap and listening to Mr. Price and his mother mumble to each other. He did not know how long it was but Mr. Price evidently left the house, within maybe twenty minutes or so. He thought, at least from his vantage point from the top of the stairs, that they might have embraced when he left. She then placed dishes in the sink and started up the stairs, presumably he thought to change into the dress that she usually wore in the house. He got onto bed and took a nap for a large part of the rest of the afternoon.

By the time school let out for Christmas vacation, there being a week until the blessed event, George happened to be playing with his dinky cars in his room. He was hoping that he would likely find a dinky car garage under the tree on Christmas day although he was not as hopeful as he had been a month before. He had noticed that his father had become strangely taciturn the last couple of weeks, seldom talking to either his mother or himself, silently sitting at either in the kitchen for dinner or in the living room reading the paper and watching the French channel on television, informing his mother, in one of his few utterances, that the T. Eaton Co. was pressing him to learn the language. For reasons that eluded his almost seven year old mind, he was worrying about not receiving anything for Christmas, as if he had committed some sort of mortal sin, a mortal sin as explained by Father

Handley during one of his sermons which he heard every morning at morning mass. George was suddenly fearful that Christmas, which seemed to be the most important day of the year to anyone in elementary school, would elude him that year. He wanted that dinky toy garage. George would be willing to go to confession every day if it meant that Christmas would turn out to be Christmas.

There were only four days left before Christmas when he overheard a conversation between his parents that was louder than usual. It was after dinner, during which time his parents only spoke to George but not to each other. With dinner being over in twenty minutes or so, George was back listening with his usual curiosity at the top of the stairs, having crept to his listening post. He could not avoid taking note of the increasing volume of the discussion downstairs after dinner was over. His father was talking loudly enough he thought to be heard by the neighbours, the Boormans. He had started to shout, asking repeatedly who he was, saying that he suspected that she was seeing someone. George immediately knew that his father was referring to Allan Price. He had seen him only that once after their initial encounter meeting with the car. The current episode suggested to George that Allan Price had been a visitor to the Gagnon house previously, perhaps a number of times, perhaps routinely. He didn't know the reason. He thought that they were just friends. He would be seven years old in less than month. He could have no other thought.

Three days later, Christmas Eve it was, his father resumed his interrogation of his mother. This time, it scared him, perhaps the approach of Christmas was the likely reason. His father did not even bother to wait until dinner was over, launching into his questioning of his mother while they were rushing through desert, apple pie that his mother announced was one of her best efforts at any kind of pastry. Not that it mattered. Right in front of him, as George felt urine running down his leg into his socks, his father threw his plate of apple pie across the room. The apple pie spattered all over the stove and the plate broke into three pieces. His mother burst into tears. She had been quietly weeping but now she seemed prepared to let herself go. George had never seen his mother cry, at least not like this. It was no surprise that George then started to cry. His pants were completely wet. His father was now yelling at the two of them, demanding to know who the male visitor was. George was scared, scared that his father knew that his son knew who his mother's visitor was although he could hardly know how his father knew. His father then went to the waist of his trousers and removed his belt. George knew that that only meant one thing. He was going to get a licking. He was waiting for his father to tell him to remove his pants, the soaked condition of which was bound to win him a few more blows on his naked rump. Instead, he used the belt on his mother, folding it in half and hitting her across the face. She screamed. His father then, at the top of his lungs, told George to get to bed. He then told his mother to stop crying, an order which he emphasized with the swing of his belt. He then got up from the table, went into the living room and turned off the lights on the Christmas tree. George continued to cry and so did his mother. He now had a headache. He fell asleep thinking about last Christmas.

The Biography of George

It was four months later. George had turned seven years old three months previously, his birthday in January. His mother gave him a birthday card and his father, who seldom was around the house anymore, didn't even mention the event. Two days later, which wasn't surprising as his mother would reflect on the development years later, his father told his mother that he intended to leave her and George. He mentioned that he was moving to a place downtown, suggesting that the two of them should start looking for another place to live. When he heard his father giving his mother the bad news, he was eavesdropping at his usual listening post. He was somehow not surprised, not really understanding why although he somehow had the fear, more like a bad dream than a fear, that his father was likely to eventually leave them anyway, his recent behaviour towards his mother peculiar enough to give George a hint of depressing things to come.

George had heard his mother receiving the news. His father had dropped in he said to gather more of his things, mainly his clothes, leaving the furniture he said to the next resident unless she and George wanted to stay on Brown Boulevard. George didn't really understand the situation. How could he? He had known that something had been wrong for some time but had no idea what it was. He had discussed it with his buddy Peter practically every day at school who had no particular advice for George aside from suggesting that he stay out of his father's way.

Peter explained, "If my father comes home grumpy, I know he's ready, you know, to hit somebody, even Mom." George was shocked, in the way that seven year old boys are shocked. "He hits your mother! He hits your mother!"

The idea that Peter's father hit his mother was something that seemed difficult, if not impossible to believe. They all were disciplined by corporal punishment, they all had been slapped, beaten with a strap, whacked with a belt, hit with a wooden spoon, or, in the case of their teacher Miss McCarthy, struck with a yardstick, which had happened several times to both Peter and himself. "And what do you and your brothers do when your father hits your mother? Does he then start hitting you?" Peter looked a little scared and a little embarrassed. He shared his secret. "We hide in our rooms and wait for my mother to stop crying. And after a while, the old man calms down, goes into the living room, lights a cigarette and turns on the television set." They looked at each other, looked a little scared at each other, and restarted the conversation they were previously conducting. On this day, the subject was gum. They talked about gum a great deal. That and toys, like his dinky cars, Tinker Toys, and the brother of Peter's most recent birthday present, a Lionel model train set. Peter said that he was expecting a bicycle or a tricycle. George forgot which.

The Kitchen

From his usual eavesdropping spot at the top of the stairs, he had heard his father notifying his mother of his own future as well as the futures of both he and his mother. As he heard the sound of his mother's tearful response to his father's statement, George felt a large knot growing in his stomach. He felt like he was about to receiving a licking, a farewell swing of his belt on his rump by a man who he thought would no longer be his father. Interestingly, that he would later be disabused of his thought although not in the circumstances that eventually would face him. Instead, his fear was overcome by his curiosity of his parents' conversation. He had crept down several steps. His father's voice was clear, his advice equally clear.

"I'm leaving you and George. That's final. You both can stay here until the end of next month. I've already sold the place so you'll have to find a place by then." The sound of his mother bursting into tears emerged again and continued. George moved down a couple of more stairs. His father had turned away from his mother and started for the front door. George tried to climb back up the stairs but was not quiet enough to avoid detection. His father was plainly enraged by his son's eavesdropping, about which he was usually aware.

He turned and started yelling at George in a frightening tone. "You little bastard. You've always been an annoying little bastard, haven't you?"

His father began to remove the belt to his trousers, a special belt for disciplining George was not in its place hanging by the kitchen sink, his mother having thrown it away after George's last strapping, his offence having removed two pennies from the change that his father usually left on the table by the front door. So he approached George with renewed anger, his folded belt in hand when Thelma, his soon to be ex-wife, hit him in the backside with a skillet. His father turned toward his mother, raised his belt and began to hit his mother with increasing ferocity, holding her with one hand and striking her with the other. His mother began to scream. George entered the kitchen and picked up the skillet which his mother had dropped after hitting James with it. He approached his father holding the skillet, intending to somehow persuade him to discontinue striking his mother. The weight of the skillet forced George to hold it with two hands. As his father continued to hit his mother with the belt, he lifted it about his shoulders and swung it at his father. George hit his knee with his first blow, a relatively soft and indirect strike. He dropped the skillet. It hit the floor with a hard noise.

His father, now noticing his son's assault, broke off his punishment of his mother, and turned to face his son. He laughed and stood before his son. George, having again picked up the skillet, managed to swing it a second time, again hitting his father in the knee, although this time landing a more direct blow. His father brought one hand to his knee and let out a quiet yelp. His mother, having sufficiently recovered from her beating to stand, told James to leave George alone, anticipating that he would likely turn his belt on George.

"Leave my son alone, you bastard, don't you touch him." she screamed. And with command, she took a couple of steps, thrust out her arms and pushed James from behind. He fell forward and hit his head on a corner of the kitchen stove. He then fell to the floor where he hit his head a second time and immediately started to bleed copiously. Within less than a minute, he was laying in a pool of his own blood. George was understandably scared by the sight and clung to his mother who, no longer screaming, held her face in her hands. "My god, George, I think your father has been badly hurt." She then revised her shaky judgment. "I can't say for sure but I think he could be dead." she exclaimed as she knelt beside her husband face down on the linoleum. George was just standing still, trembling with understandable shock. He was also partially paralyzed, waiting for his mother to exclaim to him what had just happened and what they should do next. He looked at his mother who was or maybe he thought she was reciting something, maybe a prayer, muttering unintelligibly. "What should we do?" George cried, looking at her with hopeful tears in his eyes. He was biting his lower lip, still scared but slowly recovering from the initial fright of seeing his father, who was about to leave both he and his mother for good. His mother was still muttering to herself, perhaps seeking guidance from the divine. They both just waited, George standing, Thelma kneeling, presumably waiting for the other to suggest a course of action. Neither did, at least not immediately.

Thelma broke the numbness between the two of them

within a couple of minutes. She looked over her shoulder at him. She was still kneeling over her husband, a strange panicked look on her face. His mother was also still weeping, though less so, making hardly a sound. She seemed to have made a surprisingly deduction ---- that her husband was dead, or at least close to being dead. She finally issued to him an instruction. "Go next door. Get Mark or Shirley to come over. They'll help us. Hurry." George immediately headed for the front door and climbed the stairs up to the Boorman place where he frantically pressed the buzzer to their front door. He kept his hand on the buzzer until Mr. Boorman answered the door. He looked a little annoyed, if not confused. He had brought a single finger to his mouth, signalling him to be quiet. There was a strange silence in the apartment behind him. It was his wife Shirley and the four children all in the living room listening to the radio broadcasting the rosary. George and his mother sometimes used to recite the rosary with the radio although his father never participated in what he used to call, "a dumb religious singalong".

The entire household probably heard George. "Somebody gotta come, come quick. We need somebody to help us. There's been a bad accident." he exclaimed, practically falling forward into Mr. Boorman who understandably asked George as calmly as he could. "What's the matter, George, what's happened?" It didn't take long for the rest of the family to approach the front door, waiting for George to answer. "My father, I think my father's dead. There's a lot of blood in the kitchen, it's all over the floor." George seemed to be out of breath. "My mother told me to ask you for help." The mother Shirley was clutching her husband's arm while the eldest Boorman child, thirteen year old Bob, was standing on the other side of his father, a blank look on his face. He was waiting for his father to answer George's plea for help.

Mr Boorman issued instructions. "It's okay, George, I'll phone emergency. They're will send an ambulance and alert the police. Until help arrives, you should stay here with Shirley and the kids." Then, Shirley embraced George and guided him into the house. Peter Boorman, who was knelling on a comic book while listening to the rosary on the radio, offered George an older edition of a Superman and took him upstairs with the two younger Boormans. Shirley Boorman and son Bob stayed downstairs while the father went downstairs to investigate the situation at the Gagnons.

When Mark Boorman arrived at the front door of the Gagnon place, Thelma was sitting with her back leaning across the drawers underneath the sink, her husband's body laying in a pool of blood on the floor before her. She was still weeping, barely audible but recognizable enough. When she saw Mark standing in the kitchen, she raised her arms and cried out to him. Haltingly, she started to explain. "Thank god, Mark. I need help. I'm think Jim's dead. I pushed him and he fell and hit his head, on the stove and then on the floor." She repeated herself. "He hit his head hard, twice, on the stove and the floor." She paused and then grew more agitated, almost hysterical. "Neither George or I meant anything. We never meant to hurt him." Again, another pause. "He was hitting me and then he went after George. I couldn't help it. I was worried about George. I had to do something." For some reason, she omitted George's two swings with the skillet from her commentary. She took full responsibility.

Aside from assuring Thelma that the relevant authorities

had been notified, Mark asked her to take care not to disturb the area in any way, thinking that the police would want to examine the scene for their investigation, a procedure he thought he picked up from one of the detective novels he occasionally read. He helped her up to her feet and escorted Thelma out to the living room, which was untouched by any of the events in the kitchen. He sat her down in one of the large chairs in the living room and went back to the kitchen to make Thelma a cup of tea. He took care not to step in or even near the body of James Gagnon or the pool of blood in which he lay.

The Police Arrive

The ambulance arrived first, parking right in front of the Boorman/Gagnon duplex on Brown Boulevard. Its appearance precipitated the interest of several of the neighbours who were quick to congregate on the sidewalk to the left of the steps of the duplex. Two attendants clad in white coats unloaded a stretcher and headed up the stairs with obvious haste. They knocked on the door to the top apartment and were directed into the kitchen of the Gagnon apartment by Mark Boorman. They hurried downstairs to the Gagnon flat and the police and attendants stood over James Gagnon's body for a moment and then sat at the kitchen, waiting for the police to arrive to begin their investigation. Mark was in the process of serving the hospital attendants tea when the police arrived, parking across the street from the Boorman/Gagnon duplex. The crowd on Brown Boulevard had grown slightly, several mothers pushing carriages having stopped to reconnoitre. Not surprisingly, neighbourhood witness Mrs. Gibson was on the scene, circulating among the bystanders, exchanging hearsay and theories about the situation. The arrival of an ambulance and a police car brought the crowd on Brown Boulevard to a crescendo of gossip. From across the street,

Mark could actually hear the hubbub, which was growing louder, and was beginning to wonder when a reporter would arrive. George and Peter had come downstairs, their comic book reading temporarily discontinued by the commotion across the street and their eyes were glued to the living room window. Only Thelma, sitting in a chair in the living room with a cup of tea in her lap, seemed indifferent to the cacophony gathering across the street.

Officer Bertrand and Detective Pronovost finally appeared, one in a uniform of the Verdun Police Department and the other, an older guy that was wearing a straw hat and a suit that looked like it he got it at a Salvation Army store, an old Salvation Army store. Detective Pronovost introduced Officer Bertrand and himself to Mark who pointed out that Thelma was sitting in the living room and that her son George was upstairs which was not accurate since he and Peter had crept down and were hiding behind the couch in the Boorman flat. Mark then escorted the two of them into the kitchen of the Gagnon place while the two ambulance attendants were still sitting at the table in the Gagnon kitchen sipping tea and waiting. They sat by the body of James Gagnon, which was still laying on the kitchen floor in a pool of blood that was slowly turning into some sort of custard. Detective Pronovost removed his straw hat, setting it on the counter near the sink and knelt down by the body. He turned and looked up at the four men now standing around in the kitchen.

"Now that's a head wound!" Detective Pronovist exclaimed. "If he hadn't died, he would have had a helluva headache." With that observation, which he intended no doubt as wit, Detective Pronovist chuckled, as did Officer

Bertrand and one of two ambulance attendants. Detective Pronovost, having removed a pencil from an inside pocket of his suit jacket, then used it to point out the laceration that James Gagnon had suffered from his fall to the corner of the stove. It was a significant gash that was still oozing blood. There was blood on the left front corner of the stove, which Detective Pronovost again pointed out with his pencil. Officer Bertrand had moved in closer, examining the wound on Gagnon's head. Then, Detective Pronovost made a conclusive announcement. "The man died after hitting his damn head on the corner of the stove. That is pretty well it. The only question now is how he ended up hitting his head on the stove." Kneeling by Gagnon's leg was Officer Bertrand. Detective Pronovost and the attendants joined him. Bertrand noticed a couple of small bumps on his right knee. Bertrand then pushed up his trousers and examined the bumps, saying that they were the likely result of blows from the skillet, which was still laying on the kitchen floor. Further to Detective Pronovost's request, Officer Bertrand picked up the skillet with a glove and placed the skillet in an evidence bag.

All four of them then stood up. Detective Pronovost then asked the attendants to convey the body out to the ambulance. There was a large number of people standing on both sides of the street. A second police car had arrived to control the crowd. The attendants placed the stretcher carrying James Gagnon's body in the ambulance, closed the rear door, got in the ambulance and it slowly drove away. They were headed for the Verdun General Hospital. Mark Boorman, who was standing on the Gagnon's veranda, watched another car follow the ambulance. Detective Pronovost suggested to Mr.

Boorman that he was willing to wager that the car following the ambulance was driven by a reporter. Pronovost turned back into the house to speak to Thelma Gagnon. They all walked back into the Gagnon place.

Detective Pronovost took Thelma aside as soon as they stepped inside the living room. With a serious, almost grim face, he quietly asked Thelma to report to the police station at 750 Willibrord Street within the next couple of days. It didn't sound like a request. In a nervous voice, she asked Pronovost the purpose of his request. Sensing that both he and his mother were in more trouble, George's initial shock, having faded, now reappeared. He was suddenly standing beside his mother, holding her hand, listening to Detective Pronovost's explanation. He felt like he did when he felt sick in Miss McCarthy's class. Before last Christmas.

"Well, Mrs. Gagnon, I'm convinced, based on the evidence I've seen here today, that this was clearly a case of self-defense on your part and the part of your boy here." Mrs. Gagnon looked relieved although she probably wasn't. George felt his mother's hand grip his hand more tightly. Detective Pronovost continued. "But there is a report to complete and we have to go over everything again. Details --- the Captain, Captain Chartier likes details. So I'd like to go over everything, you know, for the record." It seemed a sensible request. So Thelma did not make a comment. Still, the Detective's request did sound a little like an order. Thelma then said she would come down to the station sometime next week. Detective Ponovost nodded and then he and Officer Bertrand left the house.

As promised, Thelma Gagnon arrived at the police station at 750 Willibrord Street sometime the next week, on the Wednesday. She reported to the front counter where she told a woman officer, not a frequent sight in police stations in those days, that she was looking for Detective Pronovost. The officer, her name was Tremblay, picked up the telephone, dialed a three digit number, and announced Mrs. Gagnon's presence. She then completed her call, hung up the telephone, and asked Mrs. Gagnon to take a seat on one of the benches at the front of the station, explaining. "Detective Pronovost will be out in a few minutes." Mrs. Gagnon took a seat on one of the benches, careful not to sit beside a derelict muttering quietly to himself, which was not unusual in and of itself, but the man was also fumbling with the fly on his trousers. The other two citizens waiting to speak to a police were a middle age woman who was knitting and whistling although Mrs. Gagnon did not recognize a specific tune and a well dressed man with an umbrella and reading from a well thumbed paperback.

After providing the woman with some sort of form and informing the well dressed man with the paperback that Captain Chartier would see him shortly, she received a third telephone call and then called Thelma Gagnon to the counter to inform her that Detective Pronovost was waiting for her in Room 109 down the corridor to the left. She hurried down the corridor, found Room 109 and knocked on the door. Inside the room, she could hear the Detective on the telephone and stepped closer to the door. She heard him raising his voice and declining whatever the person on the other end of the telephone was asking or offering. So thought Thelma as she listened. Detective Pronovost forcefully hung up the telephone. Thelmas knocked on the door a second time and she then was invited into Pronovost's office. He stood up and motioned Thelma to sit in one of the two chairs positioned in front of his desk. She sat.

Detective Pronovost began the interview by thanking Thelma and explaining his purpose in asking her to visit the police station. "As I think I told you the other day, I just need some details to complete my report for the inquest." Thelma must have looked a little confused so Detective Pronovost continued. "The inquest is just a formality. In this case, the medical examiner ---- he's a guy named Gallagher --- has already agreed with the conclusion." Thelma responded predictably. "Conclusion?" Pronovost answered. He started to read from a sheet of paper that he had picked up from the desk. "There's no doubt that James Gagnon died as a result of the successive blows to the head after a fall. I should add that the fall was the result of a shove suffered during a physical confrontation with his wife Thelma Gagnon. To the officers on scene, it was clearly a matter of self defence and no further investigation is required."

Thelma sat in the chair in front of Detective Pronovost, almost dumbfounded. She wondered why the Detective had invited her down to the office. There did not appear to be any reason for her to be sitting there in front of Detective Pronovost. So she asked. "Detective, why am I here? I mean, you seem to have things pretty well lined up, right?" Detective Pronovost smiled, chuckled a bit, and then lightly slapped his desk a couple of times. "Well, Mrs. Gagnon, I have a question and a request." Thelma was a little uncomfortable but still smiled nevertheless. "What's the question?" Detective Pronovist leaned across the desk.

"The skillet. We have reason to believe that both your son and yourself hit him with that skillet. We found two fingerprints on the skillet, one adult size and one for children. While we never took either of your prints, the size of the two prints pretty well told us that both of you used it. It will not make any difference in the disposition of the case. I would just like have every detail. Just like I said to you, my Captain likes details." Thelma offered a small grin and verified the Detective's conclusion. "George was just defending the two of us. He did hit him with the skillet, twice I think, and then I pushed him into the stove. That's all I can remember." Detective Pronovost nodded and then pushed the document that was sitting in front of him across the table toward Thelma. He then pushed a pen toward her. "We would like you to initial this document, this report, in the box at the bottom right. It's a formality. It just means that we have discussed the report with you." Thelma took the pen and initialled the box. Detective Pronovost suggested that she read the document. "I don't have to, I know what it says. It says we are not guilty of anything." Detective Pronovost nodded "No, you're not."

Life Without A Father

His father was gone, dead but gone nevertheless. Convinced by Shirley Boorman, who felt that even though James had intended to leave George and Thelma anyway, it was still appropriate to see that he have a funeral, regardless of the manner of his passing. Although George's mother was understandably reluctant and unable to arrange a funeral in the circumstances, Mrs. Boorman assured her that she would make all the arrangements through Father O'Grady at Saint Willibrord's, mentioning that her husband Mark was a church deacon and would no doubt convince the church to organize a simple funeral. Shirley managed to persuade Thelma to allow a small funeral even though she remained somewhat resistant to the idea. Shirley told Thelma that she would take care of everything which, as it turned out, was not very much. Father O'Grady, who would soon turn out to be quite useful to Thelma and her son George, did not charge the Gagnons for either the funeral, the coffin in which James Gagnon slept, his grave or his headstone. As grateful as she was for Saint Willibrord's generosity, Thelma wondered why the church provided it. Shirley told her more than once that sometimes the Catholic church sometimes acts like the Catholic church. Thelma and George would soon ask this particularly Catholic church for further indulgence.

The funeral took place four days after the death of the her husband. There was no visitation, only a funeral. Aside from Father O'Grady who presided and a young altar boy with red hair who attended to him, there were only five mourners who were there for the service. There was Thelma and George, Mrs. Boorman and her eldest son Bob and neighbourhood gossip Mrs. Gibson, a surprise congregate apparently attending the event out of both curiosity and respect, not for the descendent but for the woman who helped him get there. Evidently, Shirley had informed Mrs. Gibson of the circumstances of Mr. James Gagnon's demise in so far as she knew about them, tempting Mrs. Gibson to press for more if she got the opportunity after the funeral. Unfortunately, she did not, Thelma Gagnon being too overwrought to speak to anyone after the funeral was concluded, due to guilt rather than sorrow one assumed. For his part, George was simply bored, if not agitated during the entire ritual, noting that only his mother was crying although not because she was sad, an observation that his mother confided to him when he was somewhat older. George was also surprised that Allan Price, his mother's friend who has caused all the lunacy in the first place, was not present. In fact, George never saw Allan Price again. Looking back, he didn't think his mother saw him again either. Fortunately, for her and maybe him, Mr. Price lived somewhere else in the city, the chances of an accidental meeting highly unlikely. Finally, he thought he saw Detective Pronovost saw in the parking lot outside the church. He never mentioned it to his mother or anyone else for that matter.

The morning after the funeral, the house was as quiet as it had been since James left permanently. The only sounds were occasional weeping of his mother and the general commotion of her arranging breakfast. George would sometimes crawl to the top of the stairs, expecting somehow that his father would return somehow, as if he had never died and even if he had not, had never proclaimed that he was leaving the two of them. When his deceased father did not appear, he would then creep down the stairs and then into the doorway to the kitchen where his mother was sitting over a cup of coffee, her head down, her quiet sobs interrupting her intermittent sips of coffee, a radio playing very softly, almost imperceptibly in the background, a cigarette smouldering in an ashtray. A bowl of cereal sat on the table to her left, waiting for George to arrive. He always had Cheerios or plain Cornflakes for breakfast. George preferred the former although he would settle on the latter if they were served with fruit, particularly bananas. He always wanted at least two teaspoons of sugar with plenty of milk.

He stood for a couple of moments in the doorway to the kitchen until his mother looked up from her sporadic anguish and greeted him with forced cheer. He noticed that rosary beads were wrapped around her left hand. George stepped into the kitchen, stood still again, and then asked a question that had been circulating in his head since he heard his father announce his intention to leave the house several days past. "Mom, I know Dad is gone but he had been saying that for a while, hadn't he?" His mother nodded with a sad look still on her face, tears still in her eyes. "Yes, George, he's finally gone and he won't be back. That what funerals are for. You were there." His theological question answered, George stepped into the kitchen, sat down at the kitchen table and wordlessly stared into the bowl of Cheerios. He put a spoon into the bowl and started to eat his breakfast while his mother repeated an explanation of his father's departure. She wanted George to understood, finally understand.

"Georgie, he's gone now. He said that he was going to leave, he had been saying that for weeks and now he doesn't have to say that anymore because he's dead. You know that, we went to his funeral yesterday." His mother then applied a tissue to her eyes and continued with her history. "You know your father and I had been having problems, for weeks, ever since he found out about Allan." His mother was referring to Allan Price, his mother's friend, the friend that she had not seen since the day before James died. George looked up, placed his spoon down, and then asked if they would ever see Mr. Price. It was an obvious question. "Mom, is Mr. Price? If Dad's gone, then maybe Mr. Price will come back." His mother stopping her crying and managed to offer her son a slow, sad shook of her head. "I'm afraid it doesn't look like he will be back either."

Then Thelma abruptly changed the subject, to something a little more mundane yet significantly more important. "George, you mother is worried. I don't know where we are going to live." George was puzzled. He looked at her plaintively. She knew what he wanted to know. The explanation came out intermittently, between her struggle with her words and the radio in the background. "Georgie, I don't know where we're going to go. Your father died without leaving us any money. The day he died, your father said that he had sold our flat. We have until the end of the month to leave. I don't where we are going to go after that." George was still puzzled. He didn't know what to think. Not that he was happy that his father had died, only that he was not unhappy that he had died.

"I don't know where we are going to live." And with that pitiful declaration, his mother released another avalanche of tears, bringing her hands to her face, the crucifix of the rosary almost dropping to her lap. George sat in front of his nearly finished bowl of Cheerios and drank the rest of his orange juice. With the thought of eventual eviction now brought into his mind, he thought about the loss of his dinky toys and comic books.

George finally went to Saint Gabriel Elementary the next morning, having stayed home the last five days after his father's death at her mother's suggestion, if not her insistence. She told him that she needed him for moral support, a term that she had to explain to George several times. He finally understood the term after he noticed that she had remained periodically tearful over those five days after the passing of James. Aside from constant condolence from the Boormans, Thelma tried to seek sympathy from her mother, who had moved to Toronto to live with her sister when their father died. She tried to contact her but was unsuccessful, however, when she could not reach her by telephone. It was evident that her husband had forgotten, if not outright declined, to pay the monthly phone bill. She thought of going upstairs to ask if she could use the telephone but didn't want to burden the Boormans any further. She thought that they had already done more than enough for George and herself. Besides, her financial situation, already bleak, was unlikely to get any better. Further, she simply didn't want to take on any further debt, particularly for a long distance charge.

Another responsibility, insignificant relative to acquiring another place for George and her to live was to provide George with a note to give to Miss McCarthy explaining his absence from school the last few days. She hastily drafted a note which stated that her husband, George's father had died by a domestic accident five days ago and that George should be excused from school for those days. Although he couldn't and in fact hadn't read the letter he gave to his teacher, it must have evoked a certain amount of sympathy since Miss McCarthy gave him a kindly glance after she read the letter.

Over the next week, George's mother spent most of her time attempting to find a place for her and her son to live. She had until the end of the month, hoping somehow that shelter would be available for next to nothing, whatever that meant. She was also combing through the classified advertisements of both the *Montreal Star* and the *Montreal Gazette* looking for a job. She didn't know whether she was more worried about finding another place for her and her son to live or finding employment, her last and only job serving at a diner on Hickson Street in Verdun. She was almost frantic, anxiety ridden, so much so that she turned to consulting with several of her neighbours, including Shirley Boorman, Mrs. Gibson, and Mrs. Rossenti, a disagreeable Italian woman with whom she hardly ever spoke, an understandable circumstance given that the woman did not speak English or French. When Thelma tried to explain her troubles to Mrs. Rossenti, she offered Thelma a zucchini from a basket she was carrying, apparently returning from the local farmers' market on Saint Jean Avenue. Mrs. Rossenti then took herself and her basket into her place, which was two doors down from Thelma and Shirley's duplex.

Finally, and at the urging of another neighbour, a Mrs. Inkster, who went to mass at Saint Willibrord's church practically every day, Thelma decided to make an appointment with Father O'Grady. It was Mrs. Inkster's opinion, the fact was that it was more like a belief, that the good father, or the parish priest Father Handley, might be prepared to help Thelma and her son with their problems. Two days later, it was a Saturday morning. George and his mother paid a visit to Saint Willibrord's. She had not told George the purpose of their visit, Sunday morning and the occasional weekday mass required by Saint Gabriel's his only other visits. When the two of them walked through the front doors of the church, the only sound was the murmur of a broom sweeping across the marble floor, the only light the morning illumination through the church's stained glass windows and the flickering of trays of lite votive candles in trays. The broom was in the hands of the parish janitor, a long time employee who looked like he was recovering from some sort of addiction, most likely alcohol. Thelma's mother used to say the janitor, whose name was John, was sloshed most of time, at least until he found the cure after spending a month in the rehabilitation centre operated by Jesuit priests north of the city. Now, he was sober, at least according to Fathers Handley and O'Grady, and then got his old job back looking after the church.

John the janitor didn't look up to acknowledge Thelma and George who were slowly and quietly walking up the centre aisle. George and Thelma were holding hands. They were almost creeping, which may well have explained John not noticing them. George had a funny feeling in his stomach, like the times he awaited his turn in the confessional with some genuine transgression to disclosure, even though he wasn't quite certain that he actually knew what a transgression was. He did, however, understand that feeling in his stomach. It meant something bad, something scary.

As they passed John the janitor, George noticed that the janitor's face was mildly disfigured: faded acne scares, a vague maroon colouring evocative of a man who had made drinking a career and several missing teeth. George tightened his grip of his mother's hand. They continued up to the communion rail, stopped, genuflected, and knelt on a church cushion. George noticed that his mother was still holding her rosary. She bowed and then started to recite the rosary. George recognized the prayers but really didn't know the words. She was also still handing George's hand.

They were kneeling at the rail when Father O'Grady appeared from behind the altar, walked around to the front, bowed, genuflected and continued toward his visitors. He was dressed in a plain black cassock, an informal vestment, the first time either of them had seen a priest not dressed for mass. He came down the steps and greeted his two congregants. He recognized them. It was Thelma and her son George. "Good morning, Mrs. Gagnon, Father Handley asked me to meet with you and your son here. His name is George, isn't it?" His mother nodded. Father O'Grady smiled, reached out and tousled his hair. "Father Handley told me that you two are having problems. I understand that your husband, James Gagnon, recently died and you and your son are desperate to find a place to live." Thelma looked up to gaze at Father O'Grady, tears in her eyes, and slowly nodded. "You know your husband, God rest his soul, came to see me several months ago." Thelma looked surprised. "He told me that he wasn't much of parishioner, only coming to mass the odd Sunday, to please you I would imagine, but he still came to me to discuss your situation." The Father paused for a moment and then continued with his recounting of his meeting with her husband. "He said that he wanted to leave you and George ---- he understood that the Church does not allow divorce, that the only way he could legitimately leave you and your son would be an annulment which, as you may know, is difficult to obtain." Thelma nodded again, her tears evaporating. She spoke. "I know that, Father. James and I never discussed it, that is when he was alive, but I know that annulments are hardly ever allowed. In an annulment, the church basically says that the marriage didn't really exist. But now that he is gone, I guess that doesn't matter anymore."

Father O'Grady then suggested that they continue their conversation in the front pew. Thelma and George got up to a standing position and took up seats in the front pew. Father O'Grady joined them. Thelma had stopped whimpering and was concentrating on listening to Father O'Grady. Meanwhile, George had spent most of the visit staring at the various features of the internal church architecture ----- the statutes, the paintings, the vaulted ceiling, the stained glass windows, the dimly lit lanterns which seemed to be swaying, and of most interest to George, the stations of the cross, carved reliefs depicting the fourteen acts of Christ's crucifixion. He seemed to be mesmorized by the stations, pretending to listen to Father O'Grady, who wasn't making much sense to him anyway. Neither Thelma nor Father O'Grady seemed to notice that George wasn't exactly listening to either them. He was just sitting there, his eyes still staring at the stations of the cross, as if he was searching for something.

Father O'Grady and his mother continued to discuss their situation. He wasn't listening to the conversation. Sensing that it was completely unnecessary, the good father discontinued his clarification of the canon law on the subject of the annulment of marriage. "We obviously have to concentrate on the boy and yourself. I think both of you need immediate help." There was then a lull in the conversation. George started to lean on his mother's shoulder. Thelma then responded to Father O'Grady's assurance. "Yes, Father, we need immediate help. In two weeks, George and I won't have a place to live. I don't have a job. I can't get any help from my family. My mother is elderly and lives in Toronto and my brother, well my brother, I don't know where he lives, maybe out west somewhere I think. I haven't seen or spoken to him in a year. And James, well James didn't leave me or my son with a cent. I don't know what we are going to do. I've gone to the welfare office on Notre-Dame Street. They said that they could give us a few dollars now but we would have to wait weeks for regular relief but not enough to pay for a decent place anyway. Some of the neighbours have been kind enough to pitch in but they really can't afford anything like that. My son and I have been praying a lot." Thelma then exhaled, a sound of desperation. She then put her head down on her chest. With that admission, Thelma felt like resuming her weeping but didn't. She was still shaking and holding George's hand tightly.

Father O'Grady shook his head slowly, very slowly. He then leaned forward and gently patted Thelma on her shoulder. George looked up at Father O'Grady and noticed that one of his eyes was blue and the other was green. His grey hair was thinning and he smelt of cigarettes. He had poor teeth. He then spoke again, this time sounding like he was giving one of his sermons during mass on Sunday and weekdays. George thought he was listening to a voice from heaven. "I realize that keeping a roof over your head is the most important thing to your son and yourself now. I have spoken to the sisters down at the Catholic Community Services. They told me that they have a couple of apartments available in the area. They provide temporary lodging, you know for parishioners who are in difficult circumstances, just like your son and yourself. You could move in one of them today if you want. You would have to wait a week or so for the other. We have found permanent homes for the people who were living in those places."

Thelma looked at him and, for the first time since George and her entered Saint Willibrord, she smiled. There were dried tears on her cheeks. George looked up at his mother and then joined his mother in smiling. "I can't thank you enough for anything you can do. We have been looking for a place, even a room somewhere but, as I said, we don't have any money to pay for one. I thought, I thought that maybe some kindly landlord would lend us a room, at least until we get welfare, or I get a job." Father O'Grady was looking down at the two of them with a beatific look on his face. He smiled and nodded. "Well, as I say, we have two places available, one on Willibrord and the other on 4th Avenue. As I said, you can move into the place around the corner immediately but you'll have to wait a week or so for the other." Thelma grasped the sleeve of his right arm and leaned into him. George turned his gaze toward Father O'Grady who seemed to be praying.

They moved into the place on Willibrord Street three days after it was offered it to them. They had gone over to inspect the apartment immediately after they had been informed about its availability. It was located on the first floor of a rundown Edwardian era mansion. The second and third floors of the building provided single rooms, each floor was equipped with single toilets and showers. It was much smaller than their place on Brown Boulevard, a living room just large enough for a moderately sized sofa-bed, a television set, a record player, a small coffee table, a tiny bathroom, barely bigger than a closet and an oblong shaped kitchen that barely accommodated a two person Formica table, a stove, a small refrigerator and a sink. George would sleep in a small room that also accommodated a dresser containing the clothes belonging to both of them. There was also a clothes rack by the door for their coats. The front door for their apartment featured a medium sized glass window. There was also small door in the kitchen although it was nailed shut, suggesting that it was never intended to be opened. It was windowless and faced the east side of the house. There were four wooden stairs down to the ground. Two steps away was a rusting fence and four steps away from that was an another old house in decline although it did not seem to be a rooming house.

The monthly rent on their apartment was $35, an amount that St. Willibrord's paid out of the collection plate for the first two months they lived there. In addition, for several weeks after they moved, Father O'Grady provided Thelma and her son with $10 every Sunday after mass. Within three weeks, Thelma was able to find a position as a salesperson at June's Dress Shop on Brillantine Avenue, an ironic development since James had made a living working in the Eaton store downtown. In any event, 85 cents an hour working at a job in a store in the neighbourhood was, in her words to Father O'Grady, a godsend. Overall, she appreciated her good fortune, which she attributed to the Almighty, at least in the presence of Father O'Grady.

Surprisingly, George's daily life was hardly disturbed, at least in his eight year old mind, his eighth birthday having been recently celebrated. He still walked to school at Saint Gabriel's every morning, starting at eight o'clock, fifteen minutes before his mother left for June's Dress Shop. He had been given a key to their new apartment although he usually didn't need it. Most, if not all days, he walked home from school with his friend Pete, who lived several doors down on Brown Boulevard, and stayed at his place. Pete's mother Florence, Pete's two brothers and Pete's sister took care of Pete and George until George's mother came home at five thirty in the evening. Pete's father Val usually arrived home at six o'clock after two or three quarts at the local tavern, the Dominion. George was usually gone home by then. Thelma was reluctant, however, to allow George to stay with the Butlers, seeing as how both parents were confirmed drinkers.

George's father used to call both of Pete's parents "booze hounds", slander that would have surely disqualified the Butlers from taking care of his son, regardless of his son's affection for Mrs. Butler. Although Thelma also thought them bad influences, perhaps even more so, she was still relieved that Florence Butler had offered, quite incidentally, to look after George. She needed someone to look after George now that she had a job that did not have her getting home before five thirty. She felt, even though the Butler children as well as their parents, were seldom well behaved, their reputation as neighbourhood trouble makers shared by more than just Thelma, she still felt that she didn't have a choice. Besides, as someone like Mrs. Rossenti might have said, George seemed pretty well behaved most of the time, which might have insulated him from the influence of the Butlers.

But just to make sure, Thelma would ask George for a report on the days' events before he went to bed most nights. So she was relatively satisfied that the Butler children had not exerted an undue bad influence on George. On the other hand, her son, previously as honest as he was cute, could have learned deception from the three Butler boys, two of whom were sometimes suspected of shop lifting from local stores, stealing bicycles from local parks and otherwise getting in trouble in Saint Gabriel's, Dickie being in grade four and his brother Julian in grade three. If the situation was not as difficult as it was, it was unlikely that Thelma would have allowed Florence Butler to look after her boy or allow her boy to hang around with boys like Dickie and

Julien. But she did. But as she told herself countless times, she had no choice.

Over the next few months, the daily life of Thelma and George Gagnon ran rather smoothly considering the circumstances of their new life. Thelma was relieved to realize that by the time the school year ended, the day before St. Jean Baptiste Day, George had almost forgotten his father entirely, a process that he always thought began that day when he first saw his father hit mother across the face. The summer lay ahead for George, his first summer without his mother looking after him. In this case, Florence Butler and her three boys would be supervising George's activities without the discipline of Saint Gabriel's. Thelma was understandably worried, no telling what the Butler boys would get into, the two boys who seemed unwilling or unable to control themselves. She had unpleasant, if not frightening thoughts of poor little George getting into all sorts of trouble, including ultimately landing George in reform school or foster care although she wasn't sure that the former was a possibility for someone as young as George. But again, as she had understood from the moment she allowed Mrs. Butler to take charge of her George, she knew she had no choice. She thought of again seeking the counsel of Father O'Grady but was reluctant, believing that not only had the good Father already done enough but he might involve the Butler family directly, believing that the Butler family, who also belonged to the Saint Willibrord parish, might benefit from more frequent church attendance church or more prayer. So she was left to worry about her son alone. She thought she had no option.

Strangely enough, an option that she had not considered,

even though her boss at June's Dress Shop, Gladys Denman, who had become her confidante if not her best friend, had suggested it. She suggested that Thelma she try to think about attracting another husband, a possibility that she had seldom considered. She couldn't bring herself to look for another husband although Gladys Denman insisted that it may not be too hard to find one. She thanked Gladys for her proposition but told her that she could not bring herself to look for one, a prevarication that she hoped would keep her from pestering her about the matter. She was worried, even profoundly distressed by the possibility that a stepfather could somehow influence George away from the fact that his father had been murdered by the two of them. She had a reoccurring bad dream that George would turn away from her. She could not take the chance. But that did not last long.

George Learns Something

He was eight years old and soon to enter grade three. Recently, he had momentarily befriended his two cousins, boys named Allan and Patrick Gagnon, the sons of his dead father's brother Robert. They had moved into the neighbourhood eight months ago, having previously lived in Ville LaSalle, less than several miles away. The boys were twelve and eleven years old respectively, older than George but generally comfortable with their younger cousin who basically regarded the two cousins as heroes, both of whom prompted something close to worship in George. Even before their family moved to a flat closer to his place, which was on Rielle Street, a block away from Brown Boulevard, where Thelma had rented a two bedroom about a year ago, George saw his cousins at least once a month, the two Gagnon brothers already being fairly close to each other. But now, now that they were living practically right around the corner, almost living on the same street, seeing them as often as he did, practically every day it seemed, George found himself feeling that Allan and Patrick were not only his cousins but his brothers as well. At the same time, George was no longer close to the Butler boys, mainly because the Butler family had moved away, to Dorval where they bought a new three bedroom bungalow in a new suburban development. They also were going to a new school, Saint Thomas Elementary, which was apparently constructed specifically for new suburban communities in both Dorval and Lachine.

That summer, George may have had an epiphany, as Father O'Grady might have called it, when his new friends, the cousins Allan and Patrick, took him along on a local shoplifting tour of selected Verdun grocery stores. It was a Wednesday morning in August. The two cousins were walking east along Brown Boulevard from their place on Rielle Street when they spotted George bouncing a rubber ball against the brick wall of the maintenance shed that stood on the traffic median between the two separate directions of the divided street. Patrick, the younger brother and the more mischievous of the two, stepped in front of George as they passed and caught George's three colour stripped ball as it bounced off the wall. The two brothers then laughed. Patrick held the ball and then pretended to throw the ball toward the other side of the street. George had his hands out, hoping for Patrick to throw him the ball. Allan then spoke to him, asking him if he was going anywhere. "How about coming with us? We thinking of doing a little crookin'." George had previously heard the two boys refer to this recreation, although he wasn't exactly certain that he knew what "crookin" was although he had the impression that it was something that he shouldn't do. He never thought of asking the boys to explain the activity but, on this particular day, he agreed to find out by participating in the their entertainment. Allan and Patrick both smiled and waved him up to join them. The three started to walk east on Brown Boulevard. Their destination was Laviolette's grocery store, probably the oldest grocery store in Verdun. It had been run, and was still being run by a Laviolette, the current owner being Pierre Laviolette, supposedly the great grandson of Emile Laviolette who founded a small store on the corner of Galt and Wellington, where it still stood, more than a hundred years ago.

The three of them walked into the store and stopped to talk to the cashier whose name was Claudette. Allan and Patrick were quite familiar with her, having frequented the store for a couple of years. George stood mute behind the two of them. Claudette had been working in Laviolette's for almost twenty years, a little longer than she had been married to Pierre Laviolette's best friend, whose name was Aleck Cormier. Allan handed Claudette the cashier a short note. It was signed by their mother, Diane Gagnon and asked Claudette --- actually it was addressed "To whom it may concern" ---- to provide them three packs of cigarettes. This was pretty well the normal procedure in most neighbourhoods in those days. This invariably meant that any kid holding a note from his father or mother or uncle or aunt asking for products normally limited to sale to adults, could buy beer or cigarettes without question. In some cases, particularly cases where the kids were well known in the store, notes were not necessary. In the case of Allan and Patrick, there was a certain interesting irony to some of their transactions at Laviolette's. The notes in those cases, and there were many of them, were plagiarized versions of legitimate notes given to them by their mother. Allan would try to duplicate his mother's handwriting but slowly realized that it never really mattered. Claudette barely looked at the notes anyway, whether they were legitimate or not.

On this day, George's duty, as instructed by Allan or Patrick or both of them, was to stuff as many as chocolate bars as he could in his dungarees while the two boys were distracting Claudette at the cashier counter. His technique, as instructed by Allan in particular, was to drop the rubber ball he had been playing with on the floor, go down on his hands and knees to pick it up, and steal as many bars as he could before declaring that he found the ball and stand up. Of course, George was as nervous as hell but went ahead anyway. By the time the transaction between Allan and Claudette was complete, Allan having provided 75 cents to Claudette who gave the boys three packs of Matinees, George was standing by the door, his pants bulging with maybe a six chocolate bars, equally divided between O'Henry and Snickers bars. As soon as the boys left the store, all three started to laugh, George, in addition to joining the others in laughing, had noticed that he had peed his pants sometime during the operation.

Both Allan and Patrick slapped him on the back and all three continued down Galt Street. They were headed toward the park across from Steinberg's, the largest grocery store in Verdun, if not the entire island of Montreal. George imagined that Steinberg's was the group's next target for theft. The three of them sat on a bench and shared the chocolate bars, eating two bars each, then throwing the wrappers in the park garage can. Two ladies with baby carriages went by, wondering for a moment what three boys were doing on a Wednesday morning sitting on a park bench furtively eating chocolate bars. The boys sat for maybe twenty minutes, Allan and Patrick pondering their next move, sitting there across from Steinberg's. It was getting close to lunch, George now wondering whether he would have to return home for lunch shortly. He raised the matter of lunch with his two recently established compatriots. "Don't worry about that. Your mother knows that you are with us. She told us to look after you today. She wanted to do some shopping downtown, so she wasn't going to be home until this afternoon. She gave me five dollars to buy lunch for the three of us at either Johnny's or McDermot's. " George looked a little dumbfounded but managed a small smile. Having his two cousins look after him was certainly more exciting than having his mother ordering him to stay in front of the house. He didn't realize, however, that he was going to be spending the day participating in a crime spree. It was still more stimulating than bouncing a rubber ball against the maintenance shed in front of his house on Brown Boulevard.

They entered Steinberg's and first went to the back of the store to watch the store butcher swing a cleaver. As the butcher swung a cleaver, the counter man stepped forward to serve two ladies. In the meantime, as Patrick and George watched the counter man and the butcher, Allan was quietly stuffing packaged processed meats in the waistband of his shorts. He was on his knees below the glass counter. Within a couple of minutes, he tapped Patrick on his leg below the knee, looked behind him and then away. He was now headed for the bakery department where he intended to lift three buns from the bins to accommodate the processed baloney and salami that he had just placed in his shorts. He had planned to place the buns underneath his shirt and stride casually out the front door. In the meantime, Patrick and George, alerted to step two of Allan's plan, were already out of the door.

Theft successful, all three of them walked less than a block away from the scene of the crime when Allan and Patrick broke into their usual laughter. After a short interval, George joined in their self-congratulatory merriment. Allan and Patrick thought they both had developed some of skill. After maybe six months of shoplifting and occasional breaking into houses for no reasons other than to mess the places up, they were now experienced burglars, invulnerable to capture by the apparently blind, deaf and dumb merchants. George was almost in awe of their youthful bravado. As they sat on another bench a block or so away from Steinberg's munching on their stolen lunch, Allan and Patrick started to plan their afternoon activities, presumably more felonious than stealing processed meat, stale buns and before that, morning chocolates. Allan and Patrick then went ahead and attempted to enlist George in their afternoon plans. As he sat eating his salami in a bun, Patrick had complained about the absence of mustard and butter, an observation that resulted in a shove from Allan. George just listened. They were telling him that they planned to head downtown on the city bus to the stores on St. Catherine Street, hoping to see what they could steal from Woolworth's or Simpson's or Eaton's. George did not want to accompany his two cousins. He was nervous, guilty about the chocolate bar theft, worried that his cousins would somehow persuade him, or even force him to take actions that he knew he would regret. Maybe even his mother would know. He didn't know. He was scared. Someone, aside from his cousins, would know. He guessed that his epiphany, or whatever it had been, had passed. He never went downtown with the cousins again.

As the summer and his graduation to grade three progressed, George tried to avoid his cousins Allan and Patrick. It wasn't that difficult. Even though they were impressed with his occasional inventiveness in lifting chocolate bars, dessert treats, soft drinks, comic books and cheap trinkets from a variety of local drugstores, grocery and convenience stores, they had started to believe that George was usually too nervous to continue to assist them in their felonious exploits. It took the two of them a couple of weeks to conclude that they wouldn't be inviting George to any of their future enterprises. Besides, they had successfully recruited a twelve year old boy named Gary who showed more enthusiasm than George in assisting Allan and Patrick in their endeavours. Besides, as Allan pointed out, Gary had a nice looking sister named Gwen, who he had been pursuing unsuccessfully for some time. A relationship with her brother might give him an advantage, at least he thought it would. Gary Gibson came from a large family, seven children, five girls, including Gwen, and two boys, including Gary. He used to be a relatively well behaved boy, at least in the first four or five grades of Saint Gabriel's elementary but somehow in grade six, he started to act out, almost threatening to go off the rails. The teacher, a relatively young man named Clark who was in only his second year of teaching, was expending more effort in controlling his class than teaching them anything. Gary Gibson just made things worse for Mr. Clark.

Although most of his pupils were eleven or twelve years

old, some were sixteen years old in Mr. Clark's class, boys who had failed various grades before landing in grade six. It was the procedure in those days to allow boys who failed on multiple occasions to attend the same grades several times before allowing them to leave school, the truant officers finally able to abandon them, sixteen years old being the reference point. In those days, a sixteen year old, regardless of his academic record, could actually get a job at the local brick factory, the steel works at Dominion Engineering, at the many gas stations in the area, or at the bowling alleys and pool halls in the neighbourhoods of Verdun and surrounding environs. Sometime in the spring of the year just past, Gary had started to hang around with, veneration was a more likely description of their relationship, the chain smoking Mitch Fuller, a sixteen year old classmate who drove to class on a motorcycle and had a girlfriend who sported a bee hive hairdo and worked in a local beauty parlour. Although he didn't know where Mitch ended up after leaving elementary school for the last time, which was that spring, jail was sometimes rumoured, it was Gary's theory that he was working with a guy named Norbert at the gas station on Wellington Street.

As for George, his mother was a trifle worried when she discovered that he was hanging around with Allan and Patrick, the two nephews who most of the family thought were more than a little mischievous, complaints about their misconduct often circulating at family gatherings. On the other hand, the cousins' mother Angela was the chief grumbler about her sons' supposedly unacceptable behaviour. Angela asked Thelma whether she had noticed anything unusual about George's behaviour. She had shrugged and asked her why she was asking. Angela told her that she was suspected that Allan and Patrick had persuaded George to start smoking, saying that she thought her two sons were sneaking more cigarettes from her purse than usual. Thelma smiled and nodded, telling her that she suspected that her son too was sneaking the cigarettes although she didn't think he was smoking them, suggesting that he was procuring them for classmates, particularly the older ones. Angela asked "Who would ask George to do this?" Thelma smiled again and allowed it to grow into a laugh. "Who knows? Maybe every kid older than George." Angela knew that kids sometimes were given notes from their parents asking for cigarettes or beer. So she asked Thelma: "Why don't kids wanting cigarettes just forge notes from their mothers or fathers." Thelma just looked befuddled for a moment and then answered with a certain uncertainty. "Well, maybe not every mother or father trusts their kids enough to give them notes for cigarettes or...". She paused for a moment and added, "or maybe they don't smoke." Angela smiled and come up with a slight snicker. "Who doesn't smoke?" Their conversation about their sons and cigarettes ended without further judgement. They agreed, however, that they both should watch their boys a little more closely from then on. They both knew that it was probably unlikely but they thought it was probably their responsibility anyway.

His teacher for grade three was a middle aged woman named Miss Dewan. No one in the class knew her first name. The rumour, at least among the third graders, was that Miss Dewan did not even have a first name. They were at least two dozen boys in the third grade that had been in the grade two with each other and they didn't know her first name. George's desk was three seats over in the second row, between boys named Bob Conrad and Jim Sasia, both of whom had been in grades one and two with George. He sat behind a kid named Richard Burns and in front of a kid named Mark Douglas, the latter two also classmates in his previous grades. George had started to contemplate on what basis students were assigned specific desks. In his first year at Saint Gabriel's under the dictatorial Miss McCarthy, George sat in the fourth of six rows, two from the window and three from the door while in the second grade, he was provided a desk in the second row, only a couple of feet it seemed away from the desk of his teacher, Miss Ekins. He had concluded that he had somehow displeased the school administration, mainly that he was somehow a threat to the orderly conduct of Miss Ekins' class. With the grade three architecture putting him in generally the same location as he had inhabited in grade two, a year in which he committed few, if any transgressions, he was further mystified as to the basis for the seating plan of each class. He was particularly confused since the class troublemakers, Jimmy Baker and Pat Gogarty, were seated at the rear of the room where they were able to terrorize their classmates at their leisure it seemed, that is when they weren't seated outside the principal's office, waiting for whatever penalty their most recent wrongdoings would deserve.

Over the early months of his sojourn in grade three, George joined with his seatmates Bob Conrad and Jim Sasia in developing steady friendships. The three of them became, more or less, the class clowns, an evolution that made them popular with their classmates. Their act was relatively predictable. They whispered jokes, a lot of which being lifted from newspaper comics, they emitted fart noises, which they usually pretended had come from another area of the class, made steady fun of their fellow classmates, even making fun of the teachers, particularly Miss Dewan and the principal, an unusually dour man named Malone. They also occasionally threw spitballs across the class. They would try to perform this tomfoolery while Miss Dewan had her back to her class but not always. Even Jimmy Baker and Pat Gogarty, who previously had dominated class antics, basically left them alone most of the time, their entertainment value enough to afford them a certain protection.

On the other hand, Miss Dewan did not allow them any such protection. Although she sometimes had the habit of informing her colleagues of their actions, particularly those who seemed actually humorous to Miss Dewan, their effect on their classmates was enough to prompt her to keep a careful eye on them. Every now and then, especially if their behaviour was particularly annoying, her capacity for tolerance would compel Miss Dewan to discipline at least one of them. She would send the lucky comedian to explain his wit to Mr. Malone who everyone knew was hardly appreciative of humour of any kind. Still, all three of the boys were equally culpable targets of Miss Dewan's surveillance. George was convinced that Miss Dewan suspected that he was the ringleader although he disagreed with her assessment, believing that she was biased against him because he invariably came up with the funniest comments about her, most of which were suitably moronic to easily entertain a bunch of eight year olds.

The Biography of George

The antics of three class clowns had grown tiresome however, at least to both Miss Dewan and Mr. Malone who virtually stopped disciplining them or even threatening to discipline them. The strategy was developed over a couple of months. Miss Dewan had discussed the problem posed by the three of them with not only other teachers but with Mr. Malone himself. After considering advice from them and Principal Malone, Miss Dewan came up with the idea that if she ignored the boys' antics, they would stop them. They knew that their classmate audience, who certainly had heard their routines more than once, would still laugh, no matter how many times they had witnessed their theatrics but maybe they would disregard them if they thought they weren't having much effect on the teacher. Surprisingly enough, their strategy worked to some extent. While class appreciation remained tangible enough, guffaws slowly began to fade, from roars to chuckles to little more than snickers, the lack of possible penalty having the desired effect. The class had started to believe that if Miss Dewan wasn't going to do anything about it, then whatever shenanigans the three class clowns had just pulled probably wasn't as funny as they thought they were. To the class, an appropriate reaction from Miss Dewan was like a laugh track on a television or radio show. Years later, one of George's classmates from grade three was to make that observation.

It was just after he turned nine years old, in the first week after Christmas, that Bob Conrad, thinking himself the most adventurous of the three, informed his two friends that over the holidays, he had come up with a plan to steal things from the school supply store, a small room near the principal's office that sold pens, pencils, and other scholarly utensils to pupils with money from their parents. He later said that the plan was inspired by a short story he had read in an anthology of Catholic adventure tales he had received from his parents for Christmas. Actually, it was a story of a boy who had taken to occasionally pilfering odd items from a local church for reasons that were never explained. The story was relatively simple, no particular strategy was involved in stealing the objects, small statues, candles, prayer books in the pulpit, weekly parish notices neatly stacked in the vestibule, and religious pictures of various kinds. The boy in the story never went near anything that had been left on the altar or the steps leading to the altar, again without any explanation. It had been an aside. Predictably, the story concluded when the boy, whose name in the story was Matthew, was caught by the parish priest, an unnamed liturgical lummox who punished him with six strokes on each hand with a wide cincture, a rope-like article sometimes worn around the waist by corpulent members of the clergy. Years later, when someone asked him regarding stories that may have inspired him, he mentioned the story, which was entitled "The Boy Who Stole Things in Church". That was when he also realized that the story book collection was likely published by the Catholic Church and the reason his parents had given him the book in the first place.

In any event, he managed to convince George and Jim to go along with what they may have thought in latter years to be a ridiculous and dangerous plan. But, as again they may have reflected years from then, they were in grade three and ridiculous behaviour was understandable, if not expected. But of course there was the invariable conundrum of agreeing on a strategy for actually stealing something from the school store. Bob proposed asking for a pencil or a ruler or an eraser or something generally inexpensive and, while paying for the item, dropping a coin over the bottom half of the Dutch door to the store. While the kid in charge, usually a beyond reproach seventh grader, bent down to retrieve the coin or coins, Bob would reach into the room and grab whatever was in reach, a small item, like a portable pencil sharpener for example, and stow it in his trousers while the kid was still looking for the coin or coins. George's idea was a variant of Bob's, having the buyer stepping into the supply room and offer to help look for the coin. In the meantime, one of the other two boys would sneak into the supply room and make off with whatever he could slip into his pants. With George's idea offering a broader range of articles available for theft, it was a favourite. Finally, Jim's idea was a variant of Bob's scheme. He proposed having one of them ask for an article on a back shelf and then, while the clerk's back was turned, steal whatever he could. They decided to go with Jim's proposal. It seemed simpler than the other two suggestions.

It was Tuesday afternoon at recess. They were relatively certain that they would not be interrupted that afternoon, the supply room only opened for thirty minutes before school and at the fifteen minute morning and afternoon intervals. Customers on the Tuesday afternoon were particularly few. All three of them immediately left class as soon as the bell rang for Tuesday afternoon recess, hurried to the supply room, which fortunately was also on the first floor, and waited for the seventh grader assigned to the supply room to arrive. They stood by the door a couple minutes before a tall kid who all three of them recognized from the school yard arrived. They usually saw him lingering alone staring through the fence. He wore a checked shirt and denim dungarees, an outfit that was accessorized by horn-rimmed eyeglasses and a pocket caddy. He passed by the three clowns, placed a silver key in the door, opened the supply room and turned on the light. He then closed the bottom half of the door and turned toward the three customers.

"What can I get you?" the seventh grader asked, a semi-sneer emerging on his face, the kind of contemptuous smile that someone in seventh grade usually showed someone in grade three. Jim was standing less than a foot from the door with Bob and George behind him. All three of them were apprehensive although Jim seemed the least nervous. He took one step forward and pointed at the three tan coloured knapsacks sitting on a top shelf. "I'd like to look at one of those knapsacks, the ones leaning on the back wall." The top shelf was maybe seven or eight feet from the door. A small stepladder sat against the back wall. The tall kid lost the sneer, stared at Jim and the other two boys, turned his back and headed for the knapsacks. As the tall kid walked to the rear of the store, Jim quietly pushed the half door open and crept part way into the supply room. He checked the tall kid. His back was to the door. He had pushed the stepladder to the back wall and had started to climb toward the top shelf and the knapsacks. Jim did not have too long to remove anything from the store. He glanced at the cash register which sitting to the left of the door and thought, for a fleeting moment, of trying to open it. But he quickly realized that he could not open the register without making noise. So he passed on the idea.

The tall kid was just about to bring one of the knapsacks

down from the top when he dropped it. That gave Jim additional time to select items to lift. There were several boxes of coloured crayons on a shelf. Jim picked up two boxes and threw one to each of his confederates outside of the door. He then placed several erasers in one of his front pockets, some pencils in the other and he was keeping a small math kit containing the usual equipment for himself. He started closing the half door when from the rear of the store came an exhortation from the tall kid, practically shouting. He was holding a knapsack. "Hey, where are you kids going? Hold it, I have a knapsack for you.", the latter pronouncement a ridiculous remark considering the boys' intentions. Then another exhortation. "What have you got in your hand there?" The tall kid dropped the knapsack and started towards them. All three of the thieves turned and started to flee, Jim still with the math kit still in his hand and the other two each still holding a box of crayons. Two or three steps into the hallway in front of the supply room, all three ran straight into Mr. Ascoli, a young grade six teacher, who grabbed both Bob and George by the arms and ordered Jim, in a very loud voice, to stop. A small crowd began to gather, obviously curious. Mr. Ascoli directed the three of them to hand over the items they had attempted to steal and accompany him to the Principal's office.

All three of them looked to be in shock, no tears yet, no pleas yet, as they placed the crayon boxes, the erasers, the pencils, and the math kit on the counter top of the half door to the supply room. They then turned to follow Mr. Ascoli down the hall and then right to Principal Malone's office. The crowd was growing as they walked. Just before the corner, Mr. Ascoli turned and scattered the crowd with an authoritarian glance. The three miscreants had turned the corner and had stopped in front of the Mr. Malone's office. The Principal's secretary Nelda Strobe seemed to have been expecting them. By the time Mr. Ascoli joined them, two of them, Bob Conrad and Jim Sasi, were weeping while George Gagnon had never started and was just standing there with a strange little smile on his face. He also seemed to be talking to himself. All three of them should have been expecting the worst although George did not seem to be particularly concerned, that strange little smile suggesting that Principal Malone was simply going to ignore his transgression and concentrate any consideration of penalty on the other two. Maybe it was possible that he did not seem to be scared of Principal Malone but his two partners doubted that.

In any event, all three were ushered into the office of doom by Miss Strobe who had, as always, a mildly menacing look on her face. As she left the three of them with Principal Malone, who was standing rocking back and forth with his hands behind his back. He too had a menacing look on his face. Miss Strobe closed the door as he left them with Principal Malone. She stood by the door for several moments and heard the sound of the official school belt, a hard, corrugated plastic and leather instrument of corporal punishment, being applied to the upraised hand of a nine year boy. She then heard the first of a series of relatively quiet howls of pain, sounds that she did not often hear but to which she was admittedly accustomed. They went on for at least ten minutes. Miss Strobe estimated that the three of them must have received six biffs on each hand, the final degree of punishment for elementary school infractions. She was seated at her desk when the three boys left Principal

Malone's office, holding their hands tightly underneath their armpits, muffled weeping and their faces still glistening with tears. Miss Strobe, usually inured to such displays, sat at her desk, apparently oblivious, staring. She did tell them that they could now leave school.

By the time George arrived home that day, his mother was telephoned at work to be informed of her son's encounter with Principal Malone. Miss Strobe had telephoned the mothers of the three almost immediately after George and his two friends had been released from the office. She was sitting at the kitchen table, smoking maybe the umpteenth cigarette since she got the news of George's crime. If his father was still alive, which he wasn't, an army belt, a black army belt that had hung in the kitchen by the refrigerator, would be sitting in his mother's lap. It would be waiting for his father to use it to inflict more corporal punishment on him, six on each palm would be appropriate. George remembered that his father once applied the belt to his naked buttocks for throwing a couple of peas at his cousin Patrick during Sunday dinner. But both he and his army belt were gone and his mother, his widowed mother just sat there at the kitchen table, looking sympathetic, almost contemplative. She just told him to go to his room. That was the conclusion of her consideration of the attempted robbery of the supply room of Saint Gabriel's Elementary School.

The next day, he went back to school, along with his two confederates. He met up with them maybe fifteen minutes before school started. George was certain, in so far as any kid his age could be certain about anything, that news of their little escapade would be all over the schoolyard before morning recess, the obvious source being the supply room kid. The idea that a trio of boys in the grade three attempted such an auspicious robbery was notable enough to provide gossip for weeks after the event itself. Some of the older boys were impressed enough to acknowledge George and his pals anytime they saw them in the schoolyard and the hallways. They kept saluting them for at least a week after the incident. George was quite proud of the celebration of his accomplishment, as were his two friends.

George in High School

He was in grade ten at John Grant High School, which was on Parkhaven Street in a working class neighbourhood of Lachine. He was almost sixteen years old. His mother Thelma had moved to Lachine on Notre Dame Street more than two years ago. And maybe more importantly, she was regularly seeing a man named Norman, who she met at an event sponsored by her new parish, the Resurrection of Our Lord church on 34th Street, which was a block or so away from their new apartment. He worked as a millwright at the Dominion Engineering on First Avenue in Lachine. He was making a good living, union wages, including a fair amount of overtime, a situation that allowed Norman to occasionally help out George's mother financially, her relatively new job at the Rossy Department Store on Remembrance Street in Lachine not paying much more than June's Dress Shop in Verdun did. As a result, things seemed a lot less strained at home than it had been over the past several years. For once, his mother seemed happy. They weren't on the verge of poverty anymore, his mother wasn't worrying about their next rental payment, they were now living in a house that wasn't a dump, the two of them now living in a place that was roughly double the size of the last three places in which they had lived in Lachine, all of which meant that his mother wasn't on the verge of depression most of the time. George too was relatively happy with the move to Lachine, having relocated several times in the last few years he spent in Verdun.

So George was fairly content, certainly more content than he was over the past decade or so, ever since his father James died and plunged he and his mother into poverty. He had made a number of friends in his grade ten class in John Grant, three boys he met playing bantam hockey in Carriere Park. From there, they started doing a lot of things together, playing on sports teams, sneaking smokes from their parents, hanging out at the park, and taking the bus downtown on Saturdays, where they would occasionally shoplift from the stores. They also spent a lot of time discussing the pursuit of girls, which was understandably difficult for the three boys whose experience was limited to say the least. Despite his lack of experience, the fact was that George was the playboy of the group, actually having a girlfriend, a girl named Beverly, their first date attending a school dance theatrically called the "Harvest Hop". The other two guys, Allan and Stanley did not have the same luck. They attended the occasional teen dance at the local community centre, as did George before he was involved with Beverly, leaning on the walls, a cliche of adolescent boys who spent a lot of time looking for girlfriends by staring at them.

Beverly was an attractive girl, also in grade ten but in Bishop Whelan, another Lachine high school. Amazingly enough, Beverly was also adopted, just like George had been although he believed that she was almost three years old when her parents, who were much older than most of the parents in the neighbourhood, brought her home. Their names were Hector and Irene Mills and they could not be happier. Beverly was their only child and would remain.

Strangely enough, his two friends were not envious of George. Aside from expressing disappointment when George wasn't available to join them in weekend pastimes, like attending Junior A hockey games at the Lachine Arena, going to the community dances, or going to La Cyr tavern on Notre-Dame Street where anyone of any age with a dollar could be served enough draft beers to get righteously drunk, they had to admit simple admiration. George sometimes joined them when he wasn't accompanying Beverly to the movies, to school dances, where they liked to dance every song like it was a waltz, or watching television at Beverly's place, where they spent more time making out than taking in the latest episode of *The Fugitive*. Still, for the most part, his weekends were already spoken for. On the other hand, the three of them were together most of the time during the week, that is when George wasn't with Beverly, which was seldom since she went to another high school. Allan and Stanley occasionally had a date with one girl or another although, try as they might, neither of them were able to interest them in more regular arrangements, like being their boyfriends. They occasionally thought of seeking advice from their friend George but neither of them ever got around to asking him. Besides, they never really thought that George would have any advice to give anyway. Allan and Stanley, when discussing the matter, had often concluded that George's relationship with Beverly was a matter of luck.

Regardless of the fortune that brought the two of them

together, George and Beverly were an enviable adolescent couple, puppy love at its peak. Some of his classmates, including his friends Allan and Stanley, thought that the two of them were "doing it", an extraordinary state of affairs most thought in view of their ages and the serious taboo against teenage sex, at least among Catholic teens at the time. The story was of course completely false although it did give the couple a reputation that was unwanted, particularly by Beverly. There was little doubt though that the couple was involved in a seriously passionate romance, an engagement that was almost poetic. George was almost intoxicated, madly in love with Beverly, a feeling that went well beyond adolescent infatuation, or so he thought. It was his first great love. It was as simple as that.

In late December, things changed. Winter had arrived and Christmas vacation provided the blessed couple with apparently idyllic circumstances. During the holidays, they would go skating most afternoons, they would have dinner on every second Saturday at a local restaurant named Tony's Italian with Beverly's parents who would then go to bingo night and Beverly and George would spend romantic evenings at her house. As for George, his mother liked Beverly a lot, thought she was a "nice little girl". Norman, however, did not want to encourage the besotted couple to get any closer, fearing that they would end up getting married or "doing something equally stupid" as he put it. Despite her history, Thelma did not agree with his views on marriage although she had no desire to get married again. In any event, the couple did not spend much time at George's place.

Two days after Christmas, George was invited to a party at Pat Commander's place, one of the coolest guys in grade ten at John Grant. Commander was generally regarded as a street wise guy with whom George and a bunch of other guys sometimes played pick up hockey on the rink at Carriere Park. Coincidentally, George ended up removing his skates in the shack when Commander, who just happened to be there as well, casually asked him if he was available to attend a party he and his friend Gord were throwing. Gord was another well known guy, another junior hockey player for the Lachine Maroons. Gord used to go to John Grant but quit school a year ago to devote himself to his hockey career and working at a local gas station. In any event, when George asked Pat Commander why he was inviting him, a guy he barely knew, to a party that he and his friend Gord were having, Pat laughed and told him that he was just interested in filling the house. When he mentioned the invitation to Beverly, she laughed and said that she knew Commander's sister Barbara ---- they were both in the same class at Marymount ---- and Barbara had already invited her and a date to the party. She also said that the party was liable to be quite a bit of fun since the parents would be spending the weekend at the grandmother's place in Quebec City. George wondered why any parent would allow Pat Commander to host a party without any sort of supervision. It would probably be fun observed Beverly.

❧

She introduced herself as "Bernadette" although she said that people liked to call her "Bernie". They were was standing in the kitchen of the Commander home with maybe fifty people in various states of inebriation swirling around them. There was music playing, maybe two or three different songs seemed to be playing simultaneously, and some people were dancing, some people were standing around talking to each other, others were sitting on sofas or on the floor, all were drinking or had been drinking. Although originally reluctant to engage Bernie in conversation of any kind, more shy than anything else, he could not help but stare at her long enough to convince Bernie that he was interested in talking to her. That should not have come as a surprise to her. Fact was that Bernie looked like a fox, as particularly every male he knew might characterize her. George did not have any experience upon which to base any opinion on her popularity. The girl certainly played the part. She was quite attractive, black mid-length hair enveloping a round face that looked to be almost professionally made up, piercing blue eyes, heavy mascara, assertive maroon lipstick, all the ingredients it seemed. To complete the portrait, she was was dressed all in black, black boots, black stockings, short black skirt, and finally, a low cut black sweater holding prominent breasts between which was a fountain pen, an accessory which made remembering her almost unavoidable. He didn't have to strain to remember. He had an erection. He turned away from her, to avoid her noticing, which he doubted. He asked her if she had come with anyone. She lightly laughed, telling him that she hadn't. She did say, however, that she sometimes went out with a number of guys at the party, including Pat Commander and several of his friends. He concluded then that she was, as people of his parents' generation would have observed, a fast girl. His generation may have called her something else.

He hadn't seen Beverly for maybe twenty minutes. The last time he saw her, she was huddled with three or four girls, talking and laughing. After maybe minutes of conversation, Beverly sidled to Bernie and George a little wobbly. George introduced Bernie to Beverly. The three of them then initiated a discussion of the comparative merits of the Beatles versus the Rolling Stones. Bernie was a Stones devotee. After their discussion, George and Beverly left to get a couple of beers. Bernie handed George a small piece of paper on which she had used her fountain pen to scribble her telephone number. "Maybe we can finish our discussion later. "He doubted that Beverly saw Bernie hand him the note. She glared at her anyway and walked George away.

It was ten months since they had met at the party at the Commander house. George had turned sixteen years old more than seven months ago. He had graduated from grade ten two months ago. He had been discretely going steady with Bernie for four months when they got the news in June that Bernie was pregnant. It was an astounding piece of news considering that she and George had only been intimate twice since they began going steady in February. He still felt somewhat guilty about leaving Beverly, the so-called love of his life, for Bernie earlier in the year. But he found Bernie, with her beauty, her cleavage and her stimulating disposition, undeniably attractive, so much so that, in his sixteen year old mind, he had no choice but to end his relationship with Beverly, a decision that he later grew to regret, for the new so-called love of his life.

Their relationship changed George's life significantly. His social life, his romantic life and his relationship with his mother and her common law husband were all transformed after he and Bernie become steadies. Bernie, because of her general reputation, had a circle of friends who were a little more adventurous than he was accustomed to, often going to the back room of a local supper club called the Edge on Saint Joseph where they would drink, beer for him and mixed drinks for her, any suggestion of an appropriate drinking age irrelevant, socialize with friends of Bernie and do a little dancing. His romantic life, which with Beverly had been almost spiritual, their physical expressions of love limited to French kissing and the occasional caressing of her breasts, had changed as well. Bernie was not reluctant to allow her steady companions to feel any area of her body. With George, she would strip down to her underwear whenever she got the opportunity. As for his common law parents, they met Bernie just once, an occasion that was also accidental, they having been asked to act as chaperones to a John Grant dance that George and Bernie attended. His mother, who had been so enamoured with Beverly, was not impressed, calling her "that Jane" and making an unkind reference to her outfit that evening. It was quite provocative for a high school dance. On the other hand, his mother's common law husband, who did not care much for the virtuous Beverly, took one look at Bernie and looked to be ready to compete with his son for her hand and the rest of her body.

It had been in March that George lost his virginity, an extraordinary development given his romantic history. Bernie, who had been working to add to George's experience by presenting herself to him naked every chance she got, finally managed to introduce George to full intercourse one night after an evening at the Edge. It took Bernie a fair amount of instruction and encouragement to persuade George to finally make love. It was certainly not her first time. She knew what she was doing. He didn't. As exciting as their coupling was, as it should have been, George was somehow guilty about the entire act.

It was a couple of months later when Bernie told George that she was pregnant with his baby. He almost fainted. He grew weak, his knees almost buckled, he felt like he was going to have a heart attack. Bernie told him that she had no choice but to have the baby. Her mother had had her oldest sister Lorraine, who was ten years older than Bernie, before he and her father were married. So when she told her mother, Bernie was comforted rather than chastised. At first, her mother was contemplating making arrangements for her to have her baby at Grace Haven, a maternity residence in NDG. Her mother assumed that Bernie wouldn't like the idea although she did think that Bernie would have wondered about the circumstances that faced her when she had Lorraine. So they didn't discuss any other possibility, her mother dismissing the idea before she even brought it up. So she decided that having the baby was normal, normal for the family since her mother's mother, Bernie's grandmother had her after she left grade nine. No one in Bernie's family ever asked about the baby's father. It seemed irrelevant.

It wouldn't be irrelevant to George's side of the relationship. Almost immediately after he was told by Bernie that he was about to become a father, a strange development anytime he thought about it, he resolved never to tell anyone. Not only did few people know that he and Bernie were a couple, they went to different schools and seemed so different in terms of social and sexual experience in particular, the notion that the two were about to be parents seemed almost ludicrous. Further, his common law parents, especially his mother, seldom inquired about Bernie, although his father seemed more interested in any dalliance with Bernie, not a surprising development based on that one time he met her. He did not, however, ask about her. So his fear of being discovered was likely exaggerated although it still did not tranquilize his fears of anyone, including his parents, discovering that he and Bernie were expecting. Although it may have happened occasionally, having an illegitimate child was still regarded as a serious, if not catastrophic event. While some families, like the one to which Bernie belonged, seemed inured to such circumstances, most had embarrassing, if not humiliating effects on the future of such families. George actually thought that his mother might throw him out of the house, a prospect that frightened him.

George had no choice but to hide such an indiscretion, telling his mother and his friends, including Allan and Stanley, that Bernie had dumped him and she was now going out with a guy named Roger, another guy with a serious reputation in the neighbourhood. Roger looked like a gangster, in fact many thought he actually was, He lived on his own, worked in a local factory, always dressed in leather, and drove a Plymouth Fury, the automobile alone impressing the hell out of most of the boys who knew who he was. People might have have thought that Bernie and Roger would have made a believable couple. It would have made sense. Ironically, he heard that Bernie had taken up with a guy named Louie, actually someone who worked in the same place as Roger. He may have been a friend of Roger.

Then there was the religious angle. George no longer

attended church, ostensibly devout by pretending to attend Sunday mass by going to the park or various local snack bars instead. But he was at times secretly devout to his Catholic faith, sometimes believing that the divine would somehow punish him for various sinful acts, depending on the severity of the offence. Early in his teens and even earlier, supposed wrongdoings like stealing change from his mother's purse, cheating on tests in school, lying, swearing, and self abuse, the latter being the most significant omission of all, would prompt George and most of his contemporaries to hurry to the confessional, the faithful refuge of the sinful. But as he grew older and his sins became almost habitual, he became less concerned with his faith, to the point that it seemed lost. He hadn't been to confession for several years. He may not have been a Catholic anymore. But as agnostic as George had become and had been, his belief re-emerged with the fear that the sin with Bernie might have consigned him to perdition. He even thought of returning to the confessional. He began to plan to head downtown to go to confession in an unknown church. He never went to confession anywhere.

George hardly ever socialized with anyone in Bernie's crowd, not her friends, not her family, not with anyone who may have known her. He went to a different school, he lived more than ten blocks away. He never heard about her fate, never heard about the fate of the baby. He never knew what happened to her. He knew that he would probably never forget her.

George Moves Again

George had moved to Ottawa when he was seventeen years old to play hockey for one of three junior teams in the city. His mother and his new stepfather Norman, who had moved in with the family a year before, were still concerned about his future after several minor misadventures that could have resulted in school suspensions or rebukes from a teacher or a hockey coach, the latter becoming an important individual in his teenage life. George had played hockey for a number of years, particularly after the family had moved to Lachine. He had moved from pee wee in Verdun to bantam and then midget hockey in Lachine. He was usually regarded as one of the better players on whatever teams on which he played. It was in August of his last year in John Grant high school when, trying out for a tier two junior team in Lachine, it was suggested to him by the coach of his midget team, a peculiar man named Jumbo Cormier, that he had showed marked improvement in his play and therefore deserved to move up. So he was selected to play for the Junior B Lachine Maroons, an achievement that he proudly announced to his Thelma and Norman who responded by expressing their hope that playing hockey would not affect his studies, their hope being that he would attend university. The next week, Norman notified the family that he was soon to start a new position, working for the federal government in Ottawa. Accordingly, while Norman's career had taken a fortunate turn, a move to Ottawa would mean that George's hockey career would not. He begged his mother and Norman, who he thought might be counted on as an ally, to let him stay with his uncle Richard and his family who still lived in Verdun. His mother, despite Norman's mild entreaties, declined to leave George behind in the care of his uncle. She insisted that the three of them were moving to Ottawa. In their last days in Lachine, Thelma and Norman were finally and inevitably married. Thelma's old friend Father O'Grady married the couple. As his mother mentioned a number of times, Norman was now officially his stepfather.

Over the first few weeks in Ottawa, where the family settled in the west end of the city in a house that was more spacious than their place in Lachine, George had fallen into obvious melancholy, often sitting alone in his room reading *Hardy Boys* books and old copies of the *Hockey News*, which his uncle had given him after he was finished with them. George was eventually shaken out of his torpor by his mother who reminded him that he had to register at nearly Laurentien High School, his third high school in the last several years. He also discovered that since he now lived in Ontario, he would add one year to his high school career, since Ontario prescribed at least twelve years of secondary education while Quebec only required eleven years. George was relieved. It added a year to his contemplation of his future, which would have previously required him to either enrol in college or go to work, both possibilities frightening him somehow.

It was the first week in September, the Tuesday after Labour Day. He was in line to register at Laurentien High School, standing silently in line holding his most recent report cards from John Grant. The guy behind him in line, fairly tall, muscular, the beginnings of a moustache appearing on his upper lip, asked George if he intended to try out for the football team. George replied by telling the presumed football player that he was a hockey player, mentioning that he had just moved with the family from Montreal, that he had played junior hockey there and was eager to play on a team in Ottawa. The football player told him that while Laurentien did not have a hockey team, there were four or five junior hockey teams in the area. He then suggested that he contact one of the teams and determine whether he could try out for one of them. He then named all the teams although he pointed out that a new team called Junior Rangers, which played in a relatively new arena in the southern area of the city, was looking for players. Within two weeks, after first attending one of the team's practices unannounced, he was invited to join the team. He agreed.

So it did not take long for the family, including George, to grow not only accustomed to but pleased with their new circumstances. George in particular was content. While he missed his friends at John Grant, he was pleasantly surprised when he met and started going out with a classmate named Margaret. While he was occasionally haunted with thoughts of Bernadette and their child, not having any idea of what had had happened to them, his new life had eased any regrets he may have had about his history in Lachine. He shared his new serenity with his stepfather and his mother. Norman worked for the industry department, his years of experience with Dominion Engineering qualifying him for the position he would eventually occupy, having applied for the position on the advice of his old boss. He was making more money in a more relaxing atmosphere. As for his mother, she had been saddened by her departure from Lachine although a nice house on a nice street in an undeniably pleasant neighbourhood was compensation enough, making her forget any regrets she might have had. For a time, George thought that the family were characters in a situation comedy on television.

Aside from his relationship with Margaret, whom he was now seeing regularly, he was concentrating on playing hockey for the Junior Rangers. It was a new team in the Central Junior League and as a result, most of its players were comprised of veterans who had played but were no longer regulars for other junior teams in the area. George had warmed the bench for the junior team in Lachine, an achievement of which he was surprisingly proud, at least compared to his classmates, many of whom seemed strangely disinterested in hockey. After about a month of playing on the Junior Rangers, Coach Lorne promoted him to the third line on the Ranger hockey team, mainly because he was one of few players on the team who regularly showed up for games or practices completely sober. He was not only the youngest player on the Rangers but was the only guy in Laurentien High School who he knew of who was actually playing junior hockey. As a result of his strange lack of notoriety, he was more or less compelled to socialize with his Ranger teammates, most of whom were older and certainly more experienced than he was. This placed George in a curious position. Here he was comparatively innocent, hanging with guys who drank to certain excess, smoked like crazy, and had regular relationships with young girls who some people would call "groupies". His teammates then were more than willing to acquaint this new kid with playing junior hockey, albeit bush league junior but junior nevertheless. Even Coach Lorne admitted as much, telling his charges that while they may not become professional hockey players, at least they could have a good time trying to get there. It seemed appropriate then that George started to drink, started to drink a lot, took up smoking and other things, mainly weed and other substances, and, as nervous as he was initially with this new life style, soon become comfortable with his new friends.

Naturally, all of this significantly changed George. There was no avoiding it. He occasionally stopped going to school, sometimes not going for several days, sometimes not getting out of bed until noon, the obvious result of coming home late most nights. His mother was first to notice those changes in him. While she was aware of his game schedule, it having been pasted on the door of the family refrigerator, and was aware that some of the games involved short road trips although not that many. She did not think that would involve too much time away from home. The team also practised a couple of times a week, depending on the game schedule. Regardless, George was usually not home until around midnight most nights, the explanation being, when asked, it was always related to the Rangers. His stepfather, who was understandably enthusiastic about a potential hockey career, no matter how unlikely, did not seem particularly concerned about George's newly acquired habits, excusing them because, as he put it, "He has a chance." When his mother questioned her husband's optimism, Norman shrugged and assured Thelma that pretty well anyone that plays junior hockey has a chance, as long as they stay with it. It was obvious that neither of them were going to do anything to hinder their son's newly pursued habits.

Then there was the matter of George's high school career, such as it was. Yes, he wasn't going to school much, getting up after ten o'clock in the morning wasn't particularly conducive to a successful academic career. In fact, anytime he actually attended school, it was celebrated by anyone who saw him. But more often than not, going to school was always further to constant entreaties from Margaret who hardly saw him at all after he joined the Rangers. She was about as worried about George as his parents were. Besides, Margaret had another reason, aside from his late hours and his truancy from school, to be concerned. She had heard from a close friend from school, a girl named Kathy whose brother, who no longer played hockey but still hung around with some of the guys on the Rangers, that George had developed a serious drinking problem. According to the brother, George was drunk pretty well every day, sometimes even during games and practices, a routine about which most of his teammates were aware of but coach Lorne was not. George hid his drinking in the dressing room by sneaking into the toilet with a bottle of booze, he preferred vodka as did most drinkers seeking to conceal their drinking. His teammates would roll their eyes and laugh whenever coach Lorne came into the room and asked where George was. It was the same answer every time: "He's in the can, coach." And coach would make the same observation. "Hell, that kid should go see a doctor. He always seems to be in the goddamn can." Then they would laugh louder. Every single time it seemed.

Margaret didn't think she ever saw George drunk although she admitted to herself and her closest friend Judith that she didn't have enough experience to really tell whether her soon to be erstwhile boyfriend was actually inebriated or not. One of their teachers, a Miss Gifford who taught the both of them geometry, would often ask Margaret about George, not having seen him in class for weeks at a time. Margaret was relieved that at least one of George's teachers, as far as she knew, actually cared about the whereabouts of George. Most of the teachers in grade twelve, thinking that many of their students would be in university the next year, declined to report anyone who was absent for any length of time, the point being that the truants would soon be in a position not to attend classes if they did not want to, as long, of course, as they paid their fees. Miss Gifford seemed to be one of those teachers who actually cared about the progress of her students. Margaret was disappointed that she could not have provided Miss Gifford with much in the way of information about George. Their dates, if you could have called them that, had become infrequent, so seldom that Margaret was surprised when he got in touch, maybe once every two or three weeks. Not surprisingly, George would take her to The Line, a drinking establishment on Baseline Road where barely competent musicians would attempt to impress patrons who didn't seem to like music, if that's what it was. She would watch him drink until she got drunk as well. The next day, she wouldn't remember anything, so she couldn't really say whether George had a drinking problem. She started to wonder whether she had one. She didn't like Miss Gifford asking her about George. She had come around to thinking that he was gone as far as she was concerned. Before she could figure it out, George had stopped calling her. By Christmas, he was gone.

He had stopped going to school entirely by the time students came back from their Christmas vacation. He had not told anybody, not his parents, not his teachers, not his coach on the Rangers, many of whom did not even know he was going to school, and of course not Margaret, with whom he had abandoned before Christmas. One of his buddies on the team, an older guy named Dan who was one of the few who knew that George had left school, was working in a place that manufactured aluminum siding. He suggested that since George wasn't going to school, he might consider a taking a job, which would pay him maybe two dollars an hour, which was more than he made last summer at a factory that made storm windows. Besides, as noted by Dan, who seemed to have a fair amount of experience playing the working class hero, having a regular pay cheque was better than not having one. It seemed fairly self evident. It drew a chuckle out of George, who hardly ever emitted anything that could be construed as laughter. He also thought that he might have to hide his wages from his parents who still thought he was ostensibly attending Laurentian, not having received any information to the contrary.

After a strangely perfunctory interview with a Mr. Potvin, who had introduced himself as the general manager, he started at AP Siding on Clyde Street on the second Monday in January. His initial job was to assist a guy named Raymond who operated a machine cutting sheet metal. As he had been advised by Dan, who worked in the paint shop at AP Siding, he would have to start getting up early in the morning again, suggesting that he might want to cut back on the drinking, being hung over or even still drunk not a particularly good idea when you're working with dangerous machinery. George was convinced that he was not an alcoholic, at least not yet, and therefore could reduce his consumption without undue effort. Finally, he decided that he should probably tell his parents of his change in careers. In any event, his sudden change in routine would surely be noticed at home. There was an uneven reaction when he gave them the news. It was on the Sunday, during dinner, just before they were about to sit down to watch *Bonanza* on television, when George said he had something to tell them. Both his mother and his stepfather were surprised that George not only was having dinner with them but was actually speaking with them. His parents were careful not to raise specific topics, namely school, his now former girlfriend Margaret, and of course his drinking, suspecting that their conversation would come to a swift conclusion if any of those subjects ever came up. His mother started to clear the dishes. George felt a little guilty. On the other hand, he felt like a guest who didn't have to help with the dishes.

She started to clean the table and started an aimless discussion. At first, their conversation was limited to family developments, including a fairly lengthy exposition by his mother regarding her old friend Shirley's latest surgery. Several days ago, her gallbladder was removed at the Montreal General by a doctor named Delisle. She was able to provide the two of them with supposedly the correct terminology for the surgery although she probably mispronounced the term several times before she offered to spell it. His stepfather and George both assured her that there was no need. Then there was the engagement of George's cousin Susan to a local man named Sherman Kelly who was a teacher at St. Thomas High School, a relatively new Catholic school in Pointe Claire, another suburb on the West Island. George took an interest in his mother's narrative regarding her niece's engagement. He had been infatuated with the girl's younger sister Catherine several years ago and sometimes wondered about her. Her family lived in NDG. At one time, they used to see them fairly frequently, every couple of months it seemed. But over the previous few years, they hardly ever saw them. The last time George recalled was the Christmas two years ago, before Susan was engaged. He thought that Sherman had accompanied her to the dinner that had been hosted by her parents. He remembered talking to Catherine that night. She was in grade nine at the time and went to a school called Westmore Academy. He saw his stepfather smirk for some reason. George never liked Susan and Catherine's parents.

They then briefly discussed the fortunes of the Rangers although it was clear that neither his stepfather nor his mother were particularly interested in the team. It was at that point George informed his parents that he had recently started to work at AP Siding, a firm that he said manufactured aluminum siding. His stepfather looked at him, let out a short snicker, almost a snort and made a predictable comment. "Aluminum siding? No kidding." His mother looked blankly at George, confused with her husband's observation. George wasn't surprised with his mother's perplexity although he had not spoken to her much lately. Nor did he speak much to his stepfather either. There was a gulf of silence between the three of them for a minute or so. Then George's stepfather asked the obvious question, a query that was also circulating in his mother's mind as well.

"Did you really think about it before you went ahead, quit school and applied for a job?" Both parents looked like they were actually interested in George's response. His mother had moved up in her chair and was waiting for an answer. On the other hand, his stepfather was leaning back in his chair and seemed a little bored. George started to explain. "Well, as you probably have suspected, I have not gone to school much this year. I just didn't see the point. I just wasn't interested in the few classes I did attend." George's stepfather laughed and then leaned over the table. "You weren't interested? Hell, when I went to school, I wasn't interested in any of my classes. That's what I thought school was for ---- you know, it gets you ready for real life, you know, like jobs, raising kids, that kind of thing. Right, Thelma?" Thelma offered up a sad smile and nodded.

George continued to clarify his decision to quit school and get a job. "It was all bullshit." This time, his stepfather let out a real guffaw. "I mean, at least I expected that some of my classes should be a little entertaining. They are so boring, sometimes I have found myself almost falling asleep in class." His stepfather moved forward in his chair and observed in a louder voice. "Falling asleep! You're asleep most of the time anyway. No wonder --- you're either hung over or still drunk from the night before." It was such a stunning accusation that it left his mother momentarily perplexed, sitting silently waiting for his stepfather to continue. After an interval of a couple of minutes, during which the silence was, as people say, deafening, George asked in a quiet voice. His mother was looking at him, apparently fascinated. She knew too but was waiting for Norman to tell her son what they already knew. "You were aware?" His stepfather looked at George with a strange smile. "Look, George, you stumble into the house practically every night after midnight. We know you have hockey but I don't think excessive drinking is part of the post game routine, is it?"

George was more than a little surprised, if not shocked when he received a postcard which was postmarked Vancouver. There was a small message. It said simply "We are here". It was signed Margaret and David. It was evident that his former girlfriend Margaret had moved to Vancouver and had their baby, a son named David. Based on what she had told him during their last conversation, George estimated that their son was probably around six months old. During that conversation, which was mercifully short given the subject matter, the impending birth of their child, Margaret did not mention that she was planning to leave Ottawa, let alone give him any address of her destination.

The postcard had no return address. It was obvious therefore that George could not contact Margaret, that is even if he wanted to. He wanted to contact her but, for reasons he could not explain, even to himself, he was more than interested in knowing her whereabouts. He thought of contacting her parents, who he assumed still lived somewhere in the west end of Ottawa. On the other hand, based on the fact that they had not been in touch at any time since he and Margaret broke up, he realized that it was probably not a good idea. He thought of somehow persuading his parents to get in touch with Margaret's parents but since he had never informed them of the fact that Margaret was pregnant, that too was not a sensible idea. That left her friends, that is if he could remember who they were and where any of them lived.

It took George most of the evening and part of the next morning to realize that there was one source of information that could provide him with at least the names of some of her friends. He had copies of at least two yearbooks, those of 1968 and 1969. Fortunately, for purposes of his search and previously for purposes of romance, both he and Margaret shared the grade years. He examined the appropriate home room class pictures for 1968 and 1969. He managed to come up with four names, three girls with whom George knew she was seriously friendly and a guy named Bob Coghlan who George thought might have been her boyfriend before George assumed that role. Of the three girls, Debra Monahan, Valerie King, and Wendy MacLellan, he used to be somewhat familiar with the latter. In a way, she had had been responsible for George meeting Margaret, who sat beyond Wendy MacLennan in that first day in home room 11-B in that first year in Laurentien. George had said something mildly humorous about Mr. Casey, the English teacher ---- something about the proper use of a colon. Wendy MacLennan didn't laugh, only a sight snicker. On the other hand, Margaret --- Billings was her last name --- laughed and in so doing, displayed a movie star smile. George was so enamoured by that smile that he endeavoured to impress the hell out of her every chance he got, that is, during every home room, usually by entertaining Margaret with humorous remarks about school, the teachers, and anything else he could think of.

They soon started having lunch with each other a couple of days a week, until it had grown into almost a routine. They then started seeing each other after school, their first date being a school dance on a Friday evening that did not conflict with a Ranger game. It did not take long for the two of them to begin seeing each other regularly, their relationship soon developing into almost a permanent association. Fact was they were going steady, seeing each other constantly, that is when he wasn't playing hockey. In addition, he started attending school, mainly, if not totally to see Margaret. George's improved attendance at school understandably shocked his teachers, particularly Mr. Kirk, his home room and English teacher. It soon became apparent to almost anyone who knew either George or Margaret that their relationship was the explanation for his improved attendance, if not his improved performance in school.

Their romantic relationship got better as well, their affection for each other growing it seemed daily. They began to make love as often as they could and everything changed. Though Margaret had been a virgin and George nearly so, his brief affair with Bernadette in Lachine his only experience, they soon began making love with the skill and practised enthusiasm of a couple who had been married for a decade. Anyone with any perspective on George, classmates and teammates on the Rangers, saw a considerable change in his behaviour, his drinking in particular. He had gradually become more clearheaded, actually able to participate in class, actually asking questions in class, shocking most if not all of the class, who had been accustomed to George sitting laconically toward the back of the class, looking like he was either seriously hung over or had just awoken from a long slumber. He looked better as well, his hair combed, his face shaven, his teeth brushed, all the usual features of the better regarded students. Finally, he was dressing better as well, his usual ratty sweatshirt and worn jean combination having been replaced by an outfit that could have been purchased by his mother.

However, once Margaret told George that she was with child, the precise expression she used seemingly borrowed from a Victorian novel, everything gradually returned to the way it had been. George sank into the ennui of his previous circumstances. He started drinking again, that is drinking to his customary excess, he returned to lingering after games and practices rather than changing into his street clothes and hurrying out of the arena to rendezvous with Margaret. In fact, he hardly saw Margaret after either games or practices anymore, his only consorting with her during class, after which time George always seemed to sneak out of the class room as quickly as he could, as if he was late for an appointment. Her friend Wendy MacLellan would console Margaret who would invariably begin to sob every time she saw her so-called boyfriend and future father of their child leave her presence, the obvious purpose, at least to Margaret, to avoid her.

Maybe a month after Margaret informed George that she was expecting a child and he began to avoid her, he found a note in his locker after the school day was over.

The Biography of George

He could tell almost immediately that the note was from Margaret. He recognized her handwriting. The note was short and to the point. It simply read.

"Dear George,

Not matter how you may feel now, I have to tell that I still plan to have the baby. It is due in four months. I am moving in with my aunt in Vancouver where I will have our baby. The two of us will not be back.

Love Margaret"

George stood in front of his locker, just staring. He was contemplating the last few months and rereading the note several times. He had not seen Margaret in at last month and actually had no intention of approaching her in any way in the near future. But the note changed his attitude toward seeing Margaret. He now thought that he should see her at least before she moved in with her aunt in Vancouver. Sure it was true that that he was generally reluctant, if not entirely unwilling to approach Margaret. He thought for a time of approaching her mother, a relatively progressive middle aged woman who reacted to the impending birth of her grandchild with something close to pleasure. But that was probably not a predictably good idea. Her husband Mel though was completely unhappy with the situation. Consequently, despite the comparative enthusiasm of Mrs. Billings about the birth, her husband's resistance eventually meant that George would not be approaching Margaret in the foreseeable future.

That left George with the original idea of approaching Margaret's friends, of which he had already decided that Wendy MacLellan was the best alternative he had. So George started to check the telephone book. It was either that or staking out the school for Wendy MacLellan although that approach had its drawbacks, the chief one being that Margaret would likely be present, which George wanted to avoid, at least in public. He decided, therefore, to start combing through telephone book. He got Wendy with the third MacLellan listing he came across, there being only five in total. Wendy answered the telephone directly. When he introduced himself, which was unnecessary since Wendy knew immediately who George was. Still Wendy sounded somewhat hesitant, which was understandable in view of Margaret's circumstances which George was certain Margaret had shared with her. After all, they were best friends and he found it hard to believe that Margaret would not discuss with her the pregnancy and her plans to move in with her aunt in Vancouver. He wasn't quite sure of his objective but now that he had her on the telephone, he didn't want to squander the opportunity. He immediately explained the purpose of his call. "I got a note from Margaret yesterday. It said that she was planning to move out to Vancouver to live with her aunt and have her baby there. You probably know that I haven't seen her for a month, since she told me about the baby." George paused. Wendy didn't say anything. "Well, I would like to say goodbye to her before she leaves." George paused again, his voice now lower. "Do you know when she is leaving? How long do I have?"

He heard her inhaling on the other end of the line. She slowly answered "She's leaving by the end of next week, I'm pretty sure of that. Some of the girls and I are having a little farewell party for her. It'll be at Liz Malone's place next Wednesday. Then she's planning to go out to Vancouver to move in with her aunt. So you have eight days." George asked her another question. "When's her last day at school?" Wendy told her next Wednesday, the day of the farewell party. George asked Wendy MacLellan to tell Margaret that he would be waiting for her outside the school next Wednesday. He told Wendy to tell Margaret that he would only need five minutes to say goodbye. "I'll tell her but I don't think I can guarantee that she'll want to talk to you." George then said that he hoped that she would and said goodbye.

❦

It was the next Wednesday and George was standing outside of Marymount High School nervously waiting for Margaret. He was standing with maybe a half dozen other teenage boys around his age presumably waiting for girls around Margaret's age although presumably not for the same reason. He felt like he was in some sort of lousy movie. He was waiting in a cliche, just like those stupid tragic teenage comedies he had seen on television a hundred times. He half expected it to start to rain, which it would have if it was one of those stupid movies. It didn't start to rain. The students started to emerge from the school exit. They came out in groups, enthusiastically chatting with each other, some of them applying or re-appying lipstick, some looking through their handbags, some of them holding cigarettes which they would lite as soon as they got off school grounds. Finally, Margaret appeared, walking with two other girls, happily chatting it seemed. George stood thirty feet from the entrance, just standing still and staring at the entrance. Margaret and her two friends were maybe half way to where George was waiting when the three of them turned toward the bus stop heading downtown. George had to call out to Margaret, causing a number of girls, including Margaret and her two friends, to turn towards him. Margaret looked like she was paralyzed with a surprised, if not shocked look on her face. Her two friends were pointing at George, having immediately recognized him as Margaret's boyfriend. Margaret did not point, she just started to walk toward George, slowly as if she was not convinced that she should continue to walk towards him. George just stood his ground, waiting for Margaret to come to him, which she eventually did. She was a couple of feet from him when he opened the conversation. For a moment, he looked past the advancing Margaret to observe her two friends watching her walking towards him.

His voice was almost a whisper, compelling her to take a couple of steps forward. "Hello, Margaret, I got your note and I know you'll leaving for Vancouver by the end of the week." He noticed that Margaret had allowed a surprised expression to spread across face. She interrupted George and spoke. "How, how do know when I will be leaving?" George shrugged his shoulders and turned his hands out at the waist, as if he had had something in his pockets. "Your friend Wendy told me but don't blame her. I pressured the hell out of her." Margaret looked over her right shoulder and turned back to face George. "Okay, so why did you want to know anyway?" asked Margaret, more than just inquisitive. George answered in a sort of apologetic tone. "I had to give you a proper goodbye. I happen to believe --- no, I have come to believe that with all that has happened between us, I probably will never see you again. You know, I just wanted to make sure that you'll be alright."

Margaret then surprisingly leaned forward to kiss him on the cheek. "I'll be alright or should I say, we'll be fine."

George In the Real World

Over the next few years, he did little more than drift. He had gone back to high school at night and graduated the next summer with little fanfare, wondering why he did it in the first place. He still thought about Margaret and the baby but did not do anything to contact her in Vancouver. He continued to work at AP Siding although he worked fewer shifts for the year or so he spent pursuing academia in night school. The day after he received his certificate at a brief ceremony held in an amphitheatre in city hall, he quit his job entirely to supposedly obtain a better job, thinking perhaps naively that a high school diploma could qualify him for a better job. He was also still playing hockey for the Rangers, his tenure with the team having reached its second year. Consequently, his use of alcohol had returned to pre-Margaret levels, meaning that everything about which he had previously improved due to the influence of Margaret returned to the unfortunate depths of misbehaviour he had previously explored. He barely got through night school, which was remarkable considering that he missed half the classes due to his commitment to the Rangers and was semi-drunk for the classes he did attend.

It took him less than two months to find another job,

his high school diploma showing remarkable dividends. Although he did not have any retail experience, the woman who interviewed George, who had applied at the downtown Hudson's Bay on the recommendation of one of the night school teachers, was impressed enough to hire him. He was to start in the discount clothing department of the Hudson's Bay store a month before Christmas. Mr. David Pierce, who was barely older than he was, was his first supervisor. He assigned him to discount boy's wear, where he was to sell boys' clothing to mothers looking for bargains. Aside from convincing shoppers to purchase clothing at reduced prices and then ringing their purchases through on a cash register that looked like it belonged in a museum, George was also responsible for ensuring the stock was displayed neatly. On his first day, half of which was taken up with some perfunctory training on how to make sales, provide refunds, operate the cash register, and arrange the stock properly, George served maybe a dozen customers, all but one of them were women, the other being a man who spent less than five minutes selecting a sweater for his seven year old son. He was initially confused by the operation of the cash register although with a little help from a lady from an adjoining section, i.e. women's wear, he got over his difficulties soon enough. Although he was bored occasionally, George found the job preferable, much more so than cutting sheet metal in AP Siding. He has got an employee discount and a variety of restaurants in which to have lunch.

On the home front, a week before Christmas, his stepfather Norman had a sudden heart attack at work, falling face first in front of his desk at 10 o'clock in the morning. He was pronounced dead before the ambulance arrived. He was laying in a hospital morgue when a medical examiner telephoned his mother to inform her that her husband was dead. She took the news amazing well, calmly telling the hospital that she would be in touch shortly with information on the arrangements, specifically where to send the body. She then telephoned her son George. Fortunately, she had his number at work, having been provided with it just the other day. George was saddened by the news of his stepfather's sudden death, having gotten along pretty well with Norman the last few years. He was surprised therefore by his mother's relatively calm, if not disinterested demeanour when giving him the news, at least compared to the death over a decade ago of her first husband which almost plunged her into a nervous breakdown. When he mentioned her muted reaction to Brian Jacobs, one of his friends from the Rangers hockey team, he suggested that maybe her experience of being a widow explained her rather disinterested reaction. George didn't know whether Brian was being serious.

The visitation and then the funeral of Norman drew a fairly impressive crowd. His mother's longtime priest Father O'Grady had been invited to Resurrection to officiate. According to Shirley Boorman, Thelma's friend from the old neighbourhood who came up from Montreal for the funeral, there were more than a hundred people at the funeral. She remarked that it seemed odd that her friend Thelma wasn't even fifty years old and was burying her second husband. She also wondered about her son George who now had had three fathers, including one he never met, one who adopted him and one who was his stepfather. She also commented that he seemed more despondent than his mother throughout the entire proceeding, seemingly in tears at the funeral home, in the church and even at the buffet that Thelma and a couple of her friends managed to put together at The Green Valley on Prince of Wales Drive. A couple of George's teammates came to the funeral and showed up at the buffet. George eventually cheered himself up, mainly due to his immediate interest in a girl named April Boorman, Shirley's daughter who had lived next door to George for several years before he and his mother moved. She was now going to University of Ottawa and therefore was living in downtown Ottawa, in one of the university residences. George and April had not seen each other in at least ten years but seemed to strike up a friendship almost immediately that day. Towards the end of the buffet, George asked April out. They made a date for a dinner at the Hayloft, to be followed by dancing at La Caprice, a discotheque across the river in Hull.

It would be his first date with anyone since he and Margaret parted ways. He wondered about Margaret. He thought that maybe the baby was due within weeks. But otherwise, he hardly ever thought about Margaret or the baby. Funny thing, he would start to bring up Margaret and her son almost twenty years later, prompted by a letter that Margaret was to send his mother, thinking quite correctly that George probably had moved around a bit in the twenty years since the baby was to arrive while his mother probably had not and therefore could be found. The baby was to grow up into a nineteen year old boy named Gordon.

His first date with April went remarkably well. As planned, he took her for dinner at the Hayloft on Rideau Street in downtown Ottawa, almost right around the corner from where April lived. They then went across the river to La

Caprice where they had drinks, Rusty Nails for her and beer for him, and danced until one o'clock in the morning. They then took a taxi cab back to Ottawa and then stumbled into her room in the university residence. They made out a bit but did not make love. They did, however, agree to see each other the following week. It looked like it might be a longer term arrangement. April thought he was a surprisingly good dancer, his enthusiasm his most important quality.

Fortunately for Thelma, Norman had been financially secure. His death benefit from Dominion Engineering was significant enough to not only pay for a funeral, burial at Notre Dame Cemetery to join his parents and grandparents, and a surprisingly lavish buffet dunner following the funeral and burial. He had had some savings, some predictable investments and part of a pension that ensured that Thelma would never have to think about working again. George had recently thought about moving out. With Norman gone, George's reluctance to move out would likely increase, leaving his mother alone in the place was something he wanted to avoid. His mother was generally conservative, often gently chiding George about personal behaviour about which he disapproved. So there were reasons for George to want to get his own place.

But he would not be getting his own place just yet. Fortunately though, his mother seemed to have a lot of friends, ladies that she managed to attract as friends, mainly at Out Lady of Fatima Church on Woodroffe Avenue, during the three years she had lived in the area. Thelma had joined the church ladies group, where she helped with the parish bazaar, parish supers, card evenings, and receptions for various parish events. His mother was also fairly friendly with several ladies in the neighbourhood, often taking the bus to the shops in the Carlingwood Shopping Centre, which was only one of two shopping centres in the west end. George figured that he would be in a position to move out in six months or so, by which time he thought his mother would be prepared to live on her own. In fact, she could probably live on her own before that.

Despite his theoretical expectations, all of which were self imposed, George was still living at home with his mother more than six months after his stepfather's passing. And he had no plans to move out of the house, at least no plans in the foreseeable future. April, with whom he was now romantically involved in a fairly serious way, often encouraged him to move out on his own. He would quietly dismiss her entreaties, usually by changing the subject or avoiding the subject by staring into space, effectively giving April the silent treatment, behaviour that she had come to realize was pointless and possibly dangerous, particularly if he had been drinking. In such circumstances, George was quite capable of striking April or so she was convinced. He had feigned hitting her several times although he had not actually done so. Still, for some reason that she never quite understood, April continued their relationship despite her occasional fear. She was careful, however, not to mention the possibility of getting his own place and, depending on George's mood, his mother.

Ironically, his mother was the first to move, informing George one day that she had decided to move into an apartment which was in a building not far from where they currently lived. She said that the girls, some of whom were living in the Aventura apartments, where his mother intended to move, had convinced her that she was getting too old to live alone in her current place, a three bedroom house just down Woodroffe from the Aventura Apartments. When Thelma brought up her longtime tenant, her son, they said that it was about time that George moved out on his own. The girls won the argument and Thelma had to evict her son, the obvious implication being that George could not move into an apartment with his mother. It was not surprising that George was unhappy, if not scared when his mother told him. Seeking solace, he told April of her mother's decision later that day. Not surprisingly, she told George that it was the occasion that he needed to move into his own place. She asked him how much time he had during which to look for a place. George told her a month. April assured him that she would help him look for a place. She said that she was going to university and therefore had more spare time than he did. When George mentioned study time, April kind of laughed, pointing out that this was in her first year of university, an experience with which George was not acquainted. She said that she was enrolled in the Arts program, which did not require a great deal of effort, particularly if you have a natural affinity for the courses that were normally taken in first year Arts, subjects like English, History, Social Studies, that kind of thing. April said that she found the courses relatively easy and seldom needed to invest too much time studying, volunteering that she found some of the grade twelve courses to be more difficult. She went on to mention that grade twelve required potential graduates to study science and mathematics, not exactly subjects with which April had proficiency.

George, although expressing his disappointment, if not his dismay, with the news that he would have to move into his own place, his first place living without his mother Thelma since he was living in the Notre-Dame Orphanage almost eighteen years ago, was relatively pleased that April was willing to help him looking for a place. The idea still troubled George although he did have ample experience with looking for employment. So, after discussing the matter, he and April decided that she would comb the advertisements in the paper for one bedroom apartments on a decent street downtown while George would call on the landlords of the places that the two of them were to select.

After three days of looking through the *Ottawa Citizen*, April had a list of more than a dozen apartments for rent, most of which seemed to be located in or near the downtown area. They decided to call on three places near Somerset Street below Bank Street. Because it was his first time, April volunteered to accompany George when he called on the first apartment on their list. But since they were planning to call on the three places, their appointments confirmed by telephone --- it seemed so adult to George --- the two of them agreed to see all three landlords, or their representatives, together. He and April arrived in front of a large house on Cooper Street, just east of O'Connor. The place looked recently renovated, a new porch, new windows, and what appeared to be a new roof. The two of them climbed up the four steps to the front door, opened it, and studied the four buzzers to the apartments in the house. At the bottom left of the copper plate in the lobby was a buzzer to Apartment 102, a small label identifying the occupants as the assumed custodians, the presumed Mr. and Mrs. Hutchins. George pressed it and a woman's voice answered. George identified April and himself as potential tenants, announcing that they were there to inspect the apartment that was available for rent.

The woman, in a voice that sounded sophisticated and annoyed at the same time, bid them to come in and then buzzed them up to the apartment, directing them to the left on the first floor. He and April opened the inner door, took a few steps and then faced the woman on the intercom. She was practically standing out in the hall. She looked like she was dressed for the office, a black suit over a dark blue blouse. They also noticed that the woman was wearing what looked like very expensive high heels. She looked like she was in her late thirties, which seemed to be an unusual age for an apartment custodian. Both George and April stepped forward to introduce themselves. The woman introduced herself as Ms. Hutchins and then asked if the two of them intended to move into together. After they looked at each other, April said no. Ms. Hutchins explained, "My father is the custodian. He ought to be back in a moment. He's over in 101 trying to fix Mrs. O'Brien's plumbing." April asked Ms. Hutchins for her father's first name. Ms. Hutchins looked surprised but answered anyway. "Peter." Then she continued "Oh, by the way, why don't you just walk across the hall and see how long my father will be."

The two of them were about to knock on the door to Mrs. O'Brien's apartment and its faulty plumbing when Peter Hutchins appeared in the doorway, his plumbing tools in a wooden carrying box. He greeted them casually and ushered them into his place. He put his tools down and asked them if they were there to inspect Apartment 201, looking to rent the place. George and April answered in the affirmative and then introduced themselves. Mr. Hutchins nodded and after a short pause, described the apartment: a large living room, with two windows facing Cooper Street, one bedroom with another window facing Cooper Street, a medium size kitchen with a stove with a small window with frosted glass, and a bathroom with a fair sized tub. The place sounded delightful said April but, thinking that the place was probably out of George's price range, asked Hutchins what the monthly rent was. Hutchins smiled and shook his head. He knew what April had suspected. "The rent on Apartment 201 is $350 a month. I suspect that may be a little high for you." he said, looking at George. He then put his hand out to shake their hands and said goodbye. "Thanks for coming by."

As they walked down the stairs of the large house on Cooper Street, April chuckled a bit and observed "Well, that was certainly worth it. Maybe we should get out of this neighbourhood. It may be a little pricey for you." George nodded. "Maybe we should just take a look at these other two places around here and start looking in less glamorous areas." April suggested "Hey, there are two places on Somerset that we can look at before we look at other places on your list." George agreed, pointing out that the two places on Somerset were just around the corner. "If they look expensive, we won't even call on them." April nodded and the two of them walked down Cooper, right on O'Conner and then left again on Somerset, across O'Conner. The first place, number 402, was actually a four floor apartment building that looked like there was no way in the world that George or George and April together could afford a place there. "How come these places don't advertise the monthly rents? It would be a lot more convenient for people with a budget." George asked rhetorically. April shrugged her shoulders and continued with him toward Metcalfe Street where they got a chance to inspect 310 Somerset, another renovated house that looked more even high end than the place on Cooper. They just walked past it, walked across Metcalfe, where they had lunch on Elgin Street in Abby's, a diner that was the one of the cheapest in the downtown area.

It was a Monday, a day off for George. He and April, sometimes together, sometimes only George, had spent more than a week looking for an apartment. After looking in a number of downtown areas, including in particular the Byward-Market area, before abandoning any idea of living downtown and his objective, if not his dream of renting a place from which he could walk to work. Finally, George visited a place on Laurel Avenue in the area called Hintonburg, a working class district that featured a combination of clapboard houses built in the 20s and 30s, small apartment buildings, and some small businesses, restaurants, and a variety of retail shops, including a laundry that often saw prostitutes and other street people hanging around smoking cigarettes and looking for clients and spare change. Notwithstanding such occasional inconveniences, George was prepared to overlook them for a one bedroom in the two floor apartment building. It was a square brick building that housed six apartments, three on each floor, two one bedrooms and one two bedroom on each floor. George was introduced to the landlord, a remarkably stout individual named Bouchard by an old Ranger teammate named Greg Parks. So he managed to rent a one bedroom for $160 a month, easily the most economically priced of the dozen apartments he had seen in the past ten days. That included a one bedroom apartment on Irving Street also owned by Mr. Bouchard and also being offered at $160 a month, the difference being that there had been a murder at that address a year before, there being blood stains remaining on the walls of the living room. Despite its notoriety, George declined to rent the place.

He signed a twelve month lease a day later. He first informed April, who was understandably relieved, and his mother who by that time seemed generally bored about the whole thing. He told both of them that he would be moving into the one bedroom on Laurel Avenue in less than a month. That was particularly appropriate since his mother was scheduled to move into the Aventura Apartments in about three weeks, leaving George alone in his mother's place for a week. He needed that week, not because he had much to move ---- fact was his furnishings consisted of a bed, a small dresser, and a clothing rack on wheels. George planned to outfit the rest of his place on Laurel with pieces he could pick up at the Surplus Furniture joint in the east end and have it delivered. In the meantime, for the first time in his life, he was sleeping alone somewhere, albeit in his mother's house.

Ten days later, he was comfortably ensconced in his own residence for the first time in his life. He become accustomed to a new routine fairly soon. He went to work without any apparent problem, being ten minutes closer to the Hudson's Bay store downtown by bus. Furthermore, he thought he was close enough that he could actually walk to or from work if he was inclined, which he usually wasn't. Otherwise, he went about his business with little change, the sole difference being his behaviour on his days off. On those days, he would stay in bed until the middle of the afternoon, anaesthetized it seemed by the effects of his previous night's drinking, a habit that he had quickly resumed after meeting one of the other tenants in the Laurel Street apartment building, a guy named Miller. He had reduced, if not eliminated his drinking entirely after he quit playing for the Rangers. For three years, he rode the bench for the Rangers, sometimes playing, mostly not playing, but drinking to excess most of the time, his only hiatus when he was going out with Margaret.

But as soon as he met Miller, he was back drinking to excess. Every day it seemed, he and Miller would regularly join three of Miller's friends at a local watering hole called the Elmdale, an old dumpy tavern that was two blocks away on Wellington Street. If it was evening prior to a day off, George would get absolutely drunk, often needing help from Miller and his roommate, one of the three friends, a guy named Weir, to navigate his way home. Otherwise, if he was scheduled to to work the next day, he would get only mildly inebriated although sometimes he would allow himself to go one or two quarts over the line. He would then suffer through his next day at work, avoiding customers in so far as he could and greeting his co-workers with barely a mumble. On top of that, he felt terrible. David Pearce, his supervisor, said although he looked like he hadn't slept in a week, that did not relieve him of any work related duties, including he pointed out changing some of the displays, a task that he usually avoided.

Living on his own had obviously been an unfortunate development for George, a conclusion that his mother had reached after having dinner with her son on several consecutive Sundays. Thelma also thought he looked terrible. It was a Sunday and George was, as usual, hung over, a condition that he had acquired the previous evening, a Saturday, at La Caprice with April, having switching from scotch, a libation that was usually much more effective in getting him drunk than his usual beer. April, who was drinking her Rusty Nails, was not happy with their evening, his persistent constant clutching and grabbing at her ass a constant complaint throughout the evening. Further, when they got home, April declined to spend the night, knowing that not only was he incapable of any amorous activity but would actually make sleeping unpleasant, the sound of George vomiting loud enough to disturb anyone's sleep. So George was not in particularly good shape when he arrived at his mother's apartment for Sunday dinner. Predictably, Thelma gave him a lecture about drinking, a strange complaint coming from a woman who had developed a taste for expensive wine since she moved into the Adventura Apartments. Lecture over, George could not wait to get out of his mother's apartment. He much preferred his own apartment to that of his mother's apartment.

By the time he got home that night, Miller had a party going, which was generally unusual since it was Sunday.

The door to Miller's two bedroom apartment was open and George could see that the place was jammed. It was more than a party. It was more like a Mardi Gras, albeit without the costumes. Miller saw him and motioned him into the room. Now he knew, it was a birthday party. The place was clumsily festooned with birthday greetings, those cheap inflatable things that you stuck on the wall and then had trouble removing them. Miller came over and George asked whose birthday it was. Miller smiled, took a swig of whatever it was that he was drinking and pointed across the room at a guy who looked awfully familiar. George stared hard at the guy and slowly realized that it was former best friend, Brian Jacobs from the Rangers. He had not seen him for maybe three years and here he was, dancing drunkenly by himself across the floor of the two bedroom apartment. It was mainly a male crowd, there being four women in the entire place. All but one of the women looked uncomfortable, there being four or five guys to every one of them. George noticed them but did not pay any particular attention to any of the three, there being only one of the four girls worth scrutinizing with any interest. For some reason, and a reason he could not quite comprehend, being relatively timid unless of course he had the time to consume enough alcohol to erase any cold feet he may have, he saw that the fourth girl, older and obviously less inhibited than the other three, was standing alone in the corner of the living room, pouring what appeared to be scotch or rye whisky into a tumbler. She seemed to be the only individual in the room who was not drinking beer, countless pints of which were stacked in two refrigerators and several camp coolers in the kitchen.

He approached her slowly, as he expected her to turn her

back on him. The closer he came to her, the more attractive and the more adult she seemed. This was surprising, since most, if not all of the other attendees to the party were younger and well on their way to inebriation. As he got close, she took a couple of steps toward him and stood facing him. "Hi, my name's Brenda and I know what you want to know. You want to know why I'm here, why a woman like me would be hanging around with these boys. I mean, it's obvious, isn't it, that I'm older, maybe quite a bit older that most of the people at this party." George looked intimidated, as if he expected to be. He hesitated and then mumbled his own introduction. "Hi, my name is George and you're right, I'm curious." More hesitation, more reluctance, more hesitancy, as she offered him a slight smile, a grin. He tried to continue his explanation. "I'm just wondering why I'm here." Brenda gently cut him off to basically answer his question. "I like men, especially young men with strong bodies. Look around. There are a lot of young men with strong bodies. That's why I'm here. And in case you're wondering, I live upstairs and I've know some of these boys for a while and I'm always looking for new friends, if you know what I mean." George shrugged and admitted that he didn't know what she meant. Brenda explained. "Well, this could come as a shock but I just like men. And well, this is a good place to find them. Most of these guys," Brenda waved her arm out like she was displaying items that she was about to sell. "most of these guys are young, strong and can go all night." She then started to laugh, swallowed whatever it was she drinking and then turned to greet another admirer, a tall guy with a short beard who Brenda seemed to know. George wondered if they had been intimate. By the way

Brenda touched his arm in greeting, George knew that they had been. As George drifted back into the party, Brenda, in a strange, almost conspicuously old fashioned gesture, winked, a likely invitation George thought.

It must have been two o'clock in the morning when he felt something nudge him on the shoulder. It was Miller using his foot to wake George up. He was asleep, his head half lying in an almost empty bowl of cold chili.

April and George had been discussing moving in together when the idea was suddenly abandoned when April, who had been given a key to George's apartment on Laurel Avenue less than a month before, entered his place while he and a co-worker named Cynthia were engaged in sexual congress on the living room sofa. April froze at the door, which was still open, gaped at the two of them, emitted a strange noise, which sounded a little like a child's squeal, threw George's key at the two of them, hitting Cynthia, who April had never seen or was even aware of, and then quickly backed out of the apartment and slammed its door. George was thinking about pursuing her but abandoned the idea as soon as he realized that she was out the building before he was out his own door. He stood for several moments at the open door to his apartment before closing it. Cynthia was laughing, holding the key that April had thrown at her. "I have to admit that was helluva way of ending a relationship." she observed, first holding the key up like a some sort of trophy and then placing it on the living room's makeshift coffee table, which happened to be supported by several red milk cartons, standard furniture which always added a festive touch to most apartments occupied by anybody under 25 years old. Cynthia then asked. "I know you may have told me but how long have you been going out with her? You two must be or, excuse me, must have been pretty serious. You gave her a key to your place which, as far as I know, usually means that she was going to move in with you. Right?" George nodded. "Well, you won't have to worry about that anymore."

He had met Cynthia when she was transferred to the discount women's wear section in the basement of the Hudson's Bay store. She had been working in the jewellery section on the first floor when she became the supervisor of women's wear downstairs. She was a tall, slim woman in her mid to late thirties. She was married with three children. She had gone back to work when her youngest, a boy named Thomas, entered grade one. She had worked at the Hudson's Bay store downtown in her late teens until she got married in her early twenties. It was therefore easy to return to the store given her experience, which had been in the toy and linen departments. Surprisingly, at least to her colleagues who initially regarded her as a little more than a dreary suburban housewife in her late thirties, she was seen as a fashionably, if not provocatively dressed woman who was likely to be assigned to the woman's wear, lingerie or perfume departments, such was her apparent qualifications, good looks being high on the list.

George was immediately attracted to her despite their obvious difference in age, her being at least fifteen years older than him. Still, there was something alluring about her. He was quietly enthusiastic about possibly meeting her, maybe even engaging in some sort of flirtation with her, however unlikely that seemed, given not only their ages but their respective statures in the store. It was through his supervisor, David Pearce that he was finally introduced to Cynthia who had approached the former to borrow George for a specific task. She had heard she said that George sometimes changed some of the displays that were used to advertise the clothes. She said that she wanted George to make changes to two of the displays that were currently in the women's wear department even though he did not work there. Pearce, who George thought may have had designs on Cynthia himself, had told him of his assignment. He started the first display the next day, on a weekday morning when he was not busy. It was an exhibit, or it was supposed to be an exhibit, of young men attending university. The current display had several young ladies wearing blouses and corduroy slacks. They were also wearing inexpensive loafers. George was standing before the display. Cynthia was suddenly standing behind George. She lightly touched George on the shoulder and spoke.

"What do you think? Pretty dreary, isn't it?" she observed.

George half turned toward her and admitted as much. "You're right. I don't know who thought of this exhibit but I think I can fix it." He then turned around to gaze at Cynthia. She looked unattainable. He was wrong.

Comrade George For a Time

I t was pretty well the only job he could get in the circumstances. Over the past several months, he had been asked repeatedly by his girlfriend Sharon to leave the one bedroom dump they had been sharing for less than six months. It was on Cooper Street between Percy and Lyon Streets in Ottawa. Things had not been going well between the two of them over the past six months or so, the main complication being the fact that she was working and he wasn't. It had been the subject of dispute between the two of them since he had been fired from his previous position, a job cleaning offices. He was let go from that job after his supervisor, a middle age man named Peacock, caught him drinking from a flask of scotch during his midnight shift on the tenth floor of the a building on Queen Street. It was his second dead-end job that he was forced to take after he was unceremoniously dismissed from a semi-decent position that he had held in the Royal Canadian Mint on Sussex Drive for attempting to steal a $1,000 bag of quarters.

The situation at the Mint could have been worse. Mint management, an ill- tempered man named Bridges, who was the director of the coining and metal division, had decided that while legal authorities should have been notified, he was worried that any sort of police involvement would reflect poorly on his reputation, a situation that he was always desperate to protect. So the Mint did not notify the police. It was a surprising decision, given that Bridges was a well known authoritarian and could be enthusiastically expected to turn George over to the authorities. In this case, however, Bridges was concerned that the Master of the Mint, a curious aristocrat named Ogilvy, might not consider Bridges for the job of Deputy Master, which looked to be likely when Ogilvy retired in a year or so, if there was an scandal. Bridges thought that an arrest of a Mint employee for theft would surely make the newspapers. So he settled on simply terminating Gagnon's employment. In addition to worrying about the effect that a police investigation would have on his career prospects, Bridges was concerned that any sort of broader investigation would result in revelations about other thefts, of which there were rumours of several. That would be even more disastrous Bridges thought. That was enough for Bridges to change his mind about turning Gagnon in.

Oddly enough, at the time, despite their financial problems, George was strangely pleased that he had been let go by the Mint, standing in front of a stamping machine for less than a year being hardly a compelling experience. In addition, being fired was a better fate than being placed under arrest, action that he had not encountered in his twenty four years although, in view of his troublesome history over the past few years, he probably should have been. By the time he arrived home, after stopping for a couple of drinks on a bar on Bank Street near Gilmour, Sharon was already home at their bachelor apartment on Cooper Street. She was partially high, casually sucking on a joint, a sweet cloud surrounding her. She was a part time waitress at a restaurant on Slater Street, starting at seven o'clock and punching out at ten, three days a week. Otherwise, she attended the Journalism School at Carleton University. She was to graduate in several months, after which time she was ready to start a full time position in the Industry department on Queen Street. In the meantime, he had lost his job cleaning offices.

She was trying to suppress her laughter when George walked in. He thought it would be a convenient time to tell her that he had lost another job. She offered him a toke off the joint, which he took. He then sat down, turned down the stereo, which had been playing a song that he didn't recognize, and informed her than he had just been asked that afternoon to clean out his locker the cleaning company. She looked at him for a moment, took another toke and laughed. "How many more jobs are you going to take before you stay at one for more than a year?" she said. George looked at her through a haze of marijuana and shrugged. He then went to the kitchen and returned with a beer. He then sat down on the edge of a ratty sleeper sofa and took a long gulp. "I guess you need another beer to answer, right?" she said and she then she giggled. George joined her in giggling and offered a witty, at least as far as he thought, reply. "I don't know. My usual two or three positions."

Sharon suddenly turned serious and leaned forward to the edge of the sofa bed. She then took the beer bottle out of his hand, took a sip, handed it back, pulled a cigarette out of the pack on the edge of the stereo, and lit it. "You know that I won't start at Industry for weeks and that means that I won't get a pay cheque for a month after that. Do you have any money in the bank? They owe you a couple weeks pay, don't they?" she asked. George confessed. "I only have a couple of bucks in the bank but the Mint owes me two weeks and I'll will be able to apply for UIC but that could take a month or so before I start getting cheques. At least I paid this month's rent." Sharon put her head in her hands and allowed a quiet moan to escape from her lips. "Wow. So neither you nor I have any money. Christ, I'll have to go to my parents again. You know how much I hate doing that." Unlike George, whose mother hadn't spoken to him for a couple of years, Sharon had parents who seemed to be willing to support her every endeavour, even if it seemed foolish, which did not happen that often. George shrugged his shoulders, stood up and looked out the window. He saw one of their fellow tenants, an older woman who Sharon thought was involved in something shady, talking to a young guy nicknamed Dinks. He wasn't close enough to make out their conversation.

He looked back over his shoulder at Sharon. "They're at it again, the old lady and Dinks. I wonder what she's buying now?" Sharon took her head out of her hands, looked up at George and commented. "Maybe the old lady is buying uppers --- every time I see her, she looks like she needs some help getting up the stairs." George had to agree with Sharon's speculation. Then she added a possibility. "The way things are going, I hope Dinks can sell us weed wholesale. I hope we still have enough in our stash for the next couple of weeks. I mean, I'll talk to my parents and maybe they'll sent me a cheque in a couple of days. Otherwise, we will be smoking pepper corns or something."

They smoked for a while and gradually got serious about

their situation. George would have laughed at the pepper corn remark but he had started to think seriously. He was worried about their future, their immediate future. It was looking somewhat deary. "How much do you think you can get out of your parents? You won't receive a pay cheque for maybe ten weeks and we have only enough dough to get by for three weeks tops." Sharon fired up another joint and looked at him with a confused, if not scared expression on her face. "I mean, what are we are going to do?" George looked at her with a vacant look on his face, plaintively waiting for a shot at the joint that Sharon had just lit. They were both feeling a little jittery, a little anxious, even a few tokes hadn't tranquilized them. It was clear that they needed something stronger. Aside from their pharmaceutical needs, it was also clear that they needed something more practical than weed. All they could conclude was that they needed cash.

The next day, before Sharon left for class and after gently fending off George's customary morning attempt at seduction, Sharon asked if he was heading down to manpower as well as checking the classified ads in the *Journal*. "And if you go anywhere, make sure you look halfway decent. And by the way, you sure as hell don't look decent right know." she advised, laughing. George was naked and sitting up in the sofa bed, an erection bold and visible in the sunlight streaming through the front window. She often noted that the mass of entangled curls on his head and unruly beard more often than not put off people while applying for a job. George looked a little puzzled but still nodded to Sharon. She looked a little exasperated but hopeful enough to leave the apartment with a small smile. George was still sitting up as Sharon waved, opened the door to their apartment, and left for the day. George got up, went to the window, watched Sharon go down the front stairs and head toward Bank Street where she would take the bus down Bronson to Carleton. George then went back to bed.

After maybe an hour of fitful snoozing, he took a couple gulps of scotch out of a forty ouncer that he had kept in the back of the apartment's only closet, hidden in one of his work boots. George was not particularly troubled by the possibility that Sharon was aware of his liquor stash. Sharon was aware of their other hiding place, the one reserved for weed, pot, and any other dope that the two of them managed to acquire. It was in the bottom drawer of the small desk that sat just inside the apartment entrance. For some curious reason, Sharon disapproved of George's drinking habits. George was always bewildered by Sharon's disdain for heavy drinking, particularly in view of her other appetites. They often argued about it, heavy irony on both sides of their debate, Sharon was convinced that weed was harmless, noting constantly that it was a pleasant high that wasn't dangerous and wasn't addictive. Besides, neither of them ever came home from an evening of toking in rough shape. George agreed with the assertion, claiming that he seldom had difficulty finding their apartment after an evening of the weed. At the same time, he pointed out that an evening of smoking dope often resulted in endless giggling and constant cases of the munchies but nothing else.

George finally got up, actually intending to head down to the manpower office on Bank, after which he planned to take the bus out to the UIC office on Carling. He figured that he would be out the entire day, after which he could gladly report to Sharon that he was making a responsible effort to help resolve their financial problems. Appropriately attired for a day, he never found the only tie he thought he still owned. Still, he wore a dress shirt, dress trousers, and a navy corduroy jacket that he first bought when he was still in high school. He was out of the apartment by ten o'clock and was standing in one of a half a dozen lines at the manpower office at Bank and Gilmour a half hour later. As he was waiting in line, he read the job notices that were tacked up on the boards that were scattered throughout the office. George also invested his wait time checking out his fellow job seekers. Most of the applicants were casually dressed, not as well as George he thought, but trying to look as respectable as they could, believing somewhat naively that they were more likely to impress government bureaucrats if they looked like they were making an effort. There were more men than women, most of whom looked a little depressed which was not surprising given their circumstances. On the other hand, there were several individuals who looked like they were enjoying themselves. George thought that maybe they had been drinking. That wouldn't have been surprising either.

Behind him in line, maybe five or six people back, was a guy he recognized from AP Siding, a guy with long blond hair who he barely knew but remembered as working in cutting room. He had forgotten his name, if he had known it at all. George gave him a curt nod, which was returned seemingly reluctantly, as if he didn't really recognize George. He turned and returned to face forward. He assumed that the guy no longer worked at AP Siding and was likely in line for the same purpose that he was. Before he could further contemplate the sighting of the guy from AP Siding, he was standing in front of a man who looked not only bored but entirely disinterested in his responsibilities. He looked like he was about to fall or had been asleep. So much so that George was reluctant to disturb him. He reminded George of a teacher that he had in grade seven, a relatively young man too young for his responsibilities, either then or now, too young given his obvious disposition. His name then was Mr. York. His name now was Mr. Andre Brousseau, so said the tiny name plate placed casually on the table before him.

George held a sheet of paper in hand, a form that informed manpower officials, like Mr. Brousseau, of the holder's name, address, and other personal details, including most particularly employment history, job skills, if any, and future ambitions, again if any. It was clear that the official seated in front of him, as disinterested as he seemed, had been assigned to find people jobs.

The man he had recognized, the former employee of AP Siding, had walked by him obviously disappointed, if not angered, with nothing in his hand but a cigarette which he was preparing to lite when he suddenly stopped in front of George. "Hey, I recognize you now. It took me a while but I got it now. You used to work at AP, right?" George turned toward him, then motioned the man behind in line to take his place, and answered. "Yeah, I did. I worked in the cutting room, for that guy Lawrence. I don't know where you worked but I remember you from AP. Where did you work?" His former colleague from AP looked at him, smiling. "I was on float, worked pretty well everywhere. I may have worked in the cutting room, maybe even with you though I don't remember that." George then returned his smile. They then introduced themselves, first names only.

The guy's name was Paul. He said that he would wait

for him at the building entrance on Bank Street, having suggested that they head over to the Gilmour House for a beer. It was eleven o'clock in the morning but George agreed anyway, the lure of any kind of booze too tempting to resist, despite having already consumed a couple of shots of scotch that morning. George then abandoned the line. Paul hadn't abandoned the line but probably wished he had.

It was maybe twenty minutes later and the two of them were sitting at a small table. Only Paul had received a list of possible jobs and was presently laughing at the absurdity of actually applying for any of the positions recommended to him. There were ten vacant positions, Three of them were jobs in small time manufacturing companies, making air filters, plastic bottle caps, and room fans. Two others were steel distributors or fabricators, two more being mechanic jobs at small garages, and then there was three stock room jobs in a Pascal store in the west end. Paul then showed him a list of jobs that he had received yesterday. It was the same list as he had just received. Paul then suggested that George would have received the same list had he stayed in line and they would then have the same jobs to ignore when they applied for UIC. They both laughed although George didn't really intend to ignore any of the jobs, given his dire financial situation and the fact that a UIC cheque was a month away. They then ordered the first of several quarts of beer they were to consume that day.

They exchanged life stories, routine though relatively entertaining. Whether they were being accurate or allowing themselves to take some liberties in recollecting their histories was doubtful. They were both happily surprised to learn that they both had spent their early years, including their childhood and most of their adolescences, in Montreal. Paul lived in various districts on the eastern part of the island while George, who had fascinated Paul with his recollection of his unusual origin in the Notre-Dame Orphanage on Decarie Boulevard and that he had three fathers, one unknown, one who adopted him and another who was his step-father, reported that he had lived on the western part of the island. They concluded that aside from their origins on the Island of Montreal, they never really had anything in common, no schools, no districts, no athletics, no recreations, they never even lived within ten miles of each other, a curiosity given the number of times that their respective families had moved.

They were on their third quart when, for some reason, the subject of communism was raised by Paul. They had been discussing their years in school, two years in college for Paul, which he described as basically an education in drugs and rock music, and grade eleven for George, when the former said the subject of communism was the only subject in his college career that interested him. He admitted that he had become so absorbed in the subject that he become a Communist himself, so much so that he had become a certified member of the Communist Party of Canada. Without permission, Paul then proceeded to instruct George on the fundamentals of communism, advising him on everything from the history of Karl Marx and Friedrich Engels, the basic tenets of the communist ideology, and its progress around the world, Russia, the People's Republic of China and Cuba being particularly admirable, at least to Paul. Being on their third quart at only two o'clock in the afternoon, with a plate of fries each the only substance they were able to consume during Paul's tutorial, the both of them were barely making any sense. In any event, by the time they ended their drinking session, it was three o'clock in the afternoon, both of them could hardly walk, and George had agreed that he would accompany Paul to the next meeting of the Ottawa Chapter of the Communist Party of Canada. He was home early enough to partially recover from the effects of the afternoon before Sharon arrived home. Before she had the opportunity to question him on his job seeking efforts that day, George was able to inform Sharon on his encounter with Paul and his intention to accompany him to a meeting of the local chapter of the Communist Party of Canada. She seem to immediately forget about his pursuit of employment. She said she was shocked.

One final conclusion had emerged from their meeting. George had concluded, maybe after three quarts each, that Paul bore a striking resemblance to Leon Trotsky, the beard and moustache obvious. It looked intentional, like it was some sort of masquerade. He did, however, have much longer hair than Trotsky did. All that was missing were the spectacles.

It was almost two weeks later and he still had not made any progress on getting a job. But at least he had accompanied his new friend Paul to a meeting of local communists. The meeting was held on Waverley Street, just off Bank Street, a white brick, squat building called the Ukrainian Hall. It was regularly used for various assemblies, conferences, and gatherings, of which the monthly meeting of the Ottawa Chapter of the Communist Party of Canada was one such rental. Paul, whose family name he said was

Rosenfeld, a name that George suspected had been invented to sound more Russian, introduced George to the other meeting attendees. George noted that most of the people he met seemed to have foreign names, names that sounded like they belonged in a book about the history of the Russian revolution. Most of them seemed to be university students, long and facial hair prominent features on the men and an absence of make up on the women. The remainder of the crowd, maybe two dozen or so, was composed of middle aged men. To George, a good number of them looked like they could have actually been Russian, the majority of them with greying facial hair. In total, the meeting must have held maybe eighty chapter members, which hardly filled a quarter of the hall. Facing the assembly was a table at which three individuals sat behind a tall man who was standing at a wooden rostrum. He too was sporting a full beard. Paul told George that he was the chapter president. His name was Josef Panski.

Mr. Panski welcomed the attendees and immediately introduced the speaker for the evening, the central leader of the Communist Party of Canada. Her name was Elizabeth Rotkin, who Mr. Panski called "Comrade Rotkin". At least to George, she looked like she could have been married to Stalin. She introduced the other two individuals seated with her, their names being Gapski and Nowak. Both looked to be older men who might have fought ideological struggles somewhere on the other side of the Iron Curtain. The two of them were furiously smoking filterless brand cigarettes, grim expressions on their faces, staring hard into the crowd. Rotkin began her formal presentation by announcing that the Communist Party of Canada had recently opened a new chapter in Calgary, Alberta, news that prompted applause from the crowd. Paul leaned over to whisper that the party was always enthusiastic about any improvement in their status, especially the opening of another chapter of the party, which signified improvement in its political fortunes. Regarding its fortunes, Paul had told George that the party occasionally ran for political office, whether it was federal, provincial or municipal. If the party, usually represented by the same party members regardless of the timing of the elections, were able to attract more than two or three percent of a specific vote in a specific seat, there would be a fair degree of celebration. Paul said anytime they managed such a percentage, most members thought it was a miracle. In Ottawa centre, the site of the Ukrainian Hall, the same candidate had run for the Communist Party in more than dozen elections, both federal, provincial and even municipal elections, going back to the 1950s.

Comrade Rotkin proceeded to review recent events, at least as far as the Communist Party was concerned. During her presentation regarding recent events regarding global communism, George thought he was back in high school, back in history class to be precise, trying to stay awake to listen to a teacher named Mr. Barrett. The audience seemed especially interested in current developments in Czechoslovakia, particularly the efforts of the First Secretary of the Communist Party there, a certain Alexander Dubcek, to advance liberal reforms collectively known as "Prague Spring". George, generally uneducated about current events unless they involved sports or movies, actually was aware of Mr. Dubcek. He was also aware of the Soviet response to the

Czechoslovakian efforts led by Dubcek. Comrade Rotkin concluded her address with a grim conclusion.

All agreed, prompted by Rotkin's conclusion, that Soviet action to quash Czechoslovakian reforms had led to a decrease in the Communist Party membership, both internationally and in Canada. Aside from expressions of complaint, if not disappointment, a number of suggestions to improve the party's fortunes were raised by concerned members. They ranged from handing out circulars, the cost of which was left open, to serving free alcohol at meetings. One apparently veteran member, a strange looking party member named Boris, came up with the proposal that attracted the most attention, almost all of which was negative, if not hilarious. Boris was an older man, unshaven, with bloodshot eyes, dressed in a dark, dirty coat that looked like it had been picked out of the garbage. He could barely stand up, ash dangling from a smouldering cigarette, when he proposed that the party try to persuade more bourgeois types, that is if they could find any, to join the party, if not to run for the party in elections. He reasoned that the electorate would be more impressed if the party were able to field candidates who actually had jobs rather than auditioning for a play on the Russian Revolution. The crowd laughed. Both George and Paul joined them.

Improving the political standing of the local chapter of the Communist Party of Canada was left to chapter president Panski who announced that he would form a committee to look at the issue. Mr. Panski had to shout his announcement but was ignored as people were already were lining up for drinks: rudimentary mixed drinks, wine, and a selection of Polish, Russian and Ukrainian beer. George joined Paul in the line halfway through Panski's proclamation. Paul mentioned to George that it happened every meeting that the opening of the bar immediately prompted the crowd to start to line up. The meeting organizers often tried to get the hall owners to wait until the meeting was concluded to open the bar. They usually were not successful.

Behind George in line were three women, an unusual trio for chapter meetings. They were discussing the evening's proceedings, all three of them agreeing that one of them, if not all three of them should try to volunteer for chapter president Panski's pledge to form a committee to consider ways to improve the political profile of the Communist Party in the area. Aside from eavesdropping on the women's conversation and occasionally, if not barely nodding anytime Paul made a comment on the evening's festivities, George invested much of his time in line staring at the shortest of the three women. She was the only one of the three that did not look notably serious, the other two looking as if they were participating in some sort of religious event. She had short blond hair, was mildly plumb and was sporting a little makeup, the use of cosmetics hardly a standard accessory at chapter meetings. She was the youngest and the quiet one of the three, apparently listening to her two friends debate the benefits of the suggestions for political improvements. She occasionally turned away from the conversation in which she was ostensibly engaged to offer a smirk and a quick roll of her eyes, which George thought, or more likely hoped, had been directed at him. Meanwhile, Paul had been discussing the results of the meeting with two men who were ahead of him in the line for the bar.

Her name was Hanna Skitt. She was nineteen years old and said that she was majoring in political science at Carleton University. The reason for her attraction to George remained a mystery to him. He did not, however, spend much time thinking about it. His first rendezvous with Hanna had been made that evening in the Ukrainian Hall. It was after Hanna ordered the same brand of beer as George had ordered and George had remarked on it. That prompted a brief discussion of the meeting's proceedings. She said she wanted to continue the discussion they had had that evening. George volunteered to meet her three days later, in the afternoon. She had two hours between philosophy class and a political science seminar. George was a little concerned that he would somehow run into Sharon. If he did, he was prepared tell Sharon that he was, or had been applying for a position with the university, janitorial work being the most likely excuse. For the last couple of weeks, that is since George was terminated by the Mint, he had told Sharon that he was looking for work every day, going to the extent of inventing places where he had applied. Since he had made the arrangement to meet Hanna, he spent his time in the city library reading up on the history of the Russian revolution. He had hoped to impress her.

It was a miracle. He and Hanna met in the lobby of Dunton Tower. Within ten minutes of greeting her, they were in her room in the Grenville House and they were both removing their clothing. After several frantic moments of making love on a bed that was hardly large enough for one person, George rolled off the bed, ending up on the floor where he contemplated not only his good fortune but also his misgiving. He felt guilty, however, his relationship with

Sharon the cause. He had only cheated with Cynthia and that had led to the end of his relationship with April. He did not want to endanger his relationship with Sharon, a relationship that seemed to be headed toward something a little more permanent. He mentioned his doubts to Hanna who observed, with her customary smirk, that being sexually faithful was little more than a "bourgeois fantasy", advising George not to worry about it. This led to a discussion of the Judeo-Christian views on certain types of human behaviour, including most particularly sex. Hanna observed that despite the recent sexual liberalization evident in the sixties, women in the Soviet republics were much less traditional than women in the west when it came to sex. Hanna said that she had read several academic articles on the subject.

More generally, and less specifically on the subject of sexual mores, Hanna spent much of her time, that is when they were not wrestling naked with each other in her room at the Grenville House, instructing George on Marxist and related ideologies, including Hanna's favourite political philosophy, Marxism-Leninism, the guiding discipline of the governments of places like China, Cuba and the global luminary in Communism, the Soviet Union. George barely listened to Hanna as she persisted in her political education of him. He never really understood most of her tutoring, at least when he was actually listening to her. He got the impression, however, that she never really cared whether he was listening or not, her objective it seemed was to hear herself talk. On the other hand, his main objective was to rest up for their next calisthenic on her bed. He also could never understand why Hanna was interested in him in the first place although she did compliment him at one point on his lovemaking abilities, saying that he was quite skilled for a member of the proletariat, a compliment that he sometimes received from Sharon although not in those terms. In plain language, she never connected those abilities to his membership in the proletariat.

A Gospel According to Hanna

Not surprisingly, Hanna Skitt did not believe in marriage. She often said that matrimony was a bourgeois convention and was, therefore, unwilling to even consider his proposals. It was more than a year since he had moved into Hanna's place, a one bedroom apartment that was less than three blocks north of the bachelor he had previously shared with Sharon. She had graduated with a journalism degree and was now employed in the media relations section of the Department of Industry, Trade and Commerce. Her hiring had accelerated her inevitable breakup from George, her taking less than a month to move from their place on Cooper Street into a much larger apartment on the Driveway by the Rideau Canal. George stayed in his place on Cooper Street until Hanna decided that while she had no plans to marry him, she would not mind if he moved into her place, particularly after he had started doing clerical work for the Ottawa chapter of the Communist Party of Canada. Their romance, such as it was, seem to be a secondary consideration to the both of them. Hanna, who had completed three years of university political science, had been appointed secretary of the Ottawa chapter several months previously, her main responsibilities being to produce the chapter newsletter, formulate and organize the quarterly meetings, and, most importantly, to attract new members to the Ottawa chapter. So it would be convenient to have assistance in managing her duties.

In that regard, while Hanna did not insist that George get a job, he having been unemployed for almost six months, she did encourage him to take the clerical job with Ottawa chapter of the Communist Party of Canada. Hanna had George to help her with her clerical duties. He typed out the chapter's newsletters, delivered the letters to the post office, there being around two hundred addressees, typed out the agendas for the chapter meetings, and produced pamphlets to advertise the benefits of joining the Communist Party of Canada. Aside from his clerical duties, which only required him to work maybe two to three hours a day, Hanna provided George with a number of books that she assured him would educate him on communism. Although he had studied some history in high school, he was almost entirely unfamiliar with the historical events the books covered: *The Communist Manifesto* by Marx and Engels, *Das Kapital* by Marx, *State and Revolution* by Lenin, *Ten Days That Shook the World* by John Reed and histories of Leon Trotsky, Mao Zedong, and a book entitled *Canadian Bolsheviks*, supposedly a narrative on the Communist Party of Canada. Hanna promised George that she expected to question him on his studies although she assured him, with a snicker, that she wasn't planning written examinations. For a moment and for some reason, George thought that her questions had something to do with sex. They didn't.

It was routine then that George accompanied Hanna to almost every meeting she had regarding the business of the Ottawa chapter. General meetings included officials of other chapters in Canada, students interested in communism, members of the press, as few as they were, and most frequently, the president of the Ottawa chapter Panski. Interestingly enough, Hanna was the only member of the chapter's administration who was paid. Mr. Panski as well as two vice presidents, Messrs Gapski and Nowak, had commonplace jobs --- Panski was an book keeper for a small clothing store while Gapski and Nowak worked for local factories, the former a welder while the latter drove a truck for a company that repaired small engines. All three men were committed communists, having been members of the Ottawa chapter of the Communist Party of Canada since they were teenagers. It was generally thought that all three of them were children of Russian emigres.

In discussing the Ottawa chapter executive in particular, Hanna liked to relate stories that Panski spread around the chapter. One was that before his parents immigrated to Canada, maybe thirty years ago, they had arrived in New York and lived there a few years, long enough to join the Young Communist League of the United States and befriend a man named David Greenglass, who just happened to be the brother to a woman named Ethel who eventually married a man named Julius Rosenfield. Initially, Hanna made no further explanation, looking puzzled that George seemed to have no idea who Ethel or Julius Rosenfield were. After several moments, during which both Hanna and George exchanged bewildered expressions, Hanna provided George with an historical report on the conviction and execution of the Rosenfields in New York in 1953 for spying for the Soviet Union.

"What does the execution for spying have to do with this guy Greenglass?" asked George, his interest piqued by a story that involved something that was more than academic analysis and argument. Hanna looked somewhat surprised, as if she had expected George to know the answer to his own question. "Greenglass testified against the Rosenfields, claiming that he had passed atomic secrets to Julius Rosenfield, who was a Soviet agent." Hanna then said that Ethel was convicted of espionage based on the allegations that she had typed the notes that Greenglass had given Julius Rosenfield. In any event, Hanna concluded her narrative on Greenglass and the Rosenfields by saying that the Rosenfield case was in still dispute over thirty years later. After Hanna's account of the history of the Greenglass/Rosenfield situation, George was then able to understand the reason Panski liked to relate the story of his apparent friendship with Mr. Greenglass every chance he got. George thought it had given him a certain ideological standing among local communists. When George related his opinion to Hanna, she laughed, explaining that his story about meeting David Greenglass was most likely fictional. He had a habit of inventing stories. He was capable of predictable fabrications, like picking up women, which was an extraordinary assertion given Panski's age and general demeanour, or discussing political events with local Members of Parliament who Hanna said she doubted he know any of them. While people seldom believed all of his stories, they did not seem to care, acknowledging that his general loquaciousness made him popular with the membership of the chapter. He therefore managed, Hanna claimed, to give good speeches, particularly compared to Gapski and Nowak, both of whom could barely introduce themselves without stumbling but were still outstanding members. Rumour was that Panski patterned his speeches after talks by Lenin and Trotsky.

After Hanna told him about Panski's fabrications, she mentioned that Panski had a much more available and attractive source for another tale involving a person that would be of interest to fellow communists, including most particularly members of the Ottawa chapter. In addition, this person was a local celebrity of sorts, a Soviet defector who lived a couple of blocks away from the hall where the chapter held its meetings. The defector, whose name was Igor and worked for the Soviet embassy in Ottawa, lived on Somerset Street, in an apartment building called the "Squire's Court" across the Dundonald Park. Hanna said she was surprised that Panski did not claim that he was acquainted with Igor although she did point out the Igor story was likely followed by a majority of the members of the Ottawa chapter of the Communist Party of Canada. It was continually in the newspapers, anyone reading them would be familiar with Igor and his defection. That would suggest, therefore, that any of his chapter colleagues would be able to contradict any of the anecdotes that Panski could manufacture if he were to maintain that he actually knew Igor. George agreed that Panski or anyone else would, he supposed, would be unwilling to invent stories about Igor, as tempting as it may have been.

Aside from performing his clerical duties and attempting to educate himself with the books that Hanna had recommended, George occasionally made suggestions to Hanna for attracting new members for the chapter. For no good reason it seemed, Hanna ignored most of his proposals. They included serving appetizers and drinks, showing documentary files on communist countries, the Soviet Union, China and Cuba being prominent among George's proposals, and holding seminars on specific issues related to economics for example. In regard to the latter, Hanna would eventually advocate inviting individuals who would attract interest from people who would not normally attend chapter meetings. She suggested historians, a Carleton University professor who recently published a book about Senator Joe McCarthy, other university professors, librarians, journalists, particularly those who had followed the Igor and similar stories, would be politicians, specifically individuals who have run under the Communist Party banner, debates between individuals who had opposing views, and any local personalities who had claimed or were claiming to publicly endorse communism. They would include local musicians, writers and perhaps any local people who have travelled to Soviet Union and China in particular.

While Hanna was not amendable to most of George's suggestions, believing that serving free drinks in meetings or showing documentary films were not worthwhile proposals, inviting individuals to speak at meetings, individuals who may be of interest to the chapter's members was worth pursuing. She said, however, that she would have to raise the proposal with the chapter's executive. Initially, Hanna thought that Panski may not agree with the proposal, for reasons that she guessed may have had something to do with his influence on the chapter, the fear that individuals invited to speak at meetings might be a superior attraction to the chapter membership than Panski himself. His speeches were usually rambling, sometime incoherent diatribes. He would read from books and newspaper articles.

Fact was that while Panski was hardly an inspiring speaker, he was an outstanding organizer, having increased the membership of the Ottawa chapter of the Communist Party of Canada from maybe a dozen to over a hundred in less than five years. Fact was that Panski, who become a member when a man named Feklisov, a recent Russian immigrant, founded the chapter in the early 1960's and did little, if anything to increase its membership, took over the chapter and worked to significantly increase the number of members. Panski's hold on the presidency of the chapter was therefore strong and remained strong. Hanna was worried, therefore, that Panski would oppose inviting speakers. For the simple reason that some of them could, if not would, outshine him.

It came as a surprise then when it didn't take Hanna long to convince Panski of the proposal to invite guest speakers to the chapter's meetings. In fact, Panski agreed with her that presenting guest speakers could and possibly would attract non-members to the meetings, an outcome that could result in attendees joining the chapter as new members. They then began to discuss a list of possible guest speakers and a schedule for inviting them. Hanna had not thought of proposed guest speakers and therefore was not in a position to make any recommendations to Mr. Panski. Further to her request, he gave Hanna a week to compile a list. When she arrived home, she asked George to spend a few days in the main library at Carleton University and come up with a list of speakers who might enlighten and possibly entertain people at chapter meetings. For a reason he could not quite ascertain, he was looking forward to the assignment. He guessed he would feel like a student again although that experience was limited to high school, not the superior academic pursuits available in university.

Armed with a year old student handbook from Carleton University, the last handbook that Hanna received before she retired from academics, boredom and economic hardship the causes, George identified professors working in two obvious fields; history and political science, the respective programs featuring European/Russian history and Communism. Conveniently, commentaries regarding each of the specific programs of interest identified the relevant professors. There were two professors and a lecturer with respect to the history course and one professor to inform interested students about Communism, which was a more specific topic than European and Russian history could be. He had four names: Professors Allan, Francuk, and Kamenski and a lecturer named Sarazin. Of these, Professor Francuk was the only woman, her first name was Anita.

The University of Ottawa was a larger university with a greater number of courses in history and political science. It was a bilingual school, meaning that at least half of the programs and courses could be in French, effectively disqualifying some relevant teachers from guest speaking at chapter meetings. George was able, however, to identify three individuals that could be asked to appear before the chapter meetings: Billing, Fournier, and Prudhomme, all professors and all men. Like the four from Carleton, there was no information on their scholastic qualifications and/or interests.

The Biography of George

When he told Hanna about the results of his research, preliminary as it was, she suggested that he explore the newspapers, which were archived in most libraries, including the main city library on Laurier Avenue, for information on articles on local activities of the local chapter and the Communist Party of Canada. Hanna did point out that she had already decided to invite Helen Stierman who had written a history entitled *Canadian Bolsheviks*. It was a book that Hanna had already asked George to read before she was to appear before a meeting of the chapter. He would have to visit the main city library to perform a microfilm search for articles on local communist activities, events like elections, speeches at community meetings, and letters to the editor, of which there were many. George spent almost an entire day going through the archives, so much so that he finally provided Hanna with more than four dozen newspaper articles on topics that could be related to communist activities. Hanna was pleased with George's endeavours, an assessment that ultimately resulted in sex that lasted almost all evening.

Hanna was worried that it could happen and it did at the third meeting with a guest speaker. She needed a last minute replacement for one of the guest speakers, Carleton history professor Kamenski. The substitute Hanna found had appeared on the list that George had originally compiled, but had declined Hanna's invitation. He was another teaching assistant, a recent immigrant from Russia named Aleksei Churkin. He spoke good English, passable French and had moved to Ottawa to pursue a master's degree in political science. His previous academic qualification was a degree in political history from Moscow State University. Professor Kamenski said that Churkin was likely a genius and the smartest student he had ever taught. Hanna happily accepted Mr. Churkin as a substitute speaker.

He appeared as a guest speaker on a Thursday night meeting. As advertised, he seemed articulate in both English and French. It impressed the audience even though many of them did not understand French. He was at the lectern for almost an hour. Away from the lectern, Churkin looked anything but impressive. But as he spoke, he managed to generate interest from the audience. He started his talk slowly, almost inaudibly, using sarcasm regarding the status of the students to whom he taught political science. He ridiculed the assumed privileges held by the parents of their students, their bourgeois life styles, their jobs, their money, their passing along their advantages, which he called the testament of the middle class, he called the students legacies of the privileged. The tone of his speech hardened while its volume increased. He called it entitlement.

Churkin then emphasized that the chapter should be more than a talk shop for ersatzwhile Marxists, Marxist-Leninists or plain vanilla Communists. He added members should be able to do more than sing "Le Internationale". He proposed, in fact urged action. At that point, the audience broke into applause, a reaction seldom heard during the meetings, which was not surprising, and certainly not been heard during previous meetings at which guest speakers had appeared. Churkin then turned to the need he said for advertising the chapter specifically and the party more generally. He called such efforts propaganda. Again, the room exploded into applause. It was a louder oration than previously.

George looked at Hanna. She was sitting behind Aleksei Churkin. She was staring at him like he was a statute in a holy shrine. She was enthralled. The man had charisma. He made previous guest speakers sound like grade school speakers.

Later At The Mercury Bar

It would have been around the fifth anniversary of his marriage to Elaine Mills. Both he and Elaine usually forgot the exact date. They had been living together for two years before they got married, having forgotten the exact date of that decision as well. He was married to a woman named Susan when they first met, more than seven years ago. Now, they were now faced with the practicalities of finding a larger apartment, preferably arranging for at least a two bedroom flat, purchasing furniture and clothing for an infant, ensuring that Elaine had proper medical care, and that she was able to apply for and receive unemployment insurance, maternal leave benefits not yet required from most employers, including the Mercury Bar where she worked. The Mercury Bar was a strangely furnished place where she served drinks to patrons, many of whom were usually happily inebriated within an hour of arriving. George had first met the waitress Elaine when he accompanied some of his teammates on the company slow pitch team to the place. It was after a game against Terry Industries, a company that manufactured lawn mowers. George worked for Lawrence Plastics, a company that manufactured plastic knives, forks and spoons.

The Biography of George

Both companies had teams in an eight team slow pitch league that played at Carlington Park. Players on the two teams that played each other that evening had liked to frequent the Mercury Bar. Players on the other six teams in the league, however, usually visited other local watering holes. The popularity of the Mercury Bar among the two teams was a curious, if not inexplicable phenomenon. Nonetheless, the guys playing for Terry Industries stopped going to the place after a year, reasons unknown. That left the guys from Lawrence Plastics to frequent the Mercury Bar. Unlike the more well known establishments in the area, for example the Carlton, the Elmdale, and/or the Prescott, the Mercury Bar offered an entirely different environment to customers. It had dark lightening, smooth jazz background music, black vinyl covered booths, sardonic bartenders and waitresses who all looked like they were or were about to become divorcees. The Mercury Bar couldn't be more different than the other places. The Carlton, the Elmdale, and/or the Prescott all featured bright lights, the only background entertainment being sports on the televisions on the wall, small circular tables with Formica tops with vintage tavern chairs, and the only people serving drinks being men dressed in white shirts, black pants, and white aprons. Yes, the Mercury was different.

Years later, reminiscing about their time playing slow pitch, George and one of his former colleagues at Lawrence Plastics, a guy named Butterworth, discussed the possibility that most of the denizens of the Mercury Bar were gay, public expressions of homosexuality, fairly unusual at the time. George and his friend both remembered that most of their teammates had occasionally wondered why members of the Terry Industries and the Lawrence Plastics slow pitch teams seemed to be the only recreational jocks who ever enjoyed drinks at the Mercury Bar. The two of them suspected that some of the members of the two teams were gay and liked to go there on non- game days. They then convinced their teammates to frequent the Mercury Bar. George's ex-teammate also theorized that whoever recommended the Mercury Bar for post game drinks did so several years back. Maybe the place had not been as apparently gay as it seemed years later. Both teammates ended up concluding that they had no explanation for their attendance at the Mercury Bar.

Regardless, George's regular presence at the Mercury Bar led to his making the acquaintance of Elaine who served him whenever he and his teammates came in for drinks. He was immediately infatuated with her. She was one of the younger waitresses in the place, most of her colleagues being middle aged and mainly male. He was not alone in being taken with her. Several of his teammates also had romantic designs on her, her physical attributes and vivacious disposition obvious explanations. Elaine, George and three or four of his teammates usually exchanged banter, with George and his teammates competing with each other in trying to impress Elaine with witty comments. As George's interest in Elaine intensified ----he found himself unable to escape her in his dreams --- he started to visit the Mercury Bar on evenings when the Lawrence Plastics slow pitch team wasn't playing. On those nights, George would take a table in the corner of the place, ostensibly trying to remain shrouded in the dark lighting of the place. Happily for George, Elaine was able to recognize him almost as soon as she first saw him sitting there in that corner that first night. It was a Friday when he went in there alone.

"I know you. You're usually here on Tuesday, with your buddies?" She greeted her. "But you and the guys on your team were always wearing team sweaters. And tonight, no sweater. So where's yours tonight?" With that comment, Elaine chuckled. After a brief pause, George responded, "I thought it wouldn't be, you know, proper to wear my sweater when I'm not playing. I'm just here to have a beer." Elaine smiled, walked away saying that she already knew what he wanted. George wanted her as she walked toward the bar, reflecting the fact that Elaine could have been in her mid to late thirties. Not only was he confused, wondering why he was attracted to a woman who was maybe a decade older than he but was guilty for some reason. As he sat there, contemplating his anxiety of conscience, he noticed that the bartender, a guy named Matt, glanced at him with a peculiar look on his face like he knew what was on George's mind. He thought that he winked at him.

That evening was the first time George made his romantic interest in Elaine conspicuous. His previous attempts, during those evenings when he accompanied the Lawrence Plastics slow pitch team, were hardly obvious. Fact was that his efforts were hardly efforts at all, more like implied attempts, sometimes not much more than staring. Sometimes, he would compliment her on her outfit, which was odd since her so-called outfit was pretty well identical every time he saw her, her hair, again which was odd because she always seemed to wear her hair the same way every evening he went in there or her more general appearance, all compliments of which were conveyed in the most discrete manner possible. Every now and then, one or more of his teammates would take note of his behaviour, as secretive as George may have tried to be, gently mock him although George hoped that his teammates didn't know the extent of his infatuation. On the Friday evening, without his teammates to restrain any of his amorous intentions, no matter how clumsy or futile they may have been, George had a couple of beers before he actually attempted to engage Elaine in pursuit of the real objective of his visit to the Mercury Bar.

Ordering his third beer, George took the opportunity to expand his limited discussion of his not wearing his team sweater that night. "I'm surprised you recognized me without my sweater." Elaine nodded and observed. "Well, you know that all of us, including the customers by the way, always notice you guys." She leaned in, winked and implied a compliment. "You were a particular favourite of some of the boys, if you know what I mean. Maybe you noticed but with or without your sweater, you're a favourite of a couple of the boys tonight." With that comment, she turned and looked at two guys at a table to their left. They seemed to be paying attention to their conversation although, in the Mercury Bar, George would wager that the boys were paying attention to Elaine's customer, not Elaine. Again, Elaine raised her eyebrows to go with her previous wink. There was a short silence as Elaine went to leave. George put out his hand and immediately spoke up about his true purpose. "I have to tell you. I'm, I'm....." he stuttered, stammered, nervously attempting to admit his interest in Elaine. "I wanted to talk to you. I mean, I really want to talk to you." She smiled, almost quietly chuckling. George immediately had the impression that Elaine was also expecting his admission. She had.

More than two months after George and Elaine had that first conversation at the Mercury Bar years ago, his previous wife Susan had a boy they named John. Over those months, George continued to fantasize about Elaine despite the impending birth of their first born. He had visited Elaine at the Mercury Bar every Thursday evening for the two months until Susan entered the hospital. After the birth of John, George didn't visit Elaine and the Mercury Bar until the infant was more than three months old. It that wasn't exactly his idea. Then, with the slow pitch season less than a month away, his fantasies about Elaine understandably reemerged, the link obvious. Rather than organizing indoor pre-season practice, as other teams in the league often did, team captain Foley proposed that the team get together for drinks at --- where else --- the Mercury Bar. It was no surprise then that George's reveries about Elaine understandably grew. In fact, he initially developed a heavy case of nerves, his anxiety building as the evening with the team at the Mercury Bar got nearer. Making love with Susan one night, only their third time since the birth of baby John, George somehow and surprisingly managed to imagine that he was making love to Elaine rather than Susan, a delusion that panicked him enough to make him think that Susan might suspect that he was having an affair, a circumstance that surely would have created trouble with Susan.

A few evenings later, during the Lawrence Plastics

evening out at Mercury Bar, the subject of Elaine the waitress came up after the attendees discussed the prospect of giving the team a proper name, Pirates being the most popular appellation, the possibility that two new teams, representing P C Lemaire, a plumbing supply company, and a steel fabricating company named Atlas, would be joining the league, and the retirement of Bob Tucker, a guy who played first base for the team for several years. George's teammates expressed a certain surprise when a teammate named Ron informed the meeting that he had been told by a waiter at a small local tavern called the Dominion that Elaine recently married for a third time. The table wasn't surprised by the news, most of George's teammates suggesting that a third marriage was probably predictable fate for someone like Elaine, with one member of the team calling her life a soap opera.

Elaine wasn't working that evening, somehow relieving George who wasn't sure what he would say to Elaine if he ran into her, it having been five months since he last spoke to her during one of his solo evenings at the Mercury Bar. He was still fantasizing about Elaine, impassioned dreams that were, however, becoming less memorable the longer George stayed away from her. Still, the mere mention of Elaine's name was enough to fully resurrect George's fantasy of her, so much so that he started to check the room for a glimpse of Elaine, even though he knew she wasn't there. A nervous smile spread across his face, hoping that the rest of his teammates hadn't noticed his reaction, however brief as it may have been. He sat almost transfixed, sitting staring into his dark corner of the place, apparently not paying attention to the table's conversation. The guy sitting beside

George, a guy named Dick, whacked him on the upper thigh and then made reference to Elaine. George hoped that the reference was casual and in no way specific to him. Elaine being Elaine, she was an attractive woman who may have been the object of a relaxed obsession among some of George's teammates. "Are you listening, pal?" And Dick added a sardonic remark. "Besides, she isn't here tonight."

George enjoyed the remainder of the evening, fitfully trying to banish any thought he might have had of resuming his fixation on Elaine. Although he was initially reluctant about playing for Lawrence Plastics another year, the meeting with members of the team somehow changed his mind. It wouldn't be unexpected to consider that an opportunity to run into Elaine might also be another possible reason for his change of mind, that is if the Lawrence Plastics slow pitch team continued to patronize the Mercury Bar after games. In addition, the thought of visiting the Mercury Bar on his own, as he had for several months before his son was born, also crept back into his mind. Later that evening, lying in bed with Susan, with their son John in a crib beside them, looking up at the ceiling, he considered his options, as limited as they were. His safest, in other words least troublesome, recourse was to retire from the team and avoid the entire matter of his fascination with Elaine. But lying there with an erection based on his imaginary scenario involving himself, Elaine and a nice room in the Westin Hotel downtown, George realized that that particular alternative was probably too difficult to be ignored. On the other hand, maybe he could not only stay playing with the team but immediately start a serious effort to seduce Elaine, regardless of how many times she had been married or how long she had been married to her most recent husband. Finally, there was the middle ground: continue to play for the Lawrence Plastics slow pitch team but only visit the Mercury Bar when he was accompanied by teammates which he promised himself.

He couldn't stay away from the Mercury Bar long enough to qualify himself for the commission of a mortal sin, that is of course if George still believed in that sort of thing. It must have been almost half way though the slow pitch season that he finally gave in to the temptation of returning to his passionate pursuit of Elaine. After an early game on a Monday evening, the team retired to the Mercury Bar by nine o'clock. As usual, the team sat in Elaine's section. She looked particularly attractive that evening, so much so that George seemed, at least to most of his teammates, more distracted than normal, taking time to stare at Elaine every time she passed their table, whether she was serving them drinks or not. So he decided, without too much in the way of internal deliberation, that he would resume his solitary visits to the Mercury Bar and would start a renewed campaign to seduce Elaine.

It was a Thursday evening around nine o'clock when he sort of crept into the Mercury Bar and took up an available table in a corner of the place, Elaine's usual section. She spotted George, smiled, waved and held up a finger to signify that she would be right over. The expression on her face suggested that she was somehow expecting him, which may have simply meant that she recognized him. George had brought a copy of the *Economist* to take up his time, he being the only customer in the place sitting by himself.

The Biography of George

Like most places, except for sports taverns, the Mercury Bar did not provide any television screens to entertain the solitary patron. Within three or four minutes, Elaine was standing at his table with his beer, which she placed in front of him. "Nice to see you, George, I haven't seen you in here by yourself for months though I did see you with the team the last few Mondays."

He was momentarily paralyzed, not having rehearsed any witty comments with which to impress Elaine. He managed a reply that was both feeble but veracious, adding an awkward chuckle: "Well, I'm happy that you still recognize me." Elaine waved off his admission, "Of course, I remember you from last year. I recognized you as soon as you and your baseball pals came in a couple of months ago. And now, you are in here alone, just like last year." George nodded and then looked up at Elaine, acknowledging the situation. He then repeated the confession that he first provided last year. He was almost whispering. However unlikely, it was clear that George didn't want guys at the other tables to overhear his conversation with Elaine. "Like I told you last year, I just wanted......I still just want to talk to you."

Although they were married for less than several months, her third, his second, things between Elaine and her new husband ---- his name was Al Dorn and he drove a city bus ---- were getting complicated, if not difficult. They were having difficulties, their main problems that their jobs seldom allowed them to spend much time together, she working late afternoons and evenings at the Mercury

Bar while her husband drove the city bus during the day, meaning that the two newlyweds hardly saw each other during the week. On top of that, Dorn had some interesting sexual habits, including most particularly sex with multiple partners, most of whom also drove city buses, and wife swapping, which involved Dorn's friends and their wives. Despite the fact that Elaine had worked and was still working in a bar, which George believed would have conditioned her to less conventional behaviour, including he thought the kind of sexual escapades in which Elaine and her husband were participating. Elaine was quite reluctant about her husband's erotic habits. It was a constant source of conflict between the two of them.

George was amazed, happily as it turned out, that he and Elaine were somehow able to forge a romantic relationship. Their Thursday evening conversations started casually, usually ninety minutes of George sitting at a corner table nursing a couple of beers or so with Elaine occasionally dropping by every so often. Gradually, their conversations would go beyond pedestrian chitchat, the weather and whatnot, to discussions of a more personable nature. Elaine talked extensively about her problems with her husband, mentioning every now and then her dismay about Al's sexual demands. For his part, George did not talk much too about his personal life, hardly mentioning either his own marriage or their sex life. One night, after he discovered that Elaine lived in the same general area of the city as George and that they both took the same bus route home every evening, the #51 from downtown to the west end, he decided to accompany her home. He had volunteered after she had told him that one of the drivers on the #51 evening was one of her husband's friends. She said that she was worried that she would run into him. George waited that Thursday until the Mercury Bar closed a little after midnight, no one but three waiters, a bartender, Elaine and George left in the place. They boarded the #51 bus on Slater Street. By the time he and Elaine found a seat on the bus, she had informed George that the driver was not one of her husband's friends. They were sitting together for maybe five minutes when she said that she hoped that her husband was asleep when she got home. After that confession, she took his hand, holding it tightly. She then leaned on his shoulder, whispering that she felt a lot better. That was the beginning of their affair, a discussion of proposed arrangements between George and Elaine being made after the next Monday evening, after the team had gone home. George stayed in a coffee shop, also on Slater Street, about a block west of the Mercury Bar waiting for her. He joined her at the bus stop, waiting for the #51 bus.

Coincidentally, George's wife Susan had recently registered for an evening course at Carleton University. The class was on Tuesday, starting at seven o'clock, a convenient time for a rendezvous, at least from George's perspective. Elaine said she could arrange to switch an evening off from Thursday to Tuesday with one of the waiters. Coincidentally, and fortunately, Tuesday was one of the three evenings that Elaine's husband either played hockey or went drinking with his buddies. George helpfully noted that Susan's Tuesday evening class ended by nine o'clock and was usually home by nine-thirty, by which time Elaine's husband would be either still playing hockey or ordering another beer. By the time the #51 bus reached George's stop, they had agreed that she would meet George at his place in eight days. Fortunately for the two of them, Al was usually picked up by one of his buddies on those evenings when he was playing hockey or drinking with his pals, making their car available for the evening. Her only worry was the possibility that Al would bring one of his buddies home after one of his drinking sessions for some extracurricular activities in their bedroom.

Elaine arrived at George's townhouse a little after seven o'clock on the Tuesday after next. She was dressed casually, the first time George had ever seen her in anything other than her customary waitress outfit, the black dress, the black stockings, and black pumps. Her make-up was not as eccentric as it was when she was working, her hair more shampoo advertisement than a gay nightclub look. Elaine wasn't in the place a minute before they began to remove their clothing. They were down to their underwear by the time they had reached the second bedroom, George explaining quietly that the master bedroom was out of bounds for obvious reasons. Fortunately, despite their clear passion for each other, they took their lovemaking slow, George's customary approach. Elaine was overjoyed, sex with any of her former lovers, including her three husbands, hardly approached the heights of lovemaking she was now reaching with a man named George.

As they enjoyed the afterglow of their coupling, the cliched scene of each love scene that she had read or seen, she made an unexpected statement. "You know, there are times that I wish I wasn't married. Thinking about it, there are times that I wish I wasn't ever married. I mean, like my first two hubbies, Al doesn't make love to me, he fucks me....him and the rest of his bus driving buddies. You just made love to me, my husband fucks me." George offered her a tender smile and agreed with his new lover. "I wish you weren't married either." He then softly laughed. "I wish I wasn't married either." For a brief moment, he thought of his lovemaking with Susan, both before and after the birth of John, realizing that there was nothing humdrum about their lovemaking. Sure, their lovemaking was not as frequent as it had been years ago but it was still almost as exciting. But, as George understood the mythology of adultery, the attraction of sex with a new partner was sometimes almost irresistible. Now, he believed it. And he didn't care how old she was.

More than three weeks later, during which time he and Elaine made love twice and he and Susan made love at least five times, practical considerations the main reason, George received a telephone call at home late one Wednesday night. He took the call in the kitchen. He soon discovered that Elaine's husband Al Dorn was on the line. He almost hung up, surprised, if not shocked by the call. There was a brooding kind of silence on the other end of the line, a still silence until a gruff voice asked if he was speaking to George Gagnon. He answered rather faintly. He had to introduce himself at least twice before Mr. Dorn continued with the purpose of his call. "I am Al Dorn, Elaine's husband but you're probably already know that, right?" George answered as curtly as he could. "Yes, I know who you are." There was another silence and then Al Dorn continued with his explanation. "So I guess you know why I'm calling" George could guess. "I want you to leave my wife alone or you will have a problem, a big problem." George was surprisingly composed to respond with a denial and a rather pathetic excuse. "I don't want a problem but.." Al Dorn cut him off. "But what, George?", his pronouncement of his name almost theatrically threatening. George said "Elaine and I have been together only a couple of times. I mean, we are only friends; you know from the Mercury Bar. I've known her for about a year. I used to come into the place every week with my slow pitch team and we eventually became friendly." There was a sinister laugh on the other end of the telephone. "You call what you and Elaine are doing is just friendly." George felt like saying something smart alecky but declined. Al Dorn continued. "So I want you to stop being friendly with my wife. OK. Otherwise, you and I will continue to have a problem, a big problem." With that threat, if not warning, George started to become frightened.

He then heard a rustling from the bedroom upstairs. He was suddenly concerned that Susan was awake and that she could be coming down stairs to discover who was on the telephone. He was more worried about Susan finding out who was on the telephone than he was with the fact that Al Dorn was on the telephone. He heard Susan taking the first few steps on the stairs to come down to the first floor. "Sorry, I have to go." he said. He then hung up the telephone. He left the kitchen to intercept Susan. He told her that Gary McCann, a guy who worked with him at Lawrence Plastics, had been on the telephone. He explained that McCann was drunk, was worried about his job, and wanted to talk to him. George told her that McCann, who he said was a little strange, thought they were friends and sometimes shared his troubles with him, which were well known by his co-workers at Lawrence Plastics. He doubted that Susan actually believed him. It was the beginning of the end of he and Susan.

I Found This In Your Wallet

Susan asked him to remove himself from their residence perhaps six months after she discovered his dalliance with Elaine. The proof was a weekend during which George was compelled to shelter Elaine after her husband threatened her physically. It was on a Friday afternoon. Her husband had instructed her to pack a suitcase and then physically threw her out of the house. She initially planned to seek refuge at her friend's Linda place but then remembered that her husband Al was friendly with Linda's husband John, a situation that further frightened an already nervous wife. So she thought that her only option was to seek refuge at George's place. She was simply went to his place on Westfield Drive, an address that she knew well, it being the main scene of her assignations over the past few months. It was just before dinner time on that Friday. George, who had been listening to records in the spare bedroom, answered the door and was immediately stunned. Within less than a minute, Susan shoved by her husband and stood in the door. Elaine guessed that Susan knew who she was but she introduced herself anyway. "My name is Elaine. I'm a friend of your husband. I know him from the Mercury Bar." Susan looked at Elaine as if she was a lunatic. She made a move to close the door in her face. So Elaine took a couple of steps into the apartment. George then got between the two women. Elaine explained herself to both of them. She was escaping she explained. "Al threatened to beat me and not like the previous times --- he had both fists clenched. He looked like he meant it this time, he looked crazy. I had to get out of there." George pointed to the suitcase she was holding. She nodded and explained that she had left her place once her husband started to threaten her, after it became obvious that she was having an affair. She went on to say that the main clue was a series of love notes that her husband had found in her cosmetic drawer. Then she explained her motive in calling on George's townhouse. "I don't have anywhere else to go. I need a place to stay until Al calms down. I thought that you guys could take me in for a while."

Susan looked at Elaine as if the woman had suddenly developed psychiatric problems. "You're kidding, right?" said Susan. George again interrupted and took his wife's hand. "Don't you remember all that hippie shit we used to talk about? Tolerance, communal living, free love, getting rid of all those old fashioned values, you know like marriage." He delayed for a moment and added, "We have to help her, we have to." Susan now looked at George as if her husband had also developed also psychiatric problems himself. "Remember, a few years ago, we believed in that stuff, even you." With that quiet encouragement, he took Elaine's hand and then his wife's hand and led them both into the living room. Susan didn't look happy but went along, no smile, no frown, no scowl. Elaine looked relieved but still scared.

Elaine put down her suitcase. They then sat together on

the living room couch. George sat between them and then offered them each a drink. Elaine asked for a beer while Susan requested wine. George decided on a beer himself. As George was in the kitchen fetching the drinks, he took a peek out into the living room, noticing that the two women, obvious rivals, had moved as far away from each other as they could, both leaning on the opposite ends of the couch. George returned with the drinks. He had plenty of room. As they started on their drinks, the two women stared at each other silently. Still, Elaine looked scared while Susan looked irritated, if not angry.

They drank in silence for several minutes. Then, Susan turned and asked Elaine a question that seemed almost absurdly self-evident. It was after all an accusation. "How long have you been sleeping with my husband?" she asked Elaine in a stern, almost interrogatory tone. Elaine, who should have anticipated the inquiry, sat there without an expression. She didn't know quite what to say when the truth was so obvious. In a trembling voice, Elaine replied. "For a while." Susan then turned to George, now presumably expecting him to answer. He did. "Why do you want to know, Susan? I mean, what's the point of knowing that? All I can tell you is that it has been a while." George continued. "Yes, we have been and are lovers. But I love you too." Susan looked at the two of them blankly. George continued with his explanation, an explication that Susan immediately believed was some sort of hippie fairly tale, all that stuff about open marriages and open relationships. "I may have pretended to believe in hippie bullshit like that at one time but I don't think I do anymore. I grew up you see. We got married." In response, George said that wife swapping and key clubs were becoming quite popular in certain suburbs, pointing out recent movies had taken on such themes. Susan got a funny look on her face. It faded quickly.

Again, the three of them sat in silence, seemingly waiting for one of them to speak. Finally, George suggested that each of them have another drink and plan dinner. He also proposed that Elaine stay at least one night in the spare bedroom, hoping he said that her domestic situation would improve. Susan, who had been wearing a frown and before that a scowl, looked understandably surprised and then appeared to be contemplating her husband's plan. She nodded, reluctantly, realizing that she didn't have much of a choice. No matter how upset she may have been and may continue to be with the appearance of her husband's lover at her door, Elaine's fear of her husband was so palpable as to be difficult, if not impossible to ignore. She felt she had to agree to shelter Elaine as long as she needed to be. She thought that maybe it would be the last time she would take any action that reminded her of her days as a "flower child". Anytime she reminisced about those days, she would wear bell bottom jeans, her only tie dye t-shirt, and a bead necklace, and would be rhapsodized about the effects of acid, which she had never tried. She didn't think that anyone would believe her.

They had spaghetti for dinner. Elaine and Susan had some of the cheap wine they had on hand while George had three or four pints of Labatt 50, a favourite of his ever since he began buying beer, when he was maybe fourteen years old, at the local grocery. They spent much of their dinner and the remainder of the evening talking about Elaine's daily experiences in the Mercury Bar, which she noted casually was frequented almost exclusively by gay men, patrons who she said were much better behaved than the heterosexual crowd she had served in other places she had worked. That prompted Susan to ponder the reason for the Lawrence Plastics slow pitch team to chose the Mercury Bar for post-game drinks. George told them that a guy from the team, a guy named John Stanton, recommended the place after having lunch there a couple of times a week the previous winter. He had started going there when he accompanied a colleague from the company where the two of them worked to lunch at the Mercury Bar. Stanton didn't know that the place was favoured by homosexuals but, as George pointed out in his explanation, nobody else did either. Nor did they know that the Mercury Bar lunch devotee, whose name was Rudd, was actually gay. George didn't know. There were not too many gay bars around anyway. At least, not many around where he and his teammates lived. In any event, John Stanton thought the Mercury Bar would be a pleasant place for post-game drinks and so he went ahead and recommended it. Elaine thought the origins of the team's weekly socializing at Mercury Bar humorously understandable. Reacting to the strange expression on Susan's face, George said that he had not heard any reports of any of his teammates being approached for any inappropriate behaviour, or at least inappropriate from their point of view. Elaine said she seldom heard about any unwanted incidents There were probably rumours, nothing but gossip she said.

While the three of them carefully avoided bringing up anything about Elaine's domestic troubles, which were obvious and considerable, her problems accidentally emerged during their conversation. Susan in particular wondered what prompted Elaine's husband Al to force her out of the house this day when he supposedly knew about her affair for maybe six months. After maybe an hour of drinking cheap wine, Susan finally demonstrated the indiscretion that she had been controlling since Elaine knocked on the door. "Elaine, why did your husband throw you out of your place today of all days. I mean, hasn't he known about the two of you fucking around for a while. Why did he pick today?" Elaine looked despondent, her head down, her hands almost in prayer, like she didn't want to answer. She then explained, almost in a whisper, "The bastard showed up drunk, accused me of cheating on him, as he did almost every day anyway, and started to try to rip my clothes off. He was yelling at me, saying that everyone knew. He was also in the process of taking off his clothes. He wanted to screw me but he didn't have and couldn't get a hard-on." Elaine stopped for a moment and then said that she got dressed and got out of the house. Susan asked if her husband tried to stop her. "No, he was too busy yelling and throwing things at me. I guess he had just had enough. Actually, when you think about it, it would have been kind of funny if it hadn't been so frightening. Here I was being chased out of the house by a man with his pants around his ankles, yelling and throwing things." George and Susan had to agree. It was kind of funny.

The three of them were to turn in sometime before eleven o'clock. George was reluctant about joining Susan in their bedroom, concerned that the relationship between Elaine and himself that had been made so clear that evening would have made sharing a bed difficult, if not impossible. But surprisingly, Susan invited him into their bed and actually lured him into making love to her, a gesture so unexpected that George was temporarily unable to respond, although he was able to get over that problem soon enough. George thought that maybe Susan was attempting to compete in lovemaking with Elaine, who was maybe ten years older than George and twelve years older than Susan. She was unusually passionate that evening, which left George confused and somewhat breathless although he suspected that his affair with Elaine might have been, if not was entirely based on their sexual activities, his wife's penchant for sex not as enthusiastic as that of Elaine. In addition, and perhaps more importantly, they took care not to make too much noise in pursuing their lovemaking. After all, Elaine had taken the other bedroom, adjutant to their own.

It was six o'clock in the morning, it was a Saturday when the telephone hanging on the kitchen wall rang. George got out of bed, stumbled downstairs and answered it on the fourth or fifth ring. As he should have expected, on the other end of the line was Elaine's husband Al. It could not have been anyone else. Surprisingly, Al wasn't shouting. He didn't sound angry. He sounded like he had been or was still crying. He said he wanted to speak to Elaine. He was almost pleading, disconnected, rambling. George was silent, confused, surprised, not knowing how to respond.

While George listened sympathetically, which in itself surprised him, he was also anxious, fearing that Elaine's husband would become hysterical at any moment. Elaine soon appeared in the kitchen and whispered, "It's Al, isn't it?" She was dressed only in her underwear, a light blue brassiere and matching panties. She stood close to George, almost leaning on him. Naturally, he had developed, despite the anomalous circumstances, a healthy erection which Elaine immediately grasped and started to stroke. As Elaine started to go to her knees, her favourite and most consummate sex act, George started to gently move himself away, sensing, accurately as it turned out, that they were being watched, which they were. Susan was now standing in the doorway to the kitchen, a stunned and then outraged expression on her face. After a couple of moments, during which time Elaine had disengaged herself from George's penis with a funny expression on her face, his penis quickly shrivelling from its previously excited state. George pulled up his briefs and stood stock still. Elaine then crept back a few steps and seemingly waited for Susan's reaction, a judgment that both she and George thought would likely be extreme. For his part, George hung up the telephone, waiting for Susan to pronounce his fate. He had forgotten about anything that Elaine's husband had been saying. He was frightened, his anxiety warehousing in his stomach like he was going to get sick.

Surprisingly, Susan chose sarcasm as a response. Through pursed lips, her voice seething with more than casual scorn, she spoke. "Don't let me interrupt you two. I assume that your husband was on the phone but that doesn't seem to matter." She was looking squarely at Elaine who had now gotten to her feet, "So now that you have dealt with him, you might as well go back to what were doing. I can just go back to bed and when you are finished, how about a cup of coffee?" George thought that the entire scene could have been written as perverted screenplay dialogue with Alice Kramden explaining some domestic dispute to her husband Ralph. Both Elaine and George made no reply. As she turned to go back upstairs to bed, Susan then continued with her soliloquy. "How about a threesome? After all, you both look like you're ready for some fun and maybe I could use some as well." She then started to laugh manically and headed up stairs. Elaine and George stood there, staring at each other, clasping hands nervously. Then they both heard things falling, or more accurately things being thrown down stairs. It was obvious that Susan was throwing Elaine's clothing down the stairs, her obvious intention to order Elaine out of the house. "I guess I have to go." said Elaine and walked toward the door. George followed her toward the door. He stood and watched her dress and walk out the door. She turned at the last minute, faced him with tears in her eyes and kissed him on the cheek. She then closed the front door gently and headed out the building. As George stood staring at the closed door, he heard the upstairs bedroom door slam. He would be sleeping in the spare room for the immediate future, however long that was.

❧

It was almost predictable, just like a television soap opera. After Elaine had spent that night with George and Susan at their place, George had stopped visiting the Mercury Bar to see Elaine. Since he was no longer playing slow pitch for the Lawrence Plastics team, a damaged knee the cause, he was relatively certain that he would not accidentally run into Elaine. He simply never saw her again. Although he sometimes was tempted to investigate Elaine's whereabouts, sometimes hoping to see her on a city bus or shopping downtown, he never made any serious effort to locate her. That did not mean, however, that Elaine was far from his mind. After two months or so, Susan seemingly having gradually dismissed the memory of George's affair with Elaine from her mind, she and her husband managed to reestablish a sense of normalcy, even making love occasionally, its frequency increasing with time. Sometimes, as he and Susan made love, he would imagine that he was making love with Elaine, a thought that seemed to enhance his passion for Susan. He was careful not to act in any romantic or sexual way that would suggest to Susan that he was thinking of Elaine, particularly when it came to certain actions, oral sex being a pleasure that Elaine pursued enthusiastically while Susan, for some reason that George thought was related to a previous sexual relationship, always declined. Within five months or so, George's relationship with his wife seemed to have returned to normal. In fact, Susan started to mention having another child, an ambition that she had not raised for almost a year.

It was, however, more than six months after the then apparently forgotten incident with Elaine that George was asked to remove himself from the accommodation he shared with his wife. They were having drinks before dinner one Thursday evening when Susan casually handed a small photograph of Elaine to George. She was almost naked, her only attire a pair of black stockings and a pair of stiletto heels. "I found this in your wallet." said Susan.

It took him three years to decide to move from Ottawa back to his native Montreal. After his divorce from Susan, which was finalized after about a year, the formalities handled entirely by Susan, he continued to work at Lawrence Plastics, rejoined the company softball team, accompany his teammates to the Mercury Bar, where Elaine no longer worked, and lived in a one bedroom apartment on Bank Street. He met a woman named Anna Vincent, a lawyer working for the firm's Montreal custom broker in Montreal, at a Lawrence Plastics Christmas party. At first, he and Ms. Vincent discussed their mutual appetite for devilled eggs, a common canape at social occasions, and her duties as counsel for the company's customs broker business at the port in Montreal. From there, they ended up exchanging complaints about their recent divorces.

George Going Home

He had lived with a lawyer named Anna Vincent for more than ten years when they parted company. Fortunately, a friend named Wilson had commented, they had not bothered to get married and had no children, obstacles which normally would make ending their relationship more difficult than it might otherwise be. While they had always seemed to have enjoyed each other's company, her constant drinking, her occasional promiscuity and her inexplicable interest in flamingo music eventually led to their separation, particularly after George discovered that Anna had been using Tuesday evening meetings of Alcoholic Anonymous as an excuse to conduct a number of illicit love affairs.

After he moved out of their two bedroom apartment on Melrose Avenue in Notre-Dame-de- Grace, a nice place about which visitors often expressed praise, George was forced to relocate to Harley Street near the Montreal West Train station, a much less prestigious address than Melrose Avenue. For some reason, a reason that he could not explain, he started to regularly attend the gymnasium at the YMCA on Stanley Street, usually after completing his regular shift as a salesman at the T. Eaton department store on

St. Catherine's Street. Since the winter somewhere in the late 1980s, he had been wearing the same black ski jacket every day from November to the end of March. He had purchased it with his employee discount. When he arrived in the gymnasium around six o'clock in the evening, after his normal shift, he hung his ski jacket on a makeshift coat rack that was placed just before the entrance to the locker room. He sometimes got confused as to where on the rack he had entrusted his jacket. After all, it seemed that every second coat on the rack was black.

It was a Thursday evening in February. He finished his routine, some uninspiring leg lifts, sitting cycles, triceps work, and some pull downs, the usual crap. He got dressed, picked up his ski jacket and carried his gym bag out to to Stanley Street. He then turned up to Sherbrooke Street where he caught the #105 bus going west to have dinner at Abby's, a typical greasy spoon that still featured table top juke boxes. He entered the restaurant, sat down in a booth, put down his ski jacket, ordered his dinner, hamburger steak, fries, two pints of Labatt 50 ale and coffee, pumped a quarter into the jukebox to play a couple of tunes, paid the bill with cash, put on his ski jacket and left the place. He crossed Sherbrooke Street, then the train tracks, and headed east on Harley, past the Honey Pot, another diner that he sometimes frequented, usually for breakfast or lunch if at all, dinner almost totally reserved for Abby's. He was home a little after nine o'clock.

He arrived at the door of his one bedroom flat on Harley Street. He reached into the left pocket of his jacket, taking out several keys hanging on a small key ring. He stared at it, realizing that the ring was not his. It featured a double headed eagle above a red and white striped shield. The key ring included what he thought looked like a car key, a key to the trunk of that car he assumed, an apparent house key, and what could have been a key to a safety deposit box. All very interesting he thought but he was faced with a practical problem. He had someone else's keys and presumably someone else had his. That meant that, without his key, he could not enter his own apartment. He stood with his forehead on the apartment door. Then it came to him. He would have to contact Mr. Jimmy Schmidt, the building superintendent with the well known disposition of a grouch. It was nine o'clock in the evening and superintendent Jimmy would definitely be unhappy if one of his tenants were to call on him at that time. He lived with his wife, a large woman in a wheel chair who was hardly ever seen outside the flat. Jimmy and his wife, whose name George never knew, lived in number 102, a two bedroom flat which overlooked the train tracks. George was the tenant in apartment 608.

He was downstairs facing Jimmy's door within minutes. He knocked on the door. He heard some moving inside and then Jimmy opened the door slowly. His bald head poked out of the door and rasped quietly, almost whispering an expected request. "What do you want?" George stepped back from the door. Mumbling, he introduced himself and stated his request for a spare key, which he assumed was held by the building superintendent. Jimmy answered, in a quiet but now annoyed tone of voice. "Yes, I know you. Your name is Gagnon. You're up on the top floor, in apartment 608. You're alone. You don't have many visitors" George nodded and then explained that he had left his key at the gym downtown. Jimmy continued. "And you now want me to give you a spare key, right?" George nodded, standing there like a mannequin. "Well, give me a minute, I have a spare in the cubicle in the back room." He disappeared for a moment, leaving the chain lock on, and then reappeared with a key, auburn coloured, not silver as the key he had left in the gymnasium. "Here is a spare. I only have the one. So you better goddamn well bring this back to me tomorrow. It's the only one I have" With that threat, Jimmy slipped the key between the door and the door jam to George who thanked him and backed away from the door, turned and headed to the stairs ---- the building, which was constructed probably sometime in the 1930s, was not equipped with an elevator.

It did not take George long after he used the spare key to open his apartment to wonder whether the spare key was a master key that could get into any apartment in the building. He was also disturbed about a more realistic possibility. If he had someone else's key, someone else had his key. On the other hand, if someone else had his key, he would have no idea as to which apartment door it would open. On another pragmatic latter, he made a mental note, however, to ask, if not demand that Jimmy arrange for a locksmith to change the lock on the door to apartment 608. He would talk to Jimmy when he returned the spare key. He then examined the black ski jacket he had just hung up. It was a black *Calvin Klein* ski jacket in an extra large size with two side pockets. It was identical to the ski jacket that he had been wearing every day for the last several months but he knew it wasn't his. It was obvious. George had keys that belonged to somebody else, the owner's identity unknown. He should return the keys to the YMCA gymnasium on Stanley Street he supposed and they could likely locate the owner. But for some reason, he couldn't decide. He went to bed that night without having made any decision. He was enthralled with the story of the keys. To him, the story could have been crafted by one of those short story writers that had recently become his ambition, the first of his generally indolent life. He wanted to hold on to the experience for a time.

By the next morning, he had made a decision about the keys, having realized that he wanted to know, for a reason that he could not quite understand, the identity of the rightful owner. In fact, he wanted to know more than the owner's identity, he wanted to know about the owner himself, what he looked like, how old he was, where he lived. So that was why he decided, after a cup of coffee, two slices of stale bread, and half a banana, to use his lunch hour, which was really only 45 minutes, to ask someone in the hardware department on the seventh floor of the T. Eaton department store to copy the key. On the way out of the building to work, he decided not to call on Jimmy. He would wait until the end of the day before giving him the spare key and asking him to call on a locksmith to change the lock on his apartment door. Jimmy, who was on a ladder changing a light bulb in the lobby of the building, greeted George and asked him not to forget to return the spare key. George nodded and quickly left the building. George told him that he would return by eight o'clock. He then pocketed the key, walked out the apartment building, walked west on Harley Street, north on Connauglt and then onto Sherbrooke to catch the #105 bus.

At 12:15 pm, after eating a Maywest cake for lunch on his way up to seventh floor where he found somebody from the hardware department, a small section in the north west corner of the building where Eaton's sold various power tools, nuts and bolts and such. George had a younger looking man wearing a bow tie copy the three of the four keys he found in the pocket of that ski jacket. He looked at the keys, took them, remarking that what he thought was the house key looked like it might open an older flat, an interesting observation that also seemed to belong to the double headed eagle ring that held the keys together. The younger looking man charged George $2.25 plus tax. He felt guilty somehow.

He went to the gymnasium after work, half expecting to see a notice about misplaced keys, thinking that the rightful owner would be looking for the keys, the gymnasium the most likely place to have lost them. His expectation was proven somewhat correct. So as soon as he arrived, he went to the counter and asked the woman staffing it, a relatively younger woman with a curious haircut, if anyone had asked about lost keys. The woman pointed to a cork board behind them. George walked over to the board and started to examine the notices pinned to it. The notices concerned a variety of messages, advertising gym classes, yoga classes, baby sitting, and lost possessions, including gym clothes, gym bags, and, alas, one set of lost keys. The owner of the lost keys was identified by a telephone number on an index card. To determine the identity of the owner of the lost keys, he would simply have to call the telephone number. George took the number down and asked the woman with the curious hair if he could use the telephone behind the counter. He was handed the receiver and the counter woman dialed the number for him. A female voice answered. When asked about the notice regarding the keys, she told George that her husband, who had posted the notice in the first place, had already found his keys, having left them in one of his other overcoats. After handing the receiver back, George asked for an index card. The woman handed him a card and he went to rummaging around for a pen. In doing so, he took the lost keys out of his pocket and placed them on the counter while he continued to look for a pen.

The woman picked the keys up, examined them, and then make a surprising statement. "Are these the lost keys?" she asked, a bemused look on her face. George, having found a pen in his pocket, looked up and nodded, nonchalantly. He didn't really understand the substance of her question. She then said that he wouldn't have to worry about looking for the owner of the keys. "I know who owns these keys. He's a member here." she said. She sounded astonished, as if she had just discovered some sort of treasure. George came a little closer to the counter, looked up and replied as dumbly as he could. "Huh? What do you mean?" The woman, whose name George eventually was told was Jennifer, giggled and continued. "I mean, Mr. Gagnon," looking at his membership card for a moment, "that these keys belong to Mr. Wenck, one of our members. I immediately recognized that key ring. As you see, it's quite unique."

Of course, George was startled that Jennifer or any member of the staff would be familiar with a member's keys or their key rings. "How do you know that those are this guy Wenck's keys? I mean, members don't give you their keys, do they?" Jennifer immediately responded. "For some reason, Mr. Wenck is proud of his key ring. He used to mention it occasionally. That's how I got to recognize it." She picked the keys off the counter, lifted them to the florescent lights in the ceiling and told George to examine the key ring. She then handed the key ring to George and told him to look at the tiny symbol that was where the necks of the two eagle heads met. George examined the key ring and observed that there was a small iron cross at the base of the two necks. "It's odd that Germany, and I mean Nazi Germany, abolished the double eagle symbol in the late 30s. The double eagle heads are a symbol of the Holy Roman Empire. I looked it up." explained Jennifer who was now leaning on the counter. She took the keys back from George and placed them in the drawer beneath the counter. "I'll give the keys back to Mr. Wenck."

George then turned away from the counter and started to walk into the locker room. He stopped and looked back at Jennifer. He asked her a final question. "What does Mr. Wenck look like?" He wasn't quite sure why he was asking but he did have a purpose. "Oh you can't miss him. He is short, has white hair and has a large surgical scar in his chest ---- obviously cardiac surgery. In any event, he is here if you want to meet him. He's probably in the locker room right now." George smiled, picked up his gym bag and started to head into the locker room. "Thanks." he said. Jennifer then extended the conversation. "Hey, Mr. Gagnon, why don't you return his keys to him yourself." suggested Jennifer. Towards that proposal, Jennifer reached into the drawer under the counter, pulled out the keys and handed the keys back to him. George stepped forward, accepted the keys, and headed into the locker room.

Inside the locker room, he sat in the first bay --- there were three --- and took up a position on the bench before locker #76 and begin to change into his gym clothes. Mr. Wenck's keys were sitting in the pocket of his gym shorts.

The first man that came in his area took up a position before a locker directly across from him and began to change. He was a slightly pudgy middle aged man who he had recognized. He usually worked the weights for twenty minutes and then worked the seated row machine. Two minutes later, he was certain that his target had arrived. He was white haired and looked like he might have been named Wenck. Like the pudgy man, George recognized him, coincidentally and then happily when he sat down and removed his t-shirt, revealing a surgical scar on the right side of his chest. He was sitting across from locket #34. He nodded at George who returned the gesture. George recalled that he had spoken to him before, intermittently and always briefly. George stood up from his bench, took the keys from his pocket, and wordlessly walked over and presented them to Wenck.

It was a broad smile followed by a quick laugh. Wenck immediately explained his reaction. "I was wondering what happened to these. I got home yesterday and took somebody else's keys. Obviously, they didn't work at my place." With that, Wenck reached into his gym bag, which looked more like a brief case than a gym bag, and took out George's keys and handed them to him. As expected, George smiled and also explained. "Well, they won't work at my place either, not anymore." There was a pause. Wenck had a puzzled look on his face. "I'm having the lock on my front door changed. So these wouldn't work either, at least if my building super can arrange it." George bounced the keys in his hand and tossed them into the bag in the locker. They stood looking at each other for less than a minute. Then, they introduced themselves to each other. "My name is Heinrich Wenck, I've seen you here a few times." In turn, George introduced himself. They both offered smiles.

It might have been a week later when George came across the copy of house key that he had left on his dresser. He had thought about the keys every now and then since he returned the originals to Wenck in the locker room. He had seen him in the gym twice since they exchanged keys. On both occasions, they had exchanged greetings. George had asked him about the double eagle key ring but had said little else. In any event, he picked up the key and wondered about what he was or could do about it. Laying in bed that night, he picked up the theme, deciding that he could use the key to sneak into Wenck's place, wherever he lived. He had become, for reasons he could not fathom, interested, perhaps more than that. There were things about him that captivated him, particularly that he had history in Germany before and during World War II, a reality that Wenck himself confirmed when he mentioned that his father, who was in the German army during the World War II, had given him the double eagle for joining the Hitler Youth. George had had a long fascination with the war in general and the Nazis in particular. For a moment, George thought about questioning Wenck about his activities in the Hitler Youth, which George regarded as some sort of deranged boy scout organization and a training ground for SS recruits after a thorough indoctrination. But he didn't. Somehow though, he had to investigate Heinrich Wenck. Consider it a hobby he thought. He had nothing better to do.

However, it did give him the idea that would finally involve using the key to Wenck's place, wherever it was and whenever it was empty. He lay in bed that night, contemplating a scheme to discover Wenck's home address. He could ask Jennifer at the counter although she might decline, citing some sort of confidentiality, and embarrass himself in the eyes of the staff at the YMCA. That left him with an option, to follow Wenck from the gym to his residence. George knew that Wenck was in the habit of leaving the gym when George was arriving, a convenient convergence of times. He could wait across Stanley Street until he was finished his gym routine, around 5:30 PM, and headed home. The late February weather made waiting for him outside the gym on the street uncomfortable, waiting inside being hardly a reasonable alternative. So he decided that ordering a pizza and then sitting at the window of Lucia's Pizzeria, which was diagonally across Stanley Street from the entrance to the YMCA, was likely the best way to stake out Heinrich Wenck. The next day would probably be the best alternative.

As planned, the next day at a little before 5:20 PM after placing his gym bag on one of the two seats at a window table at Lucia's, he settled into the line behind three customers to order pizza. He was able to watch the door to the Y by standing and leaning to the left. Wenck was scheduled to leave the gym in three minutes by which time he hoped that he would be sitting by the window waiting for Wenck to appear. By the time he received his dinner, two slices and a coke, his two seat table which he had reserved had been appropriated by two kids in school jackets. He panicked for a moment and then calmed down long enough to take out his wallet and offer the two of them $5 each to take another table. They agreed and took a table in the back of the place. The two guys serving the pizza from behind the glass counter looked at them, smirking and then shrugging their shoulders. He was halfway through his first slice of pizza when he saw Wenck departing from the Y. George put his pizza down, took a swig of coke, put on his jacket, and slung his gym bag over his shoulder and rushed out the door. That seemed to entertain the other patrons of the restaurant.

In the meantime, Wenck was headed south. George got within a half a block of Wenck just as he crossed St. Catherine's Street, which was about as close as he was going to get in his pursuit. He followed him down Stanley, passed the Bell Centre, across Rene-Levesque to the district called Griffintown to a street called Rioux, the area and the street both unknown to George. He was now on the other side of the street as he saw Wenck stop in front of a squat four story building with six apartments on each floor. It looked like it might have been built sometime in the late forties or early fifties. The building had not been maintained. It was shabby, the painting on the brick walls faded, its windows generally dirty. George saw a couple of people leaving the place looking like they were on something. In addition, as George stood on the sidewalk to the left of the building, George thought that the apartment building looked a lot like pictures he had seen of where he lived with his mother in Verdun maybe fifty years ago. He stared at the building, trying to remember. But he was too young then, too young to remember. Still, it was a dump.

He was now close enough to the building to witness Wenck as he entered it. He watched Wenck enter, use a lobby key to open the inner glass door and then head for the stairs towards what George assumed was the basement. Once he was certain that Wenck had entered his apartment, he approached the building and entered. He immediately consulted the alphabetical list of tenants and the apartments in which they lived. Wenck occupied apartment #108 in the basement.

George now knew where Heinrich Wenck lived and had a good idea of his schedule. He was now prepared to use the copies of Wenck's keys, to enter the lobby and then to creep downstairs into his residence. He choose a Friday, three days hence from when he discovered the man's address. During those days, he stood across the street from or near his place on Rioux and watched. He would take up a post at different stations and at different times. He wanted to be sure about one thing. Particularly, he was worried about the possibility that Mr. Wenck might have a wife, a friend or a roommate, someone who lived with him and would or could be present if George used the copied keys. On six occasions, he stood outside Wenck's place for at least thirty minutes, sometimes in the morning, sometimes in the afternoon, sometimes in the evening. They were hours of surveillance invested in ensuring that Wenck lived alone. The fact was that he did live alone although he appeared to share accommodation in the apartment building with a variety of reprobates and scoundrels, many seemingly intoxicated, some apparently mentally handicapped, others looked like simple degenerates. In fact, in the hours of watching Wenck's building, he saw few people that he would consider normal. On the other hand, he did not bother to follow Wenck after he left the building. Jennifer from the Y understood that Wenck worked as a tailor in a men's store near the YMCA on Stanley Street, a fact that he had casually mentioned during one of their brief discussions in the gym. He also told George that his father had been a tailor. Understandably he guessed, Wenck never mentioned anything specific about his father's experiences in the war, if there was anything interesting to report.

In any event, he had three days to consider a plan to enter Wenck's apartment, # 108 in the basement, without being seen or discovered by anyone. He decided that ten o'clock in the morning was probably the most suitable time to execute his scheme. Most of the people who had a reason to be out of the building were out of the building, some to work, although that number was likely fairly minimal, some to presumably procure liquor or drugs, or others to take the bus downtown to find somewhere to get stoned or annoy pedestrians for spare charge. The postman usually came by around one o'clock while deliveries, which were few, also stopped by in the afternoon. Wenck himself usually left the building by 8:15 AM or so, never speaking to anyone, taking the #107 bus north up to Stanley and St. Catherine's, where he disembarked on that corner to report to his tailor's job at a men's shop called Padar's. The rest of his schedule had been well documented, at least by George. He usually left work around four o'clock, went to the gym, and then left for home by 5:30 in the afternoon. He usually went to lunch at the Deville Diner on Stanley, usually around 11:30 AM.

Around ten o'clock on the following Friday, having taken a day off, George walked up to the outer door of 1252 Rioux Street, opened it, and then used one of his two copied keys to unlock the inner door, walked down to the basement, went left to apartment #108, and stood with the other copied key in his hand. Noticing that there was no one else in the basement, he opened the door and stepped into the apartment. He was not surprised about the decor. It was a profoundly dull beige painted one bedroom apartment that belonged in the basement of a building that was populated by many tenants that could afford to live there. Facing him as he walked in was the kitchen, a narrow room with an ancient refrigerator, a stove that looked like it was barely functional, and a small table that could seat three people. To the right was another small room, the living room which contained a well used grey coloured sofa, a brown coloured chair that looked like it had been rescued from a neighbour's garbage, a small table on which a dark glass ashtray sat, and, dominating the room, a large photograph hanging on the wall. There was a small washroom at the end of room and to the left of that, a neatly appointed bedroom that contained a three drawer dresser, a night table and a single bed that looked like it had been made up by a maid in a hotel. It looked to George like a bedroom that might have been occupied by a monk. He also noticed that there was not a television set in the apartment.

George had no doubt. It was the photograph in the living room that was the only thing worth investigating further. It was bizarre, almost surrealistic. It was a black and white photograph of Adolph Hitler greeting five members of the Hitler Youth or who he thought looked like members of the

Hitler Youth, their youthful appearances an obvious hint. Almost astoundingly, George recognized the photograph. He had seen it or a photograph closely resembling it in several of the many books he had read about Hitler. It was one of the last photographs of Hitler ever taken, probably in March or even April of 1945. George had read different biographies about Hitler, most if not all of which included a number of photographs of Hitler and his associates, from his childhood to a last photograph before his suicide at the end of April in 1945. George immediately wondered about the reason for the hanging of such an unusually large photograph, almost a poster, on the wall of the living room. It took up most of that wall across from the sofa, almost from floor to ceiling.

There was something profoundly peculiar about the photograph. Aside from Hitler himself, who looked like he was about to touch the cheek of one of five boys. Towards the end of the war, George had read that boys as young as twelve years old were drafted into the Volkssturm, the people's militia. George assumed that the five boys in the photograph were involved in defending Berlin against the advancing Russians. Aside from the unusual size of the photograph, the other peculiarity was that there was a circle drawn around one of the boys, one of the two boys who were wearing smiles, the last in the line facing Hitler. He was looking to his left at Hitler, a strangely impish grin on his face. All five were wearing caps, all five caps being in different styles, as if all five boys were responsible for their own uniforms, standard procedure for the people's militia George assumed. He sat on the sofa, contemplating the photograph and the boy with the circle around him. Who was the boy and why was he circled? Obviously, Heinrich Wenck could possibly tell him but he did not feel like admitting that he broke into the man's house. On the other hand, maybe Wenck was such a historical sycophant that the photograph was akin to a picture that teenagers like to tape to their bedroom walls. He also had the thought that Wenck had not circled the boy but had secured the photograph with the boy having been already circled. Regardless, he realized that he would have to return to Wenck's apartment and bring a camera, to photograph the photograph. It would most definitely bear further investigation.

The Picture in Mr. Wenck's Apartment

As far as the picture of Hitler and the boys were concerned, George had always been fascinated by the idea that a lot of people, common people he meant, appear in photographs with famous or infamous people, people like Hitler for example. He often wondered about those people, whether they realized that they had appeared in such a photograph and whether they remembered they had. He had always been fascinated by the idea. He remembered that years ago, one of his supervisors told him that his father had him on his shoulders to watch a parade of German soldiers marching into Vienna in March of 1938. As a ten year old boy, he said he saw Hitler walk past the two of them. He said that Hitler was no further than five or six feet from him when he passed. He also said that thousands of people, possibly hundreds of thousands of people in the crowd that day were taking photographs. Years later, he was still wondering he said whether his father and him were in any of those pictures. He thought of investigating photographs of Hitler's entry into Vienna to determine whether his father and himself appeared in any of the photographs. But he never got around to investigating any such thing. It was just something that ruminated through his mind every so often.

Most of his colleagues didn't believe the story. However, some people, including George, did. He told himself that he had no doubt that the memory of that supervisor's story of that parade in Vienna in March 1938 was the inspiration for his interest in the photograph on the wall of Heinrich Wenck's apartment. So he had spent the afternoon of the day he had entered Heinrich Wenck's apartment considering when he would return there with a camera. He decided that he would wait two days before entering the place again to take his picture. He would then rummage around the apartment looking for clues to the photograph, especially to the boy who was circled in that photograph. Ever since he saw the photograph and the circled boy, he had developed scenarios that might explain Wenck's retention of the photograph and the significance of the circle around the boy but none of them really could be proven. He had a number of questions that he wanted answered but could not figure out a way to have them answered. Why did Wenck keep and display the photograph? Who were the boys and who was the boy who was circled? Was Wenck or Wenck's father or his father somehow related to or associated with the boy in the photograph? Had the boy played a part in some activity that had been somehow important to Wenck or his father or his family? Aside from taking a photograph of the photograph, he had the hope of finding something that would answer one or more of those questions.

Two days later, as he had planned, George took a bus to 1252 Rioux Street and stood in front of Wenck's apartment building with the copied keys solidly gripped in his hand.

The Biography of George

Though he did manage to successfully sneak into apartment #108 two days previously, he still felt a little apprehensive about entering Wenck's place again. It was around one o'clock in the afternoon and, unlike the last time, when he had arrived at ten o'clock in the morning, the street was comparatively crowded, and a number of people, generally elderly, were standing on the steps of 1252 Rioux Street. He tried to act casual, like he was waiting for a taxi cab or a someone to pick him up, checking his watch and looking down the street. It took ten minutes for the people on the steps of the apartment building to depart, a small STM bus for seniors stopping to pick them up.

As the bus left, George turned and started up the apartment steps, used one key to open the lobby door, headed for the basement and used the other key to open the door to apartment #108. He entered the living room and then sat on the sofa to study the photograph just like he did two days previously. There were seven people in the picture, five boys, one of whom was circled, the one at the far left of Der Fuehrer. That boy had a smug smile on his face, a cynical smile that was less captivating than the smiles on the faces of the other four boys. The other smile in the picture belonged to Hitler who had one of his menacing old man smiles on his face. He noticed that that the collar on Hitler's overcoat was up, a curious detail since no one else in the photograph had their coat collars up. The only indication of the seventh person in the photograph was a partial picture of an officer's cap above Hitler's left. Finally, above the heads of all seven people was a partial picture of a concrete balustrade. George then snapped three pictures of the photograph on the wall. George then got up from Wenck's sofa and headed out the door.

On the way home, he fiddled with the three pictures he had taken of the photograph in Wenck's apartment. He had no success with his playing around with his camera. That lack of success was not a surprise. What did he expect? After all, the only camera he did have was a Samsung smartphone. He remembered when he had a Nikon. He wished he still had a Nikon. He also wished he had a microscope although he wasn't certain that a microscope would assist him in his investigation anyway. Although he could directly ask Mr. Wenck about the photograph, having a relationship with him from the gym, he was reluctant in view of his method of securing access to the photograph. He did not relish the idea of admitting to Wenck that he had copied his keys and used them to enter his apartment, not once but twice although maybe he would not have to tell Wenck about his second visit to 1252 Rioux Street. He needed another idea.

That night, he had a couple of revelations while struggling for sleep. He at least saw them as reasonable options. He would investigate as many books that were available on Hitler as he could, some of which he assumed would include that picture of Hitler and the boys. From there, he might be able to contact the copyright holder of the photograph and possibly uncover the identity of the boy who was circled in the photograph. In addition, he could try to find a local historian, possibly an expert on Hitler, who might be able to help him identify the circled boy in the photograph. Although success of both options seemed unlikely, if not hopeless but aside from approaching Wenck himself, they were the only possibilities.

The Biography of George

The next morning, he found the very photograph that was on Wenck's wall after a short search of Google. He also found several similar photographs on the internet. But none of the pictures showed any copyright or any publisher. He had decided that he would have to search his own apartment looking for any books he may still have on Hitler. He suspected that he had left several books on Hitler in the various residences he had occupied over the last forty years or so, particularly when for example he and a woman named Hanna, who was a committed member of the local chapter of the Communist Party of Canada, were a couple. She had encouraged him to read histories and historical biographies and such. Further to her recommendations, he remembered reading a couple of Hitler biographies, recalling at least two authors, one named Fest and the other named Toland, who had produced lengthy tomes on Hitler. He did not have either volume any more but, after a search of his current abode, he found three books about Hitler, one of which included a picture of Hitler and the five boys. That picture was identical to the picture that was attached to the wall in Wenck's apartment. It indicated that the photograph was the property of a photography studio, presumably in Germany. The author of the book, which was entitled 'Hitler Ascent 1889-1939' was a German journalist. That said, he thought that even if the photographic studios owned the rights to the photographs, they probably wouldn't know the origin of the photograph itself, specifically who took the picture and who was in the photograph. They would only know from whom they purchased the photograph.

So the only conclusion he could reach was that the only way he could identify the boy in the picture would be to find someone, a professor or a historian who was knowledgeable enough, expert enough, or even obsessed enough to identify the boy. He would be visiting McGill University, which George had discovered, through the internet of course, had the largest history department in the country. He would try to arrange an appointment to see Professor Jenkins, advertised as an authority on Hitler. In particular, he had written several monographs based on Hitler, including one entitled "Hitler's Personal Security", a subject that could possibly reflect comments and include details on photographs that could include the one in which he had an interest.

It took him a week to arrange a meeting with Professor Allan Jenkins, Associate Professor of History for McGill University. George played it straight, explaining that he was looking for ways to identify, if possible, boys pictured with Hitler in a photograph taken towards the end of the war. He told Professor Jenkins that the photograph had appeared in a number of books written about Hitler, obviously implying that he would possibly recognize it if he were shown the photograph. The professor sounded reluctant, if not suspicious. Most of the time though, he met with fellow historians, academics and sometimes graduate students to discuss the minutiae of what happened or may have happened seventy or eighty years ago. George often wondered how historians were able to document the daily activities of historical figures. He recalled that the last book on Hitler that he read was a 758 page leviathan to which was attached 212 pages of bibliography and notes, the latter made up of other books, newspaper articles, academic papers, memoranda, diaries, letters, post cards and any other written notations that might shed light on the event, period or life under study. In any event, after speaking to him on the telephone, Professor Jenkins ultimately agreed to a meeting with George, the time and place arranged by his secretary/assistant, a woman named Sara. The meeting was scheduled for the next Tuesday, five days hence.

George arrived at the Leacock Building on Sherbrooke Street at 9:45 in the morning. Professor Jenkins' office was in Room 615, which was on the second floor toward the back of the Neo-classical building that seem perfectly consistent with the pursuit of an arts education. The scent of empire style oak panelling and dusty marble floors permeated the place, reminiscent of a confessional in an old church. He arrived and stood in front of the door to Professor Jenkins' office. He knocked on the door, was invited in by Sara, and stepped into the office. She then motioned George to sit on a wooden bench against the wall facing her. George was sitting on the bench surveying the room. There were several large framed pictures on the walls of the Professor's anteroom, a portrait of the Brandenberg Gate, a view of the Bavarian Alps presumably taken from Hitler's study in the Berghof, as helpfully pointed out by Sara, and a photograph of the current German Reichstag. Sara proudly said that she had taken the picture herself. George also noticed that there were several copies of each one of the Professor's books in a book shelf standing behind Sara and her desk. He was trying to capture the titles of each one of the books. There were twelve of them, three or four of them he noted were not itemized by Google.

He had been waiting for maybe ten minutes before Professor Jenkins made his appearance, opening the door to his office. He certainly looked the part of a professor, a model for the classic liberal arts education. He was blessed with a mane of longish white hair, a kindly and wrinkled face, yellowing teeth, and a herringbone brown tweed suit with a vest. George would not have been surprised if he had a gold pocket watch somewhere in his vest. Professor Jenkins reached out and shook George's hand. "Mr. Gagnon, George, you're the guy with the photograph of Hitler, right?" George nodded and then stepped into the professor's office after the latter motioned him in. George smiled and then gazed at the walls of the professor's office. They made Sara's wall look plain and unadorned in comparison. The professor's office looked like it had been decorated to pass for a Hitler museum. There was maybe a dozen good size photographs, six on one of the walls, five on the another, and a huge photograph behind the professor's desk and his chair. The other wall held a large picture window which looked out on a grassy hill that rolled downward into one of many university quadrangles. Professor Jenkins directed him to the chair in front of the professor's desk. Jenkins almost immediately noticed George staring about the room, peering at the walls in particular. The professor then started describing each one of the photographs. All but one of the photographs were in black and white.

He started with the photograph behind his desk. It was a photograph of Hitler posed formally, presumably in his office, dressed in a business suit. "That was taken sometime in September 1936. Since he was usually dressed in the party uniform, this picture is somewhat unusual." The professor then pointed to his right and the wall with the six photographs. On the top row of the six, which were about a quarter of the size of the picture behind the professor's desk, the first showed Hitler gesticulating wildly during one of his many speeches. "That picture is fairly typical, Hitler speaking to a large audience." Next to that was another picture of Der Fuehrer speaking to a large number of military in the well known geometric patterns, all lined in perfect unison. It was taken from behind. It was the only colour picture. "This was taken at the Nuremberg Rally in 1934, one of the annual Nazi propaganda get togethers that was filmed by Leni Riefenstahl and released under the infamous title "Triumph of the Will"." The next photograph showed Hitler entering Berlin's Olympic Stadium. "This was taken at the opening of the 1936 Olympics in Berlin. He is accompanied by members of the International Olympic Committee."

Of the lower three photographs, one was a picture of Hitler's office in the new Chancellery building in 1939. Next to that picture was a photograph of Hitler speaking from the balcony of Vienna's Hofburg Palace. The audience was enormous. "The picture was taken a day after the Germans entered Austria on March 12, 1938, the so-called "Anschluss"." The final picture on that wall was a picture of Hitler and maybe thirty five other people at a New Year's Eve party at the Berghof. The professor noted that Eva Braun was standing to Hitler's left. Then, there were the five photographs on the opposite wall, three of which showed Hitler receiving accolades from various crowds of Germans. The other two pictures were identified by the professor as being among his favorites, if not his favorites. One of the photographs was a well known picture of a Russian soldier hoisting a red flay on Reichstag Parliament building. The other was a picture of lone man refusing to do the Nazi salute in a large crowd of Germans. The lone man had his arms crossed. "I love that picture. I have often wondered whatever happened to that man. I assume though that it wasn't good. I mean, if I was able to find the photograph, I am sure the Gestapo did too." With that comment, the professor got a grim look on his face and then sat back in his chair.

George then placed the manila envelope he was holding on the professor's desk, withdrew the photograph and pushed it across the desk. Professor Jenkins leaned over and examined it. He then looked up and, as expected, confirmed his familiarity with the picture.

The obvious question immediately emerged. "You want to know about the boy who is circled? Right?" George nodded and answered with a simple affirmative. Professor Jenkins then leaned back on his chair, pushed back and then opened the right bottom drawer of his desk. He reached into the drawer, pulled out a large brown folding file and laid it on the desk. He removed a stack of photographs from the file and passed them across the desk to George. There appeared to be maybe a dozen photographs in the pile.

"Take a look. They are all I have that may be of interest to you. I am sure that you may find the same picture that you have in your hand right now in the stack here." assured Professor Jenkins. George started to look through the photographs that had just been handed to him. Most of them were photographs of Hitler with members of the Hitler Youth, or who he assumed with members of Hitler Youth, young boys and adolescents, with one of them showing

Hitler with his hands on the shoulders of a young boy in uniform. Finally, there were four photographs that looked that they were taken at the same time and place as the one that hung on the wall in Heinrich Wenck's apartment. In addition, to George's great surprise, one of those four photographs was identical to the one that hung on that wall, the only difference being that there was no circle around the fifth boy on the left facing Hitler.

Professor Jenkins acknowledged George's disappointment. "I'm sorry I can't give you anything on your photograph. I just don't know who any of those boys are. You are right to think that those four photographs were probably taken in the last months of the war. By that time, the military situation was hopeless and young boys, like the boys in the picture, were being conscripted into the army defending Berlin. Hitler would take time to salute them. In fact, those pictures probably were among the last photographs ever taken of Hitler."

"So do you have any suggestions?" asked George, shaking his head. "Any other way of identifying the boy?"

Professor Jenkins answered. He had a suggestion although he seemed somewhat ambivalent about making it. "I don't know. I could give you the names of a number of other historians, professors, journalists, even amateur investigators, some of whom are with Jewish groups here in Montreal."

"Do you think any of those people will know more about the picture than you do?" quietly asked George. As soon as he posed the question, he suspected that the answer wouldn't be helpful. The only conclusion he could reach at this point was the conclusion he had probably reached as soon as he saw the photograph. He would have to ask Heinrich Wenck. Professor Jenkins may have known it as well. He looked at George with a grim look on his face. "Professor, do you think that I should talk to any of these people?" asked George, even though he thought he knew the answer. "No, I don't think any of the names I could give you would do you much good. Whoever gave you the photograph would probably be your best source. They may also be able to tell who the boy in the photograph who was circled is. But I think I already know."

"You think you already know?" said George. Professor Jenkins replied. "Yes. I think your Mr. Wenck himself circled the boy because he either knew the boy or was the boy."

A Brief Interlude, The Passing of Thelma

It was more than a month after he had completed his investigation of the photograph he had taken of the photograph in Mr. Wenck's apartment, George was informed of his mother's death when someone, and he didn't know who or in fact why, sent him a special delivery letter with an obituary page out of the November 18, 2002 edition of the *Ottawa Citizen*. It included the announcement of the passing of Thelma Gagnon at the age of 84 years. It was a brief anonymously authored account submitted by Thelma's friends at the Adventura Apartments. There was no additional text in the envelope, just the obituary. He had received the special delivery letter on December 1, 2002. He read the announcement several times.

Her friends in the Adventura Apartments in Ottawa announce with profound sadness the passing of Thelma Louise Gagnon on November 16, 2002. After a brief funeral at Saint Willibrord's in Verdun, Quebec, Thelma will be interred with her parents in Lakeview Memorial Gardens in Pointe Claire, Quebec.

George, who often reviewed obituaries in daily newspapers for no apparent reason, thought it was shortest but still poignant obituary he had ever read. George wondered but was still gratified to see that his mother was to be the commemorated or had already been commemorated in the church that had played such an important role in his family's life. He had not seen or spoken to his mother for more than three years, ever since he had moved back to Montreal. He did not have any specific reasons, at least any reasons that he could quite comprehend. Maybe it was the unhappy memory of his parents not allowing him to stay in Montreal to play hockey rather than move with the family to Ottawa after his newly assigned stepfather Norman got a job with the federal government. He had been quietly despondent about the move for a while, blaming his mother for not persuading her new husband Norman to let me stay in Montreal rather than move with the two of them to Ottawa. However, when he managed to catch on with a hockey team in Ottawa called the Rangers, his melancholy started to fade, a condition that he had put aside and then forgot completely when he started to see Margaret.

In addition, he recalled that his mother had also behaved poorly, at least from George's point of view, when George had informed her that he was moving to Montreal after having his divorce from Susan finalized. His mother, who had gotten used to George's periodic visits to her at the Adventura Apartments, was not only disappointed but almost outraged, one of the apparent symptoms he thought of her advancing dementia or Alzheimer's or whatever condition it was that made his visits to her place difficult, the possibility of saying the wrong thing a constant threat.

During their last encounter, at the moment he told her mother that he was moving to Montreal, his mother not only started to yell and burst into tears but started throwing things around the apartment. Fortunately, she had limited her projectiles to buttons from her sewing basket. In other words, it could have been worse.

The lady next door, an elderly woman with shocking white hair named Gladys, knocked on the door as Thelma continued to pitch buttons all over her apartment. George answered the door. Gladys immediately launched into an explanation of her friend Thelma's apparent aberrant deportment. "She does that all the time. Don't worry about it. I'm betting you said something that upset her. What is it today? Coins? Buttons? Spoons? Pencils? Paper clips?" she paused for a moment and then went on. "Well, at least it is not dishes. We stopped her from throwing kitchen crockery six months ago. At least I can hear her yelling. Unless she is throwing the small things, I can't hear anything unless she yells. And don't worry about the mess. Julianne will clean up." George assumed that Julianne was the apartment caretaker. George then invited her into the apartment. Gladys then went straight to Thelma, took her sewing basket off her lap and then started to stroke her hair. She nodded toward George. "Maybe you should think about saying goodbye now." George had a strange expression on his face, as if he didn't understand Gladys's request. Gladys immediately recognized George's confusion. "I think you should go now. It will take her some time to calm down."

That was the last time George saw or spoke to his mother. That was more than three years ago. Since then, he had thought of contacting Gladys. He wondered about whether her condition had worsened and contacting Gladys seemed to be pretty well the only way of ascertaining that. He had wished Gladys, his mother herself, someone from the apartment building, that is if his mother was still living there, or anyone else had told him if his mother was receiving the professional care she obviously required. In other words, George wanted to speak to a doctor about his mother.

But he had been unsuccessful and never did speak to anyone, including any doctor, about his mother, the most recent and only information he did have was the obituary in the special delivery letter he did receive on December 1, 2002. He had tried to contact Gladys, last name unknown, by telephoning the Adventura Apartments but was told that Gladys Stevenson, the only Gladys that had lived there in the last ten years, had moved into a nursing home more than a year ago. George began to think that maybe Gladys had sent him the letter from the nursing home. On the other hand, he didn't think that Gladys would have his address in Montreal, not having given it to his mother or Gladys. He also began to think that his mother may have been in touch with the Boormans, their old neighbours from their duplex in Verdun, even though they had not lived there in more than sixty years. In addition, George had no idea if the Boormans still lived in Verdun.

Aside from contemplating the source of the letter, which he had decided was not worth investigating, mainly because it seemed too difficult, he took to reflecting on his life with his mother, from the time of his adoption to the occasion of his eviction from his mother's place soon after Norman's death. For several nights after he received the letter, he would find himself laying in his bed trying to assemble an appropriate biography for his years with his mother. Reflecting on the past two decades or so, he did recollect a number of incidents involving his mother that might well changed the direction of his life, if they had happened differently or had not happened at all.

Of course, the most important incident of his early, if not entire life with his mother, was the accident on Brown Boulevard when he was a kid. Had he not hit the car driven by Allan Price, his mother would not have met Mr. Price and therefore would not entered into an affair with him. Having reached that conclusion, George then went on to the next obvious deduction, that his mother and his father would not have ended up in an altercation that ultimately resulted in the death of his father, whether it was accidental or not. When George got older, when he could possibly appreciate the implications of that incident in the kitchen, he began to believe that maybe he was finally given a reason not to feel guilty about not liking his father. He had long felt that the fact that his father, along with his mother of course, had saved him from being a ward of the Notre-Dame Orphanage ---- in other words an orphan. On the other hand, maybe his life would be better with the Grey Nuns. Or, in addition, he thought that maybe he would have done better with some other couple looking to adopt. He wondered.

While there was no doubt about the significance of the death of James Gagnon, there were several other events that could be considered influential. Prone in his bed, he lay looking at the ceiling, reflecting on the other events in his history that might have changed the direction of his life. There was his obsession with hockey and his constant intemperance, not to mention his disappointment with the move by his mother and her new husband to Ottawa. Then there were the girlfriends ---- Margaret and their baby gone wordlessly to Vancouver, Bernadette and her baby, Hanna and her bibliography of subversive literature, his marriages to Susan and Elaine of the Mercury Bar, as well as the recently departed Anna Vincent.

George's ruminations about his past exhausted, he returned to the possible source of his mother's obituary. The only conclusion he could make was a promise to himself to visit his mother's grave in the Lakeview Memorial Gardens in Pointe Claire. And maybe, he thought, that would be an appropriate farewell to his mother.

A Guy Named Frank
Passes Away

A guy named Frank passed away on a Saturday, more than one day and a month after he had moved into the small cottage on Donegani Avenue in Pointe Claire. Marian, who had gone out with Frank for several years before he got sick and sequestered himself in the small cottage on Donegani Avenue, was basically fulfilling the role of nurse. Since it was on a weekend, it was Marian who found him. She arrived at the cottage close to noon and found him laying with his eyes open and staring at the ceiling, absolutely dead. She immediately telephoned George who told her to contact the police. She sounded understandably anxious, almost panicky. In a nervous voice, she asked him to join her at the cottage. The police she expected would tell her to stay until the medics and/or the coroner arrived. She said that she just didn't feel comfortable with Frank's dead body in the room. In fact, she was scared for some reason. George assured her that someone would be there soon and that he would be right over. He pulled up to Frank's place fifteen minutes later. There were two police cars and an ambulance already there. He found Marian sitting on the only chair in the place surrounded by three officers with one holding a small note book. Two medics were in the process of removing Frank's body.

Marian had been sobbing but now seemed relatively calm. There was no doubt that she was happy to see him, to be relieved of her anxiety. After Frank was carried out and the ambulance departed for the hospital morgue, George suggested that the two of them retire to the Old Orchard Pub, which was less than a kilometre away, below the highway 2&20 and just off Sources Road. George had thought that Marian probably needed a drink, to claim her down. Once they sat down, just after they ordered drinks and were provided with menus, Marian asked Frank about possible arrangements for Frank, that is if there were to be any future arrangements. He said that he would attempt to contact his ex-wife Laura who would presumably inform their two children. But there was a slight problem with that scenario. According to George, he had not seen any of Frank's former family members for several years. He also said that he doubted that any of the three knew or cared where her husband and their father lived or had lived.

George disabused her of the notion of arrangements, assuring her that it was unlikely since Frank and Carol had been separated for ten years and divorced for six of them, and that their parting of the ways had been less than amiable. George explained. "Oh, as I said, I'll contact Laura to see if she would have any interest in having a funeral and maybe taking some sort of responsibility for his estate, that is if he had any estate. On the latter, it is my guess that he probably didn't have much of an estate. I don't think he has any assets, didn't have a job, was getting by on a little welfare, and the few bucks that I gave every month." Marian, who still looked saddened, surprisingly mentioned a death benefit that she said everyone got on their death. She also suggested that Frank might have had an insurance policy, a possibility that George said was unlikely, if not ludicrous. He pointed out that Frank had spent the last year of his life laying on a bed with his oxygen, reading and rereading yesterday's newspaper, watching the weather channel on his little television, a strange habit since he seldom went out. He subsided on lukewarm soup or Starbuck cookies donated by George when he called on him, which was pretty much daily. Otherwise, he slept and waited for the visits by George and Marian. In addition, as George pointed out with a certain soft sarcasm, Frank had no dependants and therefore no need for insurance. Then Marian posed another possibility. "Do you think Frank had a bank account?" This time, George chuckled, the irony worthy of some laughter. George then looked at Marian as if she might had taken leave of her senses. He then just shook his head.

Some time ago, maybe six months past, George and Marian had agreed that Frank's medical situation was getting worse, a prognosis that for some reason ---- George thought it was something akin to slow motion suicide ---- seemed to gratify Frank, as if he had earned his condition instead of developing it. Frank continued to present the facts of his medical state of affairs as entertainment to anyone who would listen, a dwindling group of friends who George would often invite to visit. Most of them would, however, never return after one visit, not sharing Frank's interest in discussing his seeming encyclopedic knowledge of anything to do with lung afflictions. George and Marian also now had Frank's living arrangements to consider. His landlord, a sinister man named Andre Proulx, had told Frank that he had to give up the apartment, his original week now extended to two weeks at the request of the new tenant, the idiot as George called him for paying $50 more a month for the place. In short, George had to find a new place for Frank and at probably less than the rent he was paying for the place from which he was now being asked to leave. Probably less rent was in George's interest since he had been subsidizing Frank since the latter had run out of sick leave and was now relying on unemployment insurance to sustain his pitiful living conditions.

George started to scrutinize the *Montreal Gazette* classified advertisements for appropriate accommodation. Most of the places were not even remotely within their budget, which was diminished to such a point that George had remarked, in a rhetorical way, that Frank might soon find himself living in a telephone booth. George reported his progress, or lack thereof, in seeking a new place for Frank to live out the rest of his days, his demise soon to arrive as the two of them had admitted to each other. By the time George came across a notice for a small cottage on Donegani Avenue out in Pointe Claire, Frank had three days to leave his place or be evicted, a legal procedure with which George thought landlord Proulx was likely well acquainted. Surprisingly enough, he knew the place. It was nothing more than a decrepit two room shack clad in faded clapboard with a rusted tin roof. It had one door in front and one window on the east side of the building. He frequently passed it on his way to or from work at Pointe Claire Industrial, it being on the same street as the Bank of Montreal and Johnson's Snack Bar, two places he visited occasionally. It was a kilometre from not only Frank's current lodging but also close to Marilyn's Lounge, a drinking establishment that he used to venerate but now he could no longer even consider frequenting. Despite or maybe because of the cottage's appearance, George thought that its monthly rent was likely affordable. He would have to inquire about it. After all, Frank probably only had a couple of months to live, making arrangements immediately necessary. At one point, Frank and George discussed moving him into a hotel room although the cheapest rate he could find was probably $35 a night, which was much too high for Frank's budget. So he decided that he had no choice but to pursue the cottage for rent. .

The next day, with two days to Frank's deadline, George dialed the telephone number on the classified ad for the small cottage on Donegani Avenue in Pointe Claire. An obviously older man answered in a blunt, gruff tone.

George opened the conversation in a business like manner. "Hello, I'm interested in renting the cottage you recently advertised in the paper. You know, the one on Donegani Avenue."

"Yes, I'm renting the place out at $150 a month. Electricity, water, and sewer is my business. Everything else is your business." was the answer from the gruff voice on the telephone.

"Ok but I would like to see the place before we move in." replied George. "By the way, who am I speaking to?"

The landlord on the telephone sounded like he had been

insulted. "My name is Monfils. Leo Monfils. And be there by 4 o'clock tomorrow afternoon." The telephone was then hung up.

The next afternoon, he put $200 in his wallet, anticipating that he may need it for Mr. Monfils. He drove to the place. A small, almost dwarf sized man, presumably Leo Monfils, was standing in front of the small cottage on Donegani Avenue. George noticed that the cottage did not have an address. There were no numbers anywhere on the house. It just sat on the corner between Broadview and the parking lot for Valois Park. Parking was prohibited on Donegani so George left the car around the corner on Broadview. He walked to the front of the house where he greeted Leo Monfils. He held out his hand but Mr. Monfils embargoed it away. He just stood there, glowering for reasons unknown. George looked at Monfils closely, almost inspecting him. He was a short man, barely five feet tall, almost square in stature, muscular with an obvious naval tattoo, an anchor with a small Canadian flag on his left bicep. To George, Monfils looked like a gargoyle, like he would not be out of place perched on the steeple of a cathedral in Paris. He just stood there, waiting for George to introduce himself.

"Hello, Mr. Monfils, I'm here to look at the cottage." George sounded a trifle embarrassed, even frightened. Monfils looked at him as if he didn't understand what he was saying. All he managed to produce was a grunt. It made George more uncomfortable.

"You remember we spoke on the phone yesterday." said George. "I asked if I could come by and look at the place. I'd like to rent the place today but I'd like to check out the place first."

Monfils looked at him like he had just made an unnatural suggestion. He might have thought that anyone asking to assess living quarters which went for $150 a month probably had taken leave of their senses. In fact, George thought for a moment that Monfils was about to ask him to leave. Monofils pulled on the front door and made a gesture inviting him in. George took a couple of steps forward and then climbed into the house, the door being at least a yard off the ground, as if the ground sank after the house was constructed. George stood just inside the door and looked into the place. It was immediately evident that the two rooms as advertised included a toilet, which did not have a door, as one of the two rooms. It had a shower about the size of a locker. To the left of the toilet, which was in the middle of the cottage, was a sink, a battered refrigerator, a hot plate, a cheap toaster oven, and above that were two small cabinets. On the other side of the room was a small bed, only equipped with a moth eaten mattress, a dresser that looked like it was recently liberated from the city dump, and a clothing rack. That side of the place had the small window, looking to the east. George also noted that the floor was covered with a chipped vinyl, a dreary grey.

He turned and left the cottage. Monfils was smoking a cigarette, eyes narrowed almost into a squint. After examining the inside of the house, he asked Monfils a simple question. "Does the place come furnished?" It was a sarcastic, rhetorical question. Predictably, Monfils started to laugh, as did George. They both let out incredulous laughs. "This is all you get for $150 a month. A good deal, right?" Monfils spread out his arms toward the two rooms. It was if he were presenting something he wished to sell. George knew he had no other choice. "Okay, I'll take it." Monfils nodded for a third time, stuck one hand out with a key and the other with the palm out. George reached into his pocket and handed Monfils three $50 bills. Monfils nodded for the last time and then spoke again, thanking him. George left and drove home.

Frank must have been living in the small cottage for a week when he started to discuss his impending demise seriously. It didn't surprise neither George nor Marian, both of whom were well aware of Frank's declining condition. Frank seemed to enjoy entertaining himself and presumably his guests by demonstrating an intimate knowledge of his own medical pathology, often exhibiting that knowledge for hours. That was one of the reasons, if not the chief reason that the number of his visitors gradually dwindled as they grew weary, if not completely exhausted by Frank's repetition of his various symptoms. Soon, George and Marian were his only visitors, George doing the weekdays and Marian the weekends. While both of them were just as exasperated as Frank's previous visitors had been with his patter, they were committed to taking care of Frank, no matter how annoying the task.

But as the two were left as the sole caretakers of Frank, his annoying chatter gradually to be replaced by a depressing reminiscence of his past. He would mutter about his misspent youth, his partially squandered adult years, and now the desolation of his current state. Not only was it annoying, the same depressing complaints about the pointlessness of existence, which called an "existential waste of time", a term he enjoyed repeating. On the other hand, he wasn't conscious long enough each day to say much of anything, either sleeping or struggling under an oxygen mask, having graduated from those damn cannulas.

George was relieved then when Frank's started to talk about something other than his own miserable existence. His new fixation did, however, reflect badly on his present life anyway. He had discovered, or more accurately rediscovered, his memory as he just lay there waiting for perdition. He remembered that his father served in the army in World War II, having landed on D-Day among other things. This revelation prompted Frank, in so far as he could, to complain, if not regret his failure to live a life that was as righteous as the life lived by his father. He believed that his father's war service was more important than any other detail of his life, which, in Frank's estimation, was common as hell. So Frank was admittedly envious of his father, his disappointment, if not disdain with other aspects of his father's life irrelevant in comparison. Frank often thought, if not dreamed, of the different life he would have had if he were born at a different time, specifically his father's time, the era of the so-called "greatest generation"

Frank would sometimes relate the story of the time he visited the office of the Canadian Recruitment Force Centre in Montreal. It was a long time ago, more than fifty years, when he walked in that office with the crazy notion of joining the forces, inspired by a combination of his resentment of his father's accomplishments as well as predictable difficulties he had been having at home with his father. But sitting there in the office waiting for someone to talk to, the likely attendant a corporal with a bean shave, hair scrapped to the scalp, standing on the other side of the counter with a sour look on his face. He saw several officers salute each other, he looked at the recruiting posters on the wall, he thought about his father maybe visiting a similar office when he was eighteen. But back then, his father was likely as dumb as hell and standing in line with many boys who were likely as dumb as he was. Everyone of them thought that they were doing the right thing. And they were right.

After waiting for fifteen minutes or so, the corporal with the bean shave called George to the counter and asked him to fill in a form. Frank would later say that it was then he had some sort of epiphany and left the recruitment office. He never went back.

It was two days after he was found dead that George began his search for people who might wish to mourn Frank's passing. In the early afternoon, George contacted his ex-wife Laura by telephone. She apparently worked at an apparel store in Fairview Shopping Mall, remembering that Frank had told him that his ex-wife Laura had become manager there, or so he had been told by one of her friends, having run into her one day. George got Laura on the telephone after convincing whoever had originally answered the telephone that he had a legitimate reason to talk to Laura. He felt like he was about to ask a total stranger for a date.

"Hello Laura, it's George Gagnon. I am friend of Frank, your former husband, Frank Gordon. I have important news about him." There was silence on the telephone, just a sort of quiet breathing. "Yes Mr. Gagnon. Have we ever met?"

George answered quietly. "No, I don't think so." "Why are you calling? Has Frank done something? Is he okay?" There was another brief interval of silence. Before George had time to reply, Laura continued. "You must know I haven't see or heard from Frank for a long time, for many years." George replied. "I know you haven't seen him for a while. You would have no way of knowing but Frank has passed away. He died two days ago." "Passed away?" said Laura, her tone and volume a little higher. "I don't think he was that old you know. How did he die?" To George, she sounded genuinely sad, which was surprising in view of the complaints that Frank periodically made about his ex-wife's lack of passion for him or anyone else for that matter.

George may not have wanted to but went ahead to describe, in so far as he could, the medical condition that ultimately lead to his death. "He had a lung disease, he always said that it was COPD but some people who knew him thought it was emphysema but anyway, he steadily got worse. He never wanted to go to the hospital. Fact was he just refused. So he died at home, where he was living in for a little more than a month. Anyway, only Marian, one of Frank's ex-girlfriends and I took care of him, in so far as we could. Either one of us was there every day of the week."

Laura interrupted George to make a remark that was fairly predictable. "Well, his damn drinking didn't help. Frank did a lot of it in the years that we were together. It was one of the reasons, maybe the biggest reason, that I threw him out the house."

George could not let Laura continue with any of her complaints. He basically cut her off. "Well, he wasn't drinking by the time Marian and I were looking after him, first in a dumpy apartment just below the train station on Valois Bay and then in an equally dumpy shack on Donegani Avenue in Pointe Claire. That's where he was living when he died. But before that, it was obvious that Frank was an alcoholic. He used to boast about it." There was a pause and Laura picked up the theme. "During the last few years we were together, he used to say that he was an alcoholic, like it was some sort of achievement or something. I guess that's why he accepted my throwing him out so calmly. He was resigned by then."

George then turned to the purpose of his call. "Do you know if Frank had a will? It seems unlikely but Marian thought it was possible. After all, he did work for almost thirty years, in different places, different companies. In fact, he had worked at the same place where I was working, Pointe Claire Industrial, several years before I got there, an interesting coincidence. Anyway, he had a legitimate job, more than one legitimate job, so he might had written a will. Did he ever tell you anything about a will or did you know anything about a will?" Another pause, a sound of exasperation, and then she provided the expected answer. "No, I don't think he ever had a will. Not that I knew of." George expected the answer but was still disappointed. Laura then made a suggestion. "Maybe you should talk to his last employer. They might know something. I don't know who that would be but you could try anyway."

"Thanks. Anyway, I'll let you know if we decide to have a visitation or something." George then slowly hung up. He then had a thought. He might want to put a notice in the paper, an obituary announcing a time and place for a visitation. George saw no need for a funeral, Frank never having given George any hint of any sort of religious affiliation. He was now convinced that a visitation might attract people, friends and associates who might have knowledge as to whether he had a will. Just pondering the possibility of a visitation, he then concluded that he would approach Vince, the guy who owned Marilyn's, to ask him whether his place could be an appropriate venue for a visitation for the deceased Frank Pimm. It was appropriate. This was a place where he and Frank had regularly drank, had pretended to be intellectuals, had discussed books they were trying to read, films they hadn't seen, had pretended to discuss matters they wished they understood and experiences they wished they had had. He looked up Marilyn's telephone number. Heather, the woman who was usually behind the bar arranging things for the evening, answered the phone. George asked for Vince.

"Your name is George Gagnon?" asked Vince. "That's right. I used to come in maybe three time a week, with Frank Pimm and a guy named Dan. We used to sit near the bar so we could see the television or in the corner when we didn't want to watch television." George thought he could hear Vince concentrating on the other end of the phone. And then, after a couple of minutes of presumably pondering, Vince acknowledged George. "Yeah, I think I remember you. Yeah, you and your pal Frank. The waitresses told me that you two used to talk about books, politics and all that shit. But I also know that you two may never have gone to college but were pretty good at pretending that you had." "Yeah, that was us." replied George, pleased that Vince at least remembered him. "I have a favour to ask.""A favour?" Vince laughed a bit and added a comment. "Let me guess, you owe the place money, you've been running a tab and you're a little short, right?" It was George's turn to snicker. "No, I don't owe your place any money and I don't have a tab. But I do have something to ask you." he said. Vince was ready to at least listen to his question. "Well, what can I do for you?"

George then asked. "My friend Frank, who you must have seen with me in your place a few times, died recently and I want to throw him a wake and I want to have it in Marilyn's." He paused for a moment and continued with his proposal. "I'd only want the place for an afternoon. I don't know how many people would come, but I think drinks and a modest spread of snacks would be enough. I think a couple hundred bucks for food and guests can pay for their own drinks. That should be good enough. Maybe next Monday, next week five days from now. After all, Marilyn's doesn't see too many patrons after lunch until around four o'clock or so. I know it's a favour but I would rather have Frank's wake in Marilyn's rather than in a funeral parlour. I think he deserves a proper visitation."

Having made his proposal, George nervously waited on the line for Vince. Vince came back on the line again and quickly agreed, noting that Marilyn's had hosted visitations or wakes or whatever people wanted to call them several times in the past. "Just talk to Heather. She'll set it up." George then thanked him and mentioned that he now had a date for the obituary.

Maybe five minutes after concluding his telephone call with Vince, he e-mailed the *Montreal Gazette* with Frank's obituary and paid for it with a credit card. It was absurdly brief, maybe even unholy. But George thought it appropriate.

Frank Pimm of Pointe Claire passed away on
Thursday, November 18. A visitation will be held

The Biography of George

at Marilyn's Lounge in Pointe Claire at 1 PM
on the afternoon of Monday, November 22.

Sixteen people, including Marian and himself, showed up at Frank Pimm's event at Marilyn's Lounge on that Monday afternoon. George was surprised with the number of mourners. Aside from George ex-wife Laura, there were four guys who used to work at Pointe Claire Industrial, two of whom where still working there, three guys who were working at a local chainsaw factory, the last place that Frank actually worked, two women, one named Nancy and the other Janice, a guy named Dave who said he used to play hockey with Frank and a couple of neighbours of Frank when he was living in the apartment across from Marilyn's Lounge. The most surprising attendee was Mr. Leo Monfils, the owner and landlord of the small cottage on Donegani Avenue. He announced to George, the only person with whom he spoken in the fifteen minutes he was at the visitation, that Frank had paid him rent for a year on his cottage on Donegani Avenue. Monofils also handed George a lease to the place on Donegani Avenue. The lease named Leo Monfils as the lessor, George Gagnon as the lessee, and one year as the period of the lease. Monfils had signed the lease and was waiting for George to sign as well.

George could barely say anything to Monfils. He was more than stunned. He finished his beer, from which he had just taken only one swig, and looked at Monfils with an astonished expression on his face. He initially had no idea as to how he could possibly respond to the document Monfil had just handed him. It took him maybe two minutes to come up with the obvious question. "What does this lease mean? I never asked to rent another place. I live across the street for Christ sake. I have lived there for six months and have no intention of moving anywhere else." Monfils produced a sinister laugh, not very loud but he could hear him. Monofils was explaining the lease and how George ended up with it.

"Your friend Frank was crazy, real crazy. Two weeks ago, I went over to the place on Donegani, you know just to see how things were going, you know, how the crazy bastard was settling in. Anyway, when I visited, Frank was just laying in bed, looking pretty rough. I though that he should have been in a hospital but he wouldn't go. I had to knell by his goddamn bed. He could barely talk and so I could hardly hear him. He told me that this woman Marian and yourself were taking care of him. He then asked me if I could give you a year long lease for the place. He said that you weren't doing so well and you probably would need a place to stay before long. So he gave me $1,500, every cent he had he said. He didn't say anything but I got, you know I got the feeling he expected to go any time. So I filled in the names on a lease and all you have to do is to sign." Monfils then finished his explanation and looked at George.

George was stunned, not only by the lease itself but by the suggestion that he may need to move into another place. He had to admit that it was an extraordinary example of clairvoyance. George was to be laid off by Pointe Claire Industrial within weeks. But since he had been a casual truck driver and had been paid in cash for his twenty hours a week, he could not look forward to much in the way of UIC or even welfare. That meant that he couldn't afford his current dump across from Marilyn's but would have to move into a cheaper dump, like the one that Frank had just departed. He would probably have to get some sort of day job for cash, even a paper route would do, a suggestion that made him laugh to himself. That is why moving into that derelict shack on Donegani Avenue was like a miracle. It was a lifesaver. It would take him a week to move into it.

He was 71 years old and had lived in the ramshackle shack at the unfortunate address on Donegani Avenue for several years now. He had remodelled it somewhat, mainly on the inside where he added pine panelling to separate the few parts of the place from each other, mainly to ensure that people using the toilet were granted some privacy, the addition of a door a particularly convenient addition, and, for a reason unknown, the inclusion of a bunk bed. By the door to the toilet, George had hung a small mirror, which was hardly used. George would look into it maybe once a month, mainly to ensure that he looked as bad as he felt. Over the past few years, he had grown a beard, which he always kept unkempt, allowed his bad teeth to get worse, and had effected a slight stoop that seemed to frighten most people who saw him. Over the years, he had become a collector of junk, his backyard a veritable museum of useless articles, abandoned furniture, rusted tools, and appliances that no longer worked. There was even an automobile that looked like it hadn't been drive or even moved in decades. It was a 1956 Pontiac Pathfinder, colour metallic blue.

He was still 71 years old when a man named Barnes

knocked on the door and offered George Gagnon a job for the winter. For some reason, Mr. Barnes wanted to know his family name.

Despite his promise, Daniel Small never asked Allison Coleman to review his manuscript once he had completed it. Nor did he ask her to review its first chapter. Allison Coleman never reminded Daniel of his promises.

Printed in the United States
By Bookmasters